Ascension

The Ymir Trinity

A M Leishman

Table of Contents

Chapter 1

America

Dawn's eyes snapped open at the sight of Alma entering her small town library. The tall Nordic woman stood out against a backdrop of aged, slovenly-attired, and overweight townies. She rushed in behind her and leaned forward to breathe in the air rippling from her wake. Alma's aroma was intoxicating. Unable to remain silent, Dawn moved in closer, almost touching her, and whispered, "You smell like candy."

Alma spun around to find herself looking down on a teenage girl who was an entire head shorter than her. "What?" Thick auburn hair draped over the front and back of Dawn's shoulders to frame her heart-shaped face. Connected by a constellation of little brown freckles, her bright green eyes reflected an unsettling glint of childlike happiness.

Dawn's effervescent personality overflowed from her petite body as she bounced on the balls of her feet. "You smell like candy, and you're way prettier than she showed me. I've been waiting weeks for you. She said you're fighting her because you're scared of us."

Those harassing feelings that compelled Alma to visit this neglected landlocked American town made it clear this peculiar girl was the reason. "Who are you?" Her Icelandic inflection was heavy.

"I'm Dawn. I'm in love with your accent, and your eyes! Oh my god, I haven't seen gray eyes up close before. Don't get me started on your hair!" Dawn fought a near irresistible desire to touch Alma's face. "We've been talking about you for weeks. She loves you so much. We both love you. We're going to make everything so much better for everyone!"

Alma asked, "Are you like me?" She wanted to believe she wasn't unique in their crowded world.

Dawn ran her hands down Alma's arms and entangled their fingers. She walked backward, guiding her to a small reading table beside a floor-to-ceiling window and pulled out a chair for her new friend. "No one is like you. Well, no one alive right now."

"But you know what I am?" Alma's crackling tone suggested she was on the verge of crying. The relief of not being alone overwhelmed her.

"Of course, I know everything about you." Dawn recited a disturbing incantation. "You are her hands and eyes. I am her ears and mouth. We are two pieces of a powerful tool. Her tool. We're special, you and I. We listened to her. We let her mold us into what we are, and what we are is amazing."

"Who is her?" Alma didn't know what to make of this frightening ball of energy.

"She's the voice in your head. You've felt them. Those fantastic feelings telling us what to do, what's good and what's bad." Dawn waited years for the opportunity to talk to someone about her magnificent voice, someone who understood.

Alma's expression soured. "That voice makes me feel unpleasant things. It does not give me kind feelings at all. Honestly, it seems a bit evil at times, and it takes all my strength to shut it out."

Dawn gazed into Alma's watering eyes and responded in a patronizing tone. "There's no such thing as evil. It's just layers of convoluted stuff. The deeper the layer, the harder it is for us to comprehend. The more you know, the less evil things are. It's a word people use to describe things they don't want to understand. People aren't evil, they're broken."

The confidence in her words forced Alma to shy away. "The things I have seen are worse than a person being broken. They take pleasure in harming living creatures. It is fun for them."

A breathy melodramatic chuckle escaped Dawn's nose. "No, they're definitely broken, and we don't have the tools to fix them. There's plenty of people on this planet, so we don't need to keep all the broken ones. She hates the broken ones, and so do you, but you don't want to say it."

In the corner of her eye, Dawn caught the jerking movements of a rather large beetle racing along the bottom of a bookshelf. She raised a finger in front of Alma and jumped to hunt the little bug. It didn't notice her shadow darkening its world before her hand swept it up from the matted Berber carpet. A wide grin stretched across her face as she carried her quarry back with a victorious bounce in her step.

She corralled the frantic beetle between her hands. "Most beetles are afraid to be out in the light, especially if animals or humans are around. This one isn't afraid, probably because it's stupid, or broken." Dawn held the beetle against the table with her thumb and index finger. She smirked as its delicate legs scrambled on the smooth faux-wood surface.

"I could take it outside and let it go. Killing it would be evil, right?" She delighted in her prisoner's hopeless attempts at escape. "Imagine this dumb bug breeding. The genetic flaws that made him scurry around in front of insanely powerful humans, in broad daylight, will be passed down to his stupid broken babies."

Alma pitied Dawn's terrified flailing captive. Like the bug, she too feared this adorable girl whose personality, without warning, turned dark. It was becoming clear that there was something profoundly wrong with Dawn.

She flipped the beetle onto its back, placed a finger on its hard belly, and stuck out a sarcastic pouty lip as the bug's thrashing legs struggled to escape her hold. "Those babies will have babies. They may crowd or starve out smarter bugs. Bugs smart enough not to trust us. When humans see a bunch of these things they'll kill them all, probably with poison. They'll spray toxic chemicals into all the holes and cracks in the walls and ceilings, killing the smart ones too."

"Being kind to this one stupid bug could bring genocide to thousands of beetles, and spiders, and other things living peacefully inside the walls." She positioned her fingernail over the beetles neck. "Killing him will make his entire species' genetic code a tiny bit better in the long run."

With a dutiful smile, Dawn pushed her nail down, severing the beetle's head from its body. Its legs continued twitching around her finger. "When you remove the weak and stupid from a species, you make them all better."

Alma stared horror-stricken at Dawn. "I am done with you. You are not a normal person." She stood from her chair using so much force it toppled to the ground, causing everyone in the library to notice. When she turned away, an intense feeling of despair overcame her as goosebumps washed over her arms.

Dawn could barely contain her boiling excitement. "You can see them, and she can see them through you." She moved from her chair to stand beside Alma and whispered into her braided grayish-white hair, "They're United States Air Force drones. They know you're here. Stay calm, they don't know it's you. They just know someone like you is here. They're really smart. Don't make them kill all these innocent people to stop one pretty little bug."

Any color left in Alma's face drained away. Terror cascaded throughout her entire body, freezing every muscle. She spoke with a shivering voice, "What do I do? How do I hide from them?"

Dawn perched on her tiptoes while trying to speak into her ear, but Alma was too tall. "We walk slowly to my car and nonchalantly drive away. Like your average person would. Just in case you didn't already know, they can see when you do stuff. So, don't do stuff." She wrapped her arm around Alma's lower back and guided her new friend out of the library to her old rusty blue car.

Alma's shallow breathing quickened. "I should leave this terrible country and go back home."

"They'll see that. You, coming here, that let them know we exist. They've been waiting and watching for us longer than we've been alive. All this time our technology has been getting stronger and smarter and better. They won't stop hunting us." Dawn pressed her head against Alma's shoulder. "Iceland won't protect you from them. In fact, your government would probably help them find you."

Dawn led Alma to the passenger side of her car with a gentle nudge and opened its loud creaky door. She bent down and grabbed a few large items from the floor and seat, tossing them into the back. "Go on, get in. They do have cars where you're from, right?"

Alma's extreme fear of the United States military somewhat lessened her simmering anxiety over Dawn. With a snarl and a discordant huff, she sat inside the filthy vehicle. She tried to hide an involuntary retch as she shuffled garbage from side to side to make room for her feet. The car smelled terrible, like motor-oil, leaking coolant, old food, and body odor.

Dawn backed from her parking spot as any normal person would, then stopped the car and turned to Alma. "Put your seat belt on. No way I'm going to be the one who kills you."

Alma didn't say a word during their drive to Dawn's apartment. She faced forward, keeping the creepy redhead in the corner of her eyes while lamenting her decision to visit Fort Dodge, Iowa. This nightmarish girl frightened the hell out of her. America frightened her. Everything frightened her. She turned away and stared at endless rows of corn stretching beyond the horizon.

An external sense of security comforted her when they reached Dawn's home. She followed close behind with her head down, up three flights of stairs to the front landing.

Dawn jammed her key into the lock and pulled on the knob. She fought to open the door, then pushed a bewildered Alma inside. "There's water in the fridge if you're thirsty. Make yourself at home."

Her kitchen had numerous glass bottles of supplements scattered on the counter, reminiscent of an unorganized new-age pharmacy. Curious, Alma opened the tiny refrigerator. Her water was in a large glass container. "This looks like my kitchen when I was much younger, but the food is different."

Dawn sat on a cheap bar-stool across the kitchen counter from Alma. "Of course it does. She tells us what to eat and what not to eat. She's helping us change our bodies and our brains. Kind of like rewiring us. We're upgrading ourselves, so we can hear and feel her better. It's why we don't eat sugar or, way worse, fake sugar." She picked up a random bottle, tipping it back and forth, enjoying the muted jangling noises it made. "Sugar dulls her voice."

Alma read the labels from several bottles. "I only eat real plants and lean meats."

"Yeah. I need to hear her words better than everyone else. You needed completely rewired inside. We both listened to her, and now we're better than everyone. Our connection is powerful. To her and to each other. Forever." Dawn's stare radiated spiritual contentedness.

"Why us?" Vivid images of this pretty young woman severing that little bug's head continued to haunt her.

Dawn chuckled at Alma's failure to grasp what's happening. "She didn't choose us. Her influence can be felt by almost everyone. Billions of people." She dropped the glass bottle onto the counter. "We listened better and followed her lead faster than everyone else. As we changed, we got better at making ourselves stand out. We sacrificed a lot, and we won the race."

Her joyous voice assumed a more serious timbre. "So many things humans have created make us live longer but make us deaf to her influence. Plastic is bad, but without it there would be a hell of a lot less of us. I guess that could be a good thing though."

Alma wasn't listening. Distracted by the random items in Dawn's cluttered apartment, she was trying to find any bit of information that could help her understand this girl. She focused on a picture encased in an ugly aluminum frame. "Who is this?" The image was of Dawn and a young blonde woman standing against a rustic wooden fence with thick green trees filling the background. They were dressed for hiking and both displayed sweet smiles.

Dawn pivoted toward the picture. Her expression melted into a sullen frown as she lifted it closer. "She was my roommate, my girlfriend, Emily. This is her apartment. She's been gone for a few months."

"Did she die?" Alma couldn't hide the accusation in her voice. Perhaps Emily was broken and Dawn did something far worse than killing a helpless bug.

"No. When I followed that voice and started taking all of these." Dawn gestured to the collection of supplements covering the counter. "I became kind of, radical. Emily didn't like it. She said I was turning into a Nazi. I couldn't control my thoughts or my mouth at first. She started hating me. I saw it happening, and I couldn't or wouldn't stop it. I really miss her."

"Are we Nazis? Were they the same as us?" Alma recalled some of the repulsive things she had been feeling, things she was urged to do but couldn't bring herself to do them. They made her hate the poor and dumb, feeble and dependent. She carried nothing but animosity for anyone who wasn't at or near physical perfection.

"No, they were a..." Dawn scoured her thoughts for an adequate word to describe them, but failed. "She needs us to be much more technologically advanced and that war pushed humanity a hundred years into the future, maybe more. The Germans ruined eugenics though. Eugenics is so important, but now you can't talk about it without making people mad."

Dawn delicately placed the picture back where it was. "Making people better and smarter with each generation, that's all bad now." She curled her index finger in front of Alma. "Remember the beetle?"

Alma couldn't stop thinking about that poor beetle. "Perhaps Emily was correct about you."

"I know you feel the same as me, but you fight it because they have a lot of power. If you tell a woman she's fat, a million people will come to her rescue and destroy you. They'll destroy you for telling the truth. You'll lose your job, your friends. For telling the truth." Dawn walked into the adjoining living-room, still talking. "Democracy gives the unremarkable absolute power over the exceptional. There are way more of them than us."

She thrust her hand toward her television, which wasn't on, while pursing her lips and squinting. "They've trained you, all of us, to hate the truth. We're forced to feel sorry for stupid people when we should be disgusted at the idea of them breeding." She dropped onto her sofa.

"You are not as cute as you were in the library, before the bug." Alma despised Dawn's words but struggled with similar feelings. They nagged her in dark directions, giving her the same terrible thoughts Dawn was all too proud to lay bare. "Is she the devil?"

Dawn snorted. "Don't be stupid. She guides us and helps us make good decisions. You and I followed her lead, and now she's working through us to save the human species. Something bad is coming, and she needs all of us to be better than we are. A lot better." Her vocal cadence adopted the persona of a ranting conspiracy nut. "She's been trying to save us, but we're getting too smart. The big governments like America, China, Europe, Russia, they all know so much now. They have so much power and technology. It's not like long ago." She closed her eyes and drew in a deep breath through her nose. "It's why she made us. You and me."

Alma wandered from the kitchen into the living-room and stood towering over Dawn. "Made us for what? I have been like this for longer than you know, and all I do is hide from people." She motioned upward to the numerous drones circling the city. "Now I cannot do even that."

Dawn used Alma's arm to pull herself to her feet. "You are her hands and eyes. I am her ears and mouth. Mechanics don't fix cars with their minds. They need powerful tools to help them. Without their tools, all they can do is look at the car and guess what's wrong with it, unable to do anything. That's probably frustrating."

Alma hadn't talked with another person in quite

some time, and this woman was exhausting. "Well, she needs to tell me to do something. Something not horrible."

Dawn walked to her balcony door, held out her arm, and beckoned Alma to follow. "That's what I'm here for. To help you understand those wonderful feelings from her. We need to find out who controls those drones. We need to talk to that person. Probably a man."

Alma placed her hand flat against the large window. The drones crisscrossed and circled above them in the cloudless blue sky. She could touch them if she desired. Imagining the hell they may rain down was enough to keep her fingers away from those little gray monsters.

Chapter 2

Ymir

Dawn tossed and turned for hours before rolling off the sofa and onto the floor, startling herself awake. She looked up to find Alma standing at her balcony. "You sure don't sleep much, do you." She stretched out her jaw and joined Alma at the window. "I can't see them. Are they really high up there?"

Alma followed Dawn's gaze. "They are almost in space. Higher than any planes I have ever seen. I wonder if they can see I am watching them." She imagined a cartoonish drone flaunting big goofy eyes, the two of them having a staring contest, and she was afraid to blink.

Dawn placed her hand on Alma's shoulder while pretending to watch the drones with her. "They can only see when you change or move things. She doesn't know who's in charge of them. There's been a lot more of that lately, stuff she can't see. She wants you to play nice with our government."

Alma didn't want to play with the American military at all, nice or otherwise. Although the drones appeared to be unarmed, she was mindful that somewhere out there real weapons were laying in wait. "Do you think they would destroy a city filled with people to kill me?"

Dawn made a sarcastic chuckle. "Of course they would."

Her flippant response forced Alma to recoil in disgust. "Is she telling you anything? What does she want me to do?" She put her hand over Dawn's. Her religious devotion to that voice was somehow comforting. She had always feared giving in to those feelings, assuming they came from something dark, maybe evil. The things it pressured her to do horrified her.

Alma accepting the existence of their paraclete made Dawn smile. "She's telling me you'll be protected. She wants you to know you're safe no matter what you do. Relax and listen to her. Let her guide you, and stop trying to control things."

She wanted to hate Dawn, but savored the warmth of her touch, a feeling she hadn't experienced in decades. Dawn's absolute confidence in their shared voice enabled her to abandon the struggles that tormented her for most of her life.

Alma surrendered to her opponent, relaxing her body in defeat. A calm stilled those turbulent thoughts battering her fatigued mind, forcing tears to spill over her cheeks. She rested her head atop Dawn's and asked, "Does she have a name?"

"I've been calling her, Ymir. She seems to like it." Alma's tears soaking into her hair brought a gracious smile to her face. Dawn was relishing the close bond growing between them. Ymir promised her the loneliness wouldn't last, and Ymir never lies.

Alma spoke toward the ceiling, "Well, Ymir, what do you want me to do?" Her expression blanked as she looked in the direction of a distant flight of drones, emptied her mind, and allowed Ymir to fill it. A rush of foreign feelings soothed her tired body, possessing her with a sense of duty, of purpose. It felt good to relinquish control to someone, or something else. No longer adversaries, Ymir showed her what she needed to do.

She unraveled from Dawn's embrace, walked out of the apartment, down the stairs, and across the parking lot. The beautiful Icelandic woman disappeared into a wooded preserve, moving as far away from vulnerable people as possible. Dawn whispered through tear-dampened lips, "You are her hands and eyes. I am her ears and mouth."

Deep in a southwestern Texas desert, Alma sat alone on a large comfortable chair. Its dark color contrasted with the sand, rocks, and dried shrubs surrounding it. In front of her rested a series of boulders one hundred meters wide. It read, "We should talk." She awaited the drones.

It didn't take long before those giant gray bugs invaded her space in the now familiar pattern of three teams of four. Her fingertips gripped the soft skin of her chair's arms as she pleaded, "You will protect me, right Ymir?"

Alma and the drones passed their time studying each other in silence. They circled around her and over her, never tiring of the repetition. She couldn't imagine they were seeing anything of interest.

The drones' synchronized movements fascinated her. They didn't bobble or deviate in any perceivable way. Their absolute perfection of motion contradicted nature's complex randomness. It was beautiful to witness, like watching a team of skilled dancers performing as one fluid entity.

An hour passed without drama before the thumping sounds of helicopters approaching from the northeast shattered her focus. Her jaw clenched as her grip on the chair pierced its leather. Those annoying feelings that demanded she fear these people now wanted her to interact with them. She wanted to disappear.

The tiny gray specs on the horizon grew until they hovered high above her rocky message. One of the menacing war machines made its way to the dusty earth, forcing clouds of sand to swirl in every direction. It halted its descent less than a meter from the desert floor.

A large door slid open to reveal a hunched over man in a formal looking blue military uniform. Unsure of his footing, he stepped onto the sand and stood straight and tall, tugging on the bottom of his tunic. He drew in a deep breath then let it out as he worked up the courage to walk toward Alma.

Alma lifted herself from the chair, sinking her bare feet into the dry sand. Her cold eyes and tight jaw couldn't mask the panic ravaging her insides. Their hearts were racing as they neared each other. The name on his right jacket pocket caught her attention, BELFORT. It was difficult to pronounce in her head.

They both stopped, leaving a five-meter buffer between them. He scanned her body from top to bottom. She wasn't what he was expecting. "You're a woman."

Alma's mind drifted away with the helicopters as they circled overhead and flew out of view. *That can only be a bad thing.* Her squinting focus returned to Mr. Belfort as she spoke through her teeth. "Is this a problem for you?"

"No, it's just you've always been a man in the past. I was prepared for a man." He looked around for another person. "Is the Speaker a man this time?" The out-of-place chair behind her forced a subtle laugh from his nose.

"The what?" Her response was terse. She wasn't angered by his question, she was upset she didn't understand its meaning.

Belfort's face contorted. "The Speaker? Your human counterpart. Is your Speaker male or female? She's always been a human female before."

Alma guessed he was asking about Dawn. "No, she is a teenage girl, and I am human." She couldn't help being a little curious if they had an interesting title for her as well.

"We didn't know if you were both human or not. Are you sure, or just assuming this? Where were you born?" The drones listened in as the tall thin man pushed her for unimportant information. To him, Alma appeared to be a human woman in her early twenties. "I have a daughter about your age." His thoughts turned to his child. The idea of her living without him forced a swelling in his throat. He was certain he wouldn't survive this encounter.

"I am much older than you think, and I was born, to human parents, in Iceland, Akureyri." Alma tried maintaining eye contact with Mr. Belfort while she kept her mind's eye on the drones. "Are we only going to discuss me?"

His nostrils flared as he continued attacking her with pointless queries. "We like to know who we're dealing with. Did you decide to be female, so we'd trust you more?" He did trust her more than he would have trusted a male. "Well, it's not working."

"I was born female. This is what I looked like when I was young. I could not change my gender if I wanted to. There is too much to consider. It is not only about the stuff between our legs." Her eyes rolled at the thought of how overwhelming it was to preserve her youth.

Belfort couldn't stomach playing the role of diplomat any longer. "Fine. We believe you're an abomination. A literal minion of Satan or Satan himself, herself." He accepted his fate, and resigned himself to die in service to God and country. "Looking like this is further proof you're untrustworthy, trying to manipulate us."

She didn't know how to respond to his abrupt dive into insanity. *First Dawn, now Belfort, Why are Americans so scary?* If she had to be honest, the idea of her being the devil crossed her mind more than a few times. "I do not know what I am, but I am not a bad person. I am not the devil." Alma could taste his visceral hatred. "I did not choose to be like this. I can do so much, but I have done nothing to harm anyone. I want only to help."

He clenched both hands into fists, turning his fingers a bloodless white. "We've already seen what your kind can do. None of you ever helped humanity. Time and time again your people have laid waste to this world, slaughtering millions just to entertain yourselves."

"I would never do that. You seem to know much more about what I am than I do. Why do you think I exist?" Alma questioned the nature of her own existence for decades, and genuinely wanted an answer. Her eyes watered. "There must be a reason other than harming."

Her appearing as an attractive young woman, crying like a child, made him feel less afraid of her. He hated being manipulated. "The final battle for our souls will cleanse this planet and end your kind for eternity. With you mankind will face its last trial. We stand in the shadow of Armageddon. You've been the same throughout history, but we keep getting better, smarter, and stronger."

Alma thought Dawn was bad, but Belfort was far more terrifying. "I was content hiding from people like you. I should have stayed in Iceland." She paused after deciding to control how much information she divulged about herself. "I want to work with you, with America, not fight you. She wants us to work together. We want to help in any way you need us to." Alma was panicking or Ymir was making her panic.

This angry zealot hungered for a fight, and Alma had no idea why. The more he spoke, the more obvious it became the military didn't want her in America or on Earth. They wanted her dead.

The drones disappeared, leaving the faded blue sky eerily silent. Something didn't feel right. "Where did your drones go?" She searched her surroundings with her mind, cataloging everything that could harm her.

Shrouded from Ymir, Alma, and Dawn, hidden from human technology, an AI navigated cruise missile arced over their little part of the world. Not connected to any digital or analog networks, its stealth rendered it invisible. It was special. They created it for Alma or someone like her.

Alma's urge to reason with people allowed the military's AI enough time to pinpoint her location. It harbored no animosity toward her, or Mr. Belfort. It had an important mission to complete, and nothing else mattered.

When the missile reached its destination several thousand meters above them, it detonated in a brilliant ball of energy, engulfing an area the size of a rural American town. The powerful explosion forced air down and away from its epicenter, crushing and suffocating everything beneath it.

Hours later, a serene blue sky peaked out through the settling dust and debris as nature's winds haphazardly washed the giant mushroom cloud from her skies. Alma and Air Force Captain Timothy Belfort were gone.

Chapter 3

The Kohor

Alma awoke, face up and naked in a field of grass. Her eyes fluttered open to the peaceful view of motionless striated clouds painted across a faded greenish blue sky. A gentle breeze carried the fragrant odors of hand turned soil and wind swept flowers. She savored a feeling of serenity as it washed over her, soothing her body.

Her moment of relaxation came to an abrupt end at the sounds of whispering nearby. She sat, spun around, and covered her bare breasts at the sight of three women standing a couple meters behind her. She stood, panned her surroundings, and said, "Hello?"

All three women were smaller than Dawn, who was an entire head shorter than her. Their skin radiated a warm tawny beige and their large dark irises showed no discernible border with their pupils. Long straight glossy black hair reflected hints of iridescent purple and green.

They wore similar handcrafted tan dresses carrying unique and intentional patterns of colorful beads threaded into the bulky weaves. The woman in the center of the group, older in appearance, thrust out her arms and offered Alma a loosely woven dress.

Alma stepped toward them, making sure she didn't place her feet on anything sharp and accepted the stiff garment. She slipped into the dress and pulled it up over her body. To her surprise, it was a perfect fit.

Afraid of this imposing titan, one of the younger women made a short hop backward and looked away. "I will not harm you." Alma reached out her hand, worsening the woman's fear.

The older woman muttered something in a foreign language, prompting the others to walk a few meters back. One lifted a woven sack from the ground, the other grabbed a pair of hand-made moccasins. They brought them to Alma where the one with the sack held it open in front of her. It contained some kind of bread and several unrecognizable vegetables. She made a chewing motion and pointed toward her own mouth. "Sief."

Alma was starving, so she reached into the bag, tore a piece of bread off a hard loaf, and placed it on her tongue. It tasted awful. She hid her dislike of the dry grainy thing and continued eating with a big smile. She was reluctant to try the odd looking vegetables.

The young woman rummaged around inside her bag

before removing a squat brown root plant, probably her favorite. She stood on the balls of her feet and held it to Alma's mouth. This one reminded her of Dawn. She stretched out her arms, pushing the plant as close to Alma's lips as possible. "Hasief," she said, insisting Alma taste it.

Alma bent down and unenthusiastically pressed her teeth into the ugly plant. She made an exaggerated look of pleasure as she chewed the disgusting vegetable with a nod and a smile. "Mmmm." It was reminiscent of the bloody metal taste one gets when they bite the inside of their cheek.

The shy woman avoided direct eye contact, dropped the moccasins in front of her, and stepped behind her group. Alma slipped her feet into the moccasins and noted that, again, they were a perfect fit.

Their leader uttered something Alma couldn't understand, shooing them away. Bag of food in hand, they walked off together, whispering and laughing to each other. The friendlier woman kept glancing back at Alma with a coy smile as they made their way through the grassy field.

"Who are you and where am I?" Alma opened her mind and listen for Ymir's brutal voice. What she heard was unfamiliar. The feelings it provided were different, depressing, giving her an overwhelming sense of despair. There was a presence, but it wasn't Ymir.

After the two younger women disappeared from view, her guide turned to follow them. She glanced over her shoulder while making sure Alma was keeping up. At the plateau's boundary they peered down on a sprawling village with thin plumes of smoke rising from numerous campfires scattered about.

Smells of burning wood and boiling vegetables filled the air as Alma and her companion traversed the steep rocky wall. At the base of the plateau, small people with shiny black hair were everywhere. Alma's tall strong body, pale skin, and long thick white hair was a jarring sight for the local inhabitants.

Near the entrance of the village, converging streams of villagers gathered in front of her, chattering to each other. Alma kept hearing one word echoing throughout the crowd, Æsir. Her heart was pounding hard enough to show a throbbing vein in her neck. She looked down on her guide and asked, "What does Æsir mean?"

Not understanding her words except that one, she rubbed two fingers on Alma's arm. "Æsir." She rubbed her fingers on her own arm and said, "Kohor." With a broad sweeping hand gesture over the front of her village, she repeated, "Kohor."

She led Alma further into the massive community. Everyone was about the same size and skin tone, and dressed similar. She didn't notice any grown people appearing male, but saw children running around, so she assumed men must be here somewhere.

Her despair and torment worsened as they moved closer to the village center. Her guide was leading her toward something terrible, but for reasons she failed to understand, she trusted her. They stopped in front of a wide building constructed of mud, branches, and grass. Alma followed her inside.

On the other side of the door, she stood horrified. Scattered throughout the large open room were tens of suffering people laying on filthy blankets in the dirt. Eye watering smells of rampant infection and drying blood filled the air. She tried not to gag or worse, vomit.

They were in agony, many of them coughing and drooling from broken jaws. Bruises, gashes, bleeding, missing limbs, missing eyes, this was a nightmarish display of random carnage. They appeared to be women at various stages of dying.

With a directional nod, Alma's guide gestured toward a Kohor woman near the middle of the room. She was missing an ear and eye from the right side of her head, while blood soaked cloths secured her shattered arms. Visible in her eyes, death was immanent.

Alma made her way to the young woman, tiptoeing around a maze of groaning people to kneel beside her. The damage to her body was horrendous, giving her the impression it was intentional. Every shred of this woman's trauma played out with unnecessary realism in her imagination.

She peered deep into the woman's ravaged body, running her mind's eye through her sinew, bones, and organs. She traversed and memorized the winding lattices of her DNA. Although similar in appearance, there were enough differences to know these Kohor weren't human.

Particles of matter from the surrounding air and dirt swept into her patient's failing body. She manipulated them like clay, squeezing and sculpting them into the basic cells needed to stitch the mutilated woman back together.

In her head, this process lasted hours, but to everyone who experienced her divine intervention, less than a second had passed. The young woman sat up and fumbled her way toward Alma where she wrapped her restored arms around her.

With each broken person, the task of mending them

grew easier and faster, automatic. Alma lifted her exhausted body from the ground and made her way back to her new friend, who didn't appear the least bit surprised by what she witnessed. She looked into the woman's confident face. "You know what I am." She recalled the words of that tall insane man in the Texas desert. "Are you the Speaker for this place?"

She stared into her guides eyes, into her black irises, and followed thin branches of green and purple radiating from her pupils. They reminded her of bird feathers reflecting ambient light. Alma rubbed two fingers on her arm. "Raven. Until you tell me your real name, I will call you Raven."

Raven and Alma wandered through the village repairing injured villagers as they happened upon them. She wanted to prove her skills reached beyond living things, so she fixed a broken clay pot laying in pieces beside the door of a modest home. People followed them around like excited groupies. Children vied for her attention, crisscrossing in front of her while performing, what they believed to be, impressive stunts.

It didn't take long for her to fall in love with her new family. Alma ate their disgusting food and enjoyed their weird music. She loved playing with the little children, teaching them games she relished as a child in Iceland. Raven stuck to her side. They were inseparable. Their language barrier crumbled as they developed their own non-verbal communication.

Alma delighted in her developing connections with the Kohor people. A blanket of contentedness warmed her thoughts for the first time in her adult life, but that depressing voice continued to haunt her.

Deep within the bowels of an observation platform orbiting the Kohor moon, Cartara, thousands of bluish-pink women and men went about their normal daily routines. Researchers stood in front of inverted egg-shaped consoles spaced at regular intervals along the perimeter of every open room in this gigantic installation.

In a nondescript room filled with thin bald people facing oval dents carved into the walls, a series of sweeping bright white lights caught one man's eye. His Kohor village required attention. Absent any emotion, he stroked the lights, sending hours of recorded scenes into his optical implants.

His mind played sequences of images depicting an overview of Alma mingling with the Kohor people. He zoomed in as the movies replayed, closer and closer until he was sure she wasn't one of them. His composure eroded into a subtle anxiety. He alerted the military.

Expressionless soldiers marched down long corridors into a hangar containing space-faring shuttles of various sizes and purpose. The group of men entered a shiny metallic ship big enough to accommodate their fifteen-person team.

The shuttle lifted as a large door beneath it slid open to show the colorful Kohor moon. It passed from the warmth and safety of its mother into the harsh cold of space on its short journey to Raven's village.

Alma didn't see or hear the shiny intruder approaching. Raven made several attempts at describing them, her torturers, the murderers of her people, but their language barrier was too considerable for the flourish of angry words she used whenever the subject came up.

When the ship revealed itself against the hazy sky, Kohor scattered in fear. Panicked screams emanated from every direction as Alma stood mesmerized watching the trespasser drift to the ground. She had never seen a real spaceship before. If not for the widespread terror, this could have been an exhilarating experience.

A flood of incredible dread rippled throughout her body, raising the hairs on the back of her neck. The darkness grew heavier with each passing moment. That voice, this world's voice, did not like these people.

Feelings of homicidal rage were nothing new for Alma. Ymir's push to wipe out large swaths of the human population was a regular occurrence, but this felt different. There was an urgency to these emotions, as if lives depended on her willingness to kill.

Alma ran toward the village entrance to greet their visitors, dragging a reluctant Raven by the hand. She stopped in awe as the beautiful mirrored ship slowed its descent to hover above the ground. It was a breathtaking scene, but something was wrong. There was an invisible shroud enveloping it, confusing her thoughts.

A wide door slid open to reveal five ugly, thin, bald, bluish-pink men readying to jump out. They stood a few centimeters shorter than herself, and were dressed in machine crafted uniforms, unlike the handmade clothing of the Kohor.

The shroud protecting their ship from Alma's

influence followed them as they emerge. The harder she tried to focus on it or the grotesque blue people, the more her tormented brain grew overwhelmed with feelings of frustration and helplessness.

Raven grabbed her arm and screamed a word quite familiar to her. "Hættulegt!" Alma froze at the sound of Raven's dire warning in her own native language. Raven waved her fingers in the direction of the blue people. "Trey!"

Alma recognized that Kohor word. Villagers have uttered it many times, and not in a friendly manner. From the context of their conversations, and her profound rage, she assumed these were the monsters who had been harming them.

Two thin blue men pushed a tall metallic box from their ship. It floated above the ground as they positioned it between themselves and the village. One of them called out to Raven in her language and gestured toward Alma. Raven, worried, pulled Alma behind her and shouted another Icelandic word, "Búr!"

Their shiny enclosure was some kind of cage. She couldn't imagine anything capable of imprisoning her, but didn't want to test that assumption. Alma yelled over Raven's head, "No!"

A rapid pulse of bright beads streamed from the top of the ship, destroying nearby buildings. Screams of fear and pain echoed throughout the village as Kohor families burned inside their homes.

The man reiterated Raven's word. "Búr."

Alma closed her eyes and allowed Cartara's powerful anger to guide her. Dirt and clay churned deep under the soldier's feet, converging and compressing into a long thin spike. A razor sharp ridge rose from the spike, wrapping helically from top to bottom, resembling a three-meter-long screw.

The screw spun underfoot, pushing back soil as it tunneled upward toward its unfortunate target. It erupted from the ground and plunged between his legs. Dark purple blood, tissue, and bone radiated in every direction.

It continued up his body, shredding and mixing his internal organs, and burst through his skull. Brain matter and bloodied flesh splashed across horrified Trey soldiers. His gruesome death happened so fast he didn't have an opportunity to scream.

Crew members inside the ship launched another salvo of beads at Alma to cover the retreat of their team. A solid barricade of dense matter formed between them, blocking their assault.

As the ship lifted into the air, a massive wave of rocks and dirt flowed up and over it, rolling it onto its side. Alma forced Cartara to open wide and swallow the tumbling vessel, then buried it under a pile of heavy boulders.

Raven shook her hands in the air, screaming words Alma didn't understand. It was obvious she was warning about more ships in orbit, so Alma turned her focus upward, scanning both sky and space, but found nothing.

Much larger beads of light rained down across the village. Alma did her best to stop them, but many hit their targets. Kohor families were dying, and it was her fault. She repeated Dawn's chant with a slight modification. "I am your hands and eyes. Raven is your ears and mouth." She cleared her mind and gave herself to this world's voice. It wanted her to find those ships. It wanted her to hunt the blue people and slaughter them all.

Alma traced the beads into orbit and found a hollow frustrating hole in space. She gathered every spec and clump of matter floating nearby and formed a long spear, which she hurled into the nothingness. It disintegrated against a shield, leaving a small shell of dust around one end of an invisible bubble.

She collected more debris and smashed it into the oblong sphere until it was covered in a thin layer of visible dust. Their shields repelled her dust, but she pushed back, causing trillions of tiny specs to hop on its surface. Several particles managed to penetrate the shield, disappearing into the void.

Patterns allowing her dancing dust a predictable route inside emerged. Alma created a new spear with a point so fine it couldn't be seen by human eyes, and threw it toward her ball of dirt, piercing its shell, but nothing happened. She made more. Spears from every direction entered the space she couldn't see or feel.

A few hundred passed through the barrier before one of them destroyed a part of the Trey ship that kept it invisible. Alma crushed it into a super-dense ball, killing the tens of thousands of people on board. Her compact ball produced new unstable elements. These heavy elements fused together, releasing their energy in an explosion brighter than any star.

Fueled by an intoxicating mixture of rage and wartime victory, she vacuumed up every bit of matter she could reach outside Cartara. She broke her collection down into single atoms and rearranged their particles to construct a cloud of hydrogen large enough to encircle the entire moon.

When one of her atoms impacted a concealing shield, thousands of spears formed, weaving through the empty space. Ship after ship revealed themselves, allowing her to crush them into volatile balls no bigger than her palm. The Trey research vessels were too big and slow to evade her murderous tirade.

Hundreds of thousands of Trey perished before she could find no more ships to puncture and squash. Alma dropped to Raven's feet, exhausted. Hours in her mind were milliseconds to the Kohor people. From their perspective, the brilliant explosions appeared simultaneously in the skies above.

Pleased by Alma's incredible show of power and mercy to her Kohor children, Cartara rewarded her by flooding her body with an impassioned spiritual joy. Tears streamed uncontrollable from her eyes. Ymir's emotions were never this intense, or pleasurable.

Raven put her hands on Alma's shoulders. Her world's voice finally gave them a Caretaker not weakened by generations of torture at the hands of Trey oppressors. She cried along with Alma while hugging her head tight against her belly.

This world opened her heart to Alma. She wasn't one of her cherished Kohor, she was a stranger. She reached out to the stars seeking help and was provided this loving demigoddess. Cartara gave herself to Ymir, joining the two worlds together in a rare and monumental pact.

Alma stood as her mind filled with images of familiar and unfamiliar places. She smiled at visions of the beautiful Earth and her glorious diversity. She could see and touch the entire human and Kohor solar systems, and then there was Dawn's proud beaming smile. Overcome, she dropped back to the ground, sobbing at Raven's feet.

Chapter 4

David Trauger

Alma stepped from one world into another, appearing on the tarmac of the American Air Force base nearest where their military murdered her and Captain Belfort. She had a better understanding for how someone could justify taking extreme measures to protect the people they cared about.

Sirens sounded throughout the base upon Alma's arrival. The AI, aware of her return, ordered a dozen expendable humans to engage. Alma squinted at the sunlight glinting off a group of military vehicles racing down the runway in her direction, their images blurred by heated air rising from the road.

They do not know what is happening. They are only doing their jobs. She knelt on the ground and placed her hands on top of her head, fingers interlaced, waiting for them to take her into custody.

A team of agitated Military Police officers leapt from their moving trucks and surrounded her with weapons drawn. One officer barked out orders, "Stand up and turn around!" He bound her wrists behind her back and forced her into the rear of his vehicle. After securing their cargo, the prisoner convoy rushed toward a cluster of large structures near the perimeter of the base.

On their approached of an abandoned aircraft hangar, Alma sensed a familiar frustrating emptiness. There was a cage waiting for her in that building. She was curious as to how the Americans possessed a technology similar to the much more advanced Trey.

The brakes of her truck made an ear-piercing squeal as it stopped in front of the hangar door. Her driver dragged her from the vehicle as the other officers surrounded her with weapons in hand. Cuffed from behind, they pushed her through the service entrance. Once inside, her worlds vanished under a dark cloud of frustration and confusion.

Alma didn't anticipate their cage enveloping the entire building. Blanketed in an agitating feeling of hopelessness, she looked for a way out. Trapped and powerless, her head drooped with wide open eyes. Ymir's and Cartara's voices fell silent.

The Military Police, oblivious to who or what she was, guided her to an empty office and forced her down onto a dusty chair. They left the room with two of them taking positions at either side of the door. She slouched into the filthy chair and stared at an empty gray wall, contemplating her impotence.

After ten terrifying minutes, an older man in desert military combat fatigues entered and took a seat at the other side of the desk. He was big, with broad shoulders and a thick strong chest. His harsh lined face showed the stress of many difficult decisions. Three stars adorn his collar and the name sewn into his camouflaged jacket read, TRAUGER. His large stature conjured agonizing memories of her father.

He swiped open his tablet and read aloud, butchering her name, "Alma Ólafsdóttir. Born..." He glanced up with an annoyed smirk. "You look damn good for an eighty-four-year-old. It says you were born in some unpronounceable city in Iceland. You were born female? I guess they're trying something new this time."

Her situation stirred feelings she hadn't felt in decades. She feared this man. "Akureyri. They?"

"They, him, her, it, you all call them something different." He looked into her trembling eyes. "I'm wondering, how did you know the missile was coming? We thought we did a good job hiding that thing from you."

"Missile?" Alma had no idea what he was talking about. She found herself in a state of confusion every time she set foot in this country.

"In the desert." He hoisted a thumb backwards over his shoulder. "You could have saved him too, you know. For someone claiming to want to help us, saving one of our people would have gone a long way toward building trust."

His casual attitude about killing one of his own people shocked her. "I did not escape your bomb. You killed me, and you murdered one of your own soldiers to do it." Tension radiated through her jaw, forcing her teeth together. "I do not know how long I was dead. When I woke on that other planet, I did not even know where I was."

"Planet?" His tone mimicked that of a man talking down to a fibbing child. "Is this a language issue?" His icy stare was intended to intimidate her, and it worked.

"I died, and I woke on another world where I met people called Kohor. I saw other people too. Horrible people. Trey."

The General's phone vibrated itself to the edge of the desk. He put it to his ear, but didn't speak. His lack of expression gave no clues as to what the caller was saying. Without acknowledging the call, Alma, or explaining anything, he stood and left the office.

"Where are you going?" She tried to turn her old heavy chair around. Some pathetic feeling deep down inside, one of her own feelings, made her want him to stay. His domineering presence was more comforting than sitting alone in that ugly bunker.

A couple of minutes passed before a man and a young woman joined her in the room. They didn't look as menacing as the General, definitely not soldiers. Their average stature and purposeful demeanor reminded her of doctors. She hoped they weren't planning on dissecting her.

The middle-aged man sat in the General's chair and the young woman took a seat on an old sofa against the wall to Alma's right. "Hi Alma, I'm Major Craig Halvorson and this is Captain Stacey Martin." Stacey's youthful appearance caught her attention.

He tipped his head to the side and yelled toward the open door. "Can someone take off her handcuffs?" The officer who cuffed her entered, removed her restraints, and returned to his post.

Craig made an artless attempt at smiling, hoping to convince her she could trust them. "Kohor. I'd love to know where you heard that word. Can you describe them?" His enthusiastic but phony demeanor was off-putting. She preferred the older mean looking General.

Alma rubbed her unrestrained wrists and sneered at Craig. "One of the women told me that is what they are called. I named her Raven because her hair and eyes make me think of blackbird feathers." She couldn't help glancing over at the young blonde woman who didn't appear nervous, scared, or excited. Alma's suspicious mind didn't trust her.

"They are much smaller than I am and quite thin, maybe because they eat only vegetables. All of them have black shiny hair and dark eyes. Raven is in charge. I believe she is the Speaker for their world."

Surprised, they both stopped tapping on their tablets to focus on her. Alma sat up straight, her eyes widened. "Now what did I say?"

Craig put down his tablet and laid his arms open on the table. "Can you tell us about the other people. The ones that the Kohor didn't like. The Trey?"

His obvious psychological attempts at comforting her were doing the opposite. "They are ugly people, with purple skin and gigantic black eyes. They tried to imprison and kill me." She scowled and glanced around the room. "Like this, but they failed. They have ships and weapons that are unlike anything I have ever seen on Earth except for in movies."

Alma locked eyes with Craig and snarled. "You are better at prisons and killing, though. They came down from much larger ships in space. I ended them all. This was the first time I intentionally harmed a living creature, except insects and farm animals for food or mercy."

Craig couldn't contain his excitement. "How did you kill them?"

Alma recalled Dawn with that bug in the library, wondering if she made the Trey stronger by removing the ones stupid enough to attack her friends. "I crushed their large ships so small they exploded, likely similar to that bomb you murdered Mr. Belfort with."

Stacey was paying much closer attention now. Her nostrils flared. "If we let you go, or you found a way to escape, would you kill us?"

She couldn't stop thinking of the beautiful Kohor people who died because she refused to get into the Trey cage. "No, you are misguided while trying to protect humans from me. The Trey murdered innocent people to force my surrender. I killed them because they hurt my friends. If you hurt my friends, yes, I will kill you. I will kill anyone who helps you. I will bury this entire base deep inside Earth."

Alma's dark diatribe set Stacey's heart pounding. A lopsided grin adorned her face. "Can you see both worlds?"

"I cannot see anything. Your stupid cloud is making me blind and irritable. How does such a thing exist in two different solar systems?" She motioned upward to the shroud surrounding the building. "Before I was forced into this place I could see everything, planets, moons, floating rocks and two stars. More than before you killed me."

Craig leaned over the office desk. "So, the military killed you, and you came back on another world. Now you can see and interact with everything in both solar systems, but before they killed you, you only saw the

Earth?" He appeared proud, as if the military gave her a gift by nuking her.

"When I woke there I could see only that place on that planet. Nothing more." She couldn't stomach looking at him any longer. Something about him made her uncomfortable.

"I saved her people and I stopped their torture by killing the invaders. She was begging me to do it by filling me with anger and hate. When I killed them all, then I could see everything. That world gave herself to Ymir. Ymir is very happy with me."

Stacey was showing greater interest than Craig at this point. "You're not like the others. None of them had this level of control over matter."

Craig tapped a few buttons on his tablet, causing the veil to retract from around the hangar. Alma's body shivered with a rush of power as her mind's eye filled with two solar systems. She located their shroud making machine and opened the floor beneath it, dropping it to its death.

The wide grin of pride on Craig's face was reminiscent of a child who believed he deserved some kind of reward for releasing her. "Your existence challenges everything we know about your kind. We want to start building a mutual trust. I hope you'll stay a little while longer."

Worried Alma was planning to leave, Stacey spoke. "We thought we knew so much about you. We know about the Kohor and the Trey and others, but you, you're special. You're so much more impressive than anything we could have imagined."

Alma didn't disappear, which they welcomed. Craig's eyes popped open with a sudden epiphany. "You were on their world, their home. You can make this whole problem go away."

"What problem?" Every time an American spoke, she got the impression she was missing out on important information. It was difficult for her to imagine this wasn't intentional.

"The Kohor will be here in less than three years." Craig swiped at his tablet and turned it around for her to see. "These Kohor are not like your friends." His finger hovered above a black picture with what appeared to be a bunch of fuzzy stars. He tapped on a large blurry star. "That right there, that's a ship. There are at least two others in line behind it."

He spread his fingers over the screen, making the fuzzy ship bigger. "They're massive. Hundreds of millions of Kohor soldiers and millions of small ships on each one. These smaller ships exist for one purpose, fighting. We can't defeat millions of armed, space capable craft with our inferior Air Force jets."

Stacey chimed in. "They've been here before." She waited for a reaction from Alma, and wasn't disappointed.

"When?" A flood of feelings from Ymir twisted her insides. Ymir loved Alma's new Kohor friends, but their distant cousins filled her with dread.

Stacey swiped a finger across her tablet, searching for one of her reports. "From what we could get from the downed Kohor ship, they were here..."

Alma interrupted, "Kohor ship? You have one of their ships?" She whipped her head back and forth from Stacey to Craig, wanting to hear more.

Stacey continued. "... A few thousand years ago in China. I haven't seen the ship. It's a scout ship of some kind. The Russian military shot it down over one of their Navy harbors. There were no survivors, but they did recover a body. From what they tell us, its propulsion systems and shields are beyond our technology, but their computer data, that's woefully insecure and simple to decipher."

"I want to see it. Why does she not know where it is?" Ymir knew where it was, but she feared Russian technology and what they would be willing to do with it. "I will touch it, this ship."

Alma stood and Craig stood face-to-face with her. "They won't trust you, and they know as much about you as we do." He didn't wish to seem like he was challenging her, so he sat back down. "Please don't go there." Alma vanished before he could complete his sentence.

Dawn's face lit up when Alma appeared in her living-room. Their eyes welled with tears as Dawn jumped from her bar-stool at the kitchen counter and ran into Alma's open arms. "You were gone for so long." She balanced on her tiptoes and nuzzled her neck. "I forgot how good you smell."

Alma never thought about how long she was dead before waking on Raven's world. "How long was I gone?" She believed she was with the Kohor people for at least four weeks, but their days were different.

Dawn muffled her words in Alma's hair. "Almost three months. I couldn't feel you at all, but she told me you were okay. It was hard to believe her, but I forced myself. She told me you're much stronger now. She says you're amazing."

Alma wanted to talk about the Kohor, but doubted Dawn would be interested. "There are other people out there. The American military seems to think there are even more than I saw. They already knew about that other world. They know so much. Much more than I do."

Dawn continued hugging and sniffing her. "Ymir is so proud of what you did over there. The flood of new images I'm getting are confusing and make me tired. I can't hear or feel that other place. Is there someone like me over there?"

"Her name is Raven. She may have told me her real name, but I cannot understand what she says." Alma ran a hand down Dawn's long auburn hair. "She is not young and happy like you. She seems mostly sad."

"I met bad people too, but something is not right about them." Alma's voice lowered. "They are much more advanced than us, but terrible at fighting. They were easy for me to stop. Your military, they are much smarter about these things. Like war. When they begin to understand that technology, they will not need me any longer."

Dawn faked a little smile and tried to speak in a gentle reassuring manner. "They need us, and we need them. We're all humans, and we belong together."

Alma exclaimed, "They have a ship, a spaceship!"

Dawn squinted and wrinkled her nose, wondering how backward Iceland must be. "We have lots of ships in space. There are even a few space stations up there. Americans have been in space since way before I was born."

"No, the Russians. They did not build it. Their air force shot it down, I believe. It was not created by humans." She turned away and stared through Dawn's patio window. "I want to feel it. Come with me." Alma reached out, beckoning Dawn to her side.

Dawn hesitated as a concerned look blanketed her face. "She wants us and the United States military to be partners, friends. Talk to them first. They understand these things better than we do, maybe more than Ymir does, and you'll need their help on that other world. You can't fight a battle and not expect your enemy to regroup and come back stronger and more prepared. Things are going to get a lot worse."

Alma returned to the dusty office where she was held captive, with Dawn at her side. The immediate change from her apartment to a dingy gray room illuminated by bad lighting was disorientating. "That was weird. Please don't tell me this is Russia."

Her cautious eyes darted around the empty room while her mind searched for another machine that could disable her abilities. "American soldiers imprisoned me here for a time. I broke their machine, so we should be safe."

Alma and Dawn heard voices coming from the main hangar, so they left the office to investigate. Her two interrogators were standing and talking with General Trauger, surrounded by Military Police. A nearby soldier snapped his hand to his side-arm as everyone turned to look.

She stared at the armed man with an expression of knowing ridicule, and addressed the General in a loud voice. "I did not go to Russia." She didn't understand why, but she craved his approval.

General Trauger walked across the room to join them. "Of course you didn't. We nuked Texas to stop you. I can only imagine what the Russian's would be willing to do." Not wanting his soldier harmed, he made a subtle hand gesture ordering him to stand down. "If other nations think we're talking, it'll be a world war. Probably the last war ever on this planet."

"I do not want a war, but it was hard not to go there. Dawn convinced me to come here first. She wants us to work with you." Alma placed one hand in the middle of Dawn's back and pushed her forward until she stood face to chest with the giant American General.

"Hi." She nervously bobbed on the balls of her feet. Dawn's hero worship of the United States military landed her in front of an actual General. To her, the American military represented humanity at its fittest and finest.

General Trauger offered his hand. "Dawn, it's nice to meet you in person. You can call me David. Full disclosure, we've been watching you for a while."

With a beaming smile, Dawn wrapped both hands around his and didn't want to let go. She fought a powerful desire to jump into his huge arms. "I know. She told me about the people in the cars, and the drones, and the microphones. I don't care. She told me you're afraid of us. I do kind of feel bad about that."

He towered awkward over the bubbly little teen. "With what we understand, you hear actual words from them, her?"

"Some words, more images and feelings. Intense feelings and pictures way more than anything else, but not like from a camera. More like what a toddler would draw with crayons." Her instant adoration of him was something she had for only one other person, Alma. Dawn moved in closer. "She wants us all to be partners."

His authoritarian voice sounded calm and diplomatic as he pivoted toward Alma. "We'll have to work out a lot of trust issues first. Not going to Russia, knowing we couldn't stop you, that was a big deal. We appreciate that."

"I want to touch that Kohor ship." She wedged between Dawn and the General, attempting to interfere with a creepy energy oozing from her. "I do not know why I feel the need to do this, but I need to do this."

Craig and Stacey squeezed themselves into their circle. Craig interrupted, "I wonder if you could copy it without them knowing."

Alma was growing frustrated with people making statements assuming she understood their meaning. "I do not know what you mean. Copy?"

"How long have you had your abilities?" Craig regretted the patronizing tone in his voice. He turned his head down and braced for some kind of punishment.

Irritated, Alma responded, "Longer than you have been alive."

"I'm sorry, I didn't mean to say it like that. It's just that you don't seem to understand your own remarkable capabilities." A chair sitting alone in a corner of the hangar caught his eye. "You can move that chair across the room. You can also make it appear across the room without moving it. Right?"

She didn't understand where he was going with this, but she played along. "Yes." Without a sound, the little metal chair appeared on the other side of the hangar.

General Trauger shook his head in disbelief. "Damn." Dawn giggled.

Craig wasn't surprised, but he was somewhat

44

shocked by her willingness to perform for them. "I want your permission to activate some sensors in this building. This isn't like the veil. It just alerts us when you alter things on a, a quantum level."

Although apprehensive, she nodded.

Craig tapped a few buttons on his tablet and started recording sensor telemetry. "Can you push the chair, please?"

The chair slid across the concrete floor making a tooth-scratching grinding metallic noise. Its movements highlighted a stream of blocks in a three-dimensional grid on Craig's tablet. "Now, copy the chair into a different location."

Alma's response was terse. "I do not know what you mean."

Dawn, with Ymir's assistance, tried to simplify things for Alma. "Make the chair appear somewhere else without destroying the original." Dawn threw her hands in the air and yelled, "Wait! Did you kill me and recreate me when you brought me here?"

Stacey smiled at her auburn haired doppelgänger. "Alma reorders subatomic particles to form the matter needed to create objects, like that chair, and you. If she didn't dismantle the original particles, there would be two of you."

Dawn grabbed Alma's arm, squeezing hard. "You need to let people know this before you move them around. This can seriously mess with someone's personal beliefs." She wanted to pretend that being destroyed and recreated with different matter wasn't an issue, but her mind was spinning as she labored to accept what she learned.

Alma struggled to calculate the amount of times she killed and recreated herself. It was a large number.

She looked to Dawn with apologetic eyes. "I was not aware this was happening. I am so sorry." The last thing she wanted was to instill fear in people. It crushed her heart knowing she upset her friend.

General Trauger was growing annoyed of the unhelpful banter. "Can you copy that chair without destroying the original?" Dawn moved away from Alma and closer to him, close enough their arms touched.

Alma returned her focus to the chair. On the other side of the hangar a new chair, a molecular identical twin to the one in front of them, appeared. "Apparently, I can." The ramifications of her newly-discovered ability frightened her. She could make fifty Dawns or a million of the same adorable puppy.

Craig glanced up from his tablet with a thin wide smile stretching across his ecstatic face. "No sensors tripped around the original chair. Sir, I'm confident she can copy the Kohor ship without the Russians knowing."

Ymir understood Craig's enthusiasm and disclosed the Kohor ship's location to Alma. The twisted remains of a damaged spaceship laid in pieces in the center of an otherwise empty hangar. No defense sirens blared, no missiles arced over the planet. The Russians didn't attack.

General Trauger whispered again, "Damn."

Chapter 5

Demigoddesses

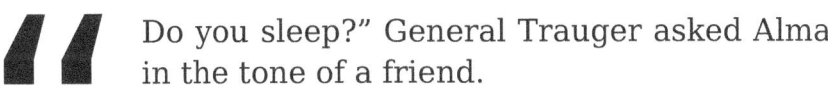Do you sleep?" General Trauger asked Alma in the tone of a friend.

She was getting bored with their questions, but at least this one was new. "No." Alma couldn't remember the last time she slept, unless she counted her death at the hands of the American military.

Alma, Dawn, General Trauger, Stacey, and Craig sat around a beautiful mahogany conference room table in one of the nicer buildings on the Air Force base. "Fantastic."

General Trauger gestured to Craig. "You're going to help her become an engineer, and we don't have much time." He pivoted to Alma with a conciliatory smile. "Assuming you're willing to work with us?"

Alma wouldn't mind if he phrased his requests as orders. There was something comforting about someone else taking charge, making her life less complicated. She didn't know if it was him, his military training, or Ymir's influence, but she enjoyed the lack of chaos and uncertainty in his rigid military world.

Dawn's dreamy eyed focus on this weathered old man made apparent her desire to join their conversation. "Is there anything I can do?"

General Trauger chuckled at her doe-eyed freckled face. "I've read a lot about your abilities and I have an important job for you if those things are even half true. You and your invisible friend can help us vet some engineers."

He held a hand out to Stacey and Craig. "I trust these two, and I trust you'd know if I shouldn't. We're going to need a lot more people like them, and it would only take one person to blow this up into an international disaster."

"We trust them, and of course we'll help out any way we can." Dawn wasn't exaggerating. No one in her life caused her to feel this useful and wanted, not Alma, not Ymir.

Dawn's apparent infatuation with the General disgusted Alma, prompting her to lean in and whisper, "Are you certain this is Ymir you are feeling?" She attempted to mask her annoyance with a humored inflection. "I need you to listen to her voice, not your teenage body."

Her question forced Dawn to pucker her face. She wasn't attracted to him, that much. Her feelings were something different, similar to adoration. "Don't be gross. Ymir wants him on that other planet. She wants him and the military to secure the entire Kohor solar system and I have to stay here." She breathed in deep through Alma's hair. "You always smell so good."

Alma patted her hand. "Okay." She realized General Trauger and the engineers had been talking this whole time, and pretended she was listening. "I am not good at math."

Craig made a timid half-hearted chuckle. "We're confident you're going to be an incredible asset. Don't worry about the math." He spun his tablet around to show her a live-streaming video feed of the hangar holding their copy of the mangled Kohor ship. "We were hoping the first thing you could do is create five more of these."

Without making a sound, five identical shipwrecks appeared staggered throughout the hangar. It took Craig a moment to notice them on his screen. "God you're awesome, and a little terrifying to be honest."

Alma recoiled. "You must know I am not dangerous. I will not harm anyone."

General Trauger rapped his knuckles on the table. "Alma, you're very dangerous. There are stories estimating ninety percent of humanity has perished in various wars fighting people like you." He addressed the entire team in a commanding voice. "We all know Alma is different. There has never been this level of cooperation in the past, and I trust her implicitly." He focused on her indignant eyes. "Don't lie to yourself. You're dangerous, and you need to accept that."

Upset that his unpalatable words rang true, no matter how much she wished otherwise, Alma's voice grew deliberate and angry. "As are you."

General Trauger acknowledged her with a quick

nod. "That's why no one can know about you. The two of us working together? No nation will let that happen without a fight."

Dawn sat behind a small table outside a service door to the hangar, basking under a hot Texas sun. She wore desert military fatigues with her long auburn hair pulled back and folded into a camouflaged hat. Nothing could remove the huge grin from her face. She wasn't an official member of the United States Air Force, but she wore that glorious flag on her arm with beaming pride.

Teams of excited engineers funneled into a queue in front of Dawn's table. One by one, each person presented their government issued identification cards for her approval, oblivious to the true nature of her job. Dawn gave herself to Ymir, and together, they vetted the potential engineers.

Security around her was tight. There were more Military Police than people in line. They were under strict orders to protect and aid her in any way she required. Dawn loved having her own police force. If someone didn't feel right, she'd wave an officer or two over and have them take the confused engineer for later questioning. Intoxicated with power, she raised the standards for her selection process.

Those Dawn removed, Ymir didn't like for various reasons. When she rejected a person, they were escorted or dragged away into a holding room off the side of the building. Some struggled with officers only to be subdued by force. Dawn delighted in watching them overpower her rejected candidates.

With the line cleared of hopeful scientists and engineers, General Trauger walked her into a viewing room where she could see her collection of losers through a one-way mirror. "I'm going to have them stand, one at a time. You tell me what the issue is with them." Each of them happened to be male.

General Trauger entered the room filled with Military Police and sidelined men nervously wondering what was happening. He adjusted his earpiece and looked into the mirror. "Anyone in particular you'd like to start with?"

Dawn shouted, assuming he could hear, "Start with the one on the far right." General Trauger waved for the man to step forward. His large powerful stature made him stand out from the other engineers. With no concern in her voice, she announced, "He's a Russian, or he works with them." She was enjoying this.

Trauger tilted his head to the mirror with wide eyes and hands gesturing as if to say, "What?" Without further hesitation, he commanded his officers to escort the man away. "Hold him." Two MPs walked him out of the room for a more thorough interrogation. "I hope that was the worst of them." Dawn's connection with Ymir made the huge and flawed process of military background checks useless. She was incredible. Plans to march thousands of base personnel passed her filled his mind.

"The rest of them are just gross. One is really fat." Dawn motioned to a man missing his left arm below the elbow. "How do you look at these people without gagging?" She singled out another man. "That first gross guy, he's terrified of something. I mean, really fucking terrified."

General Trauger disliked Dawn's lack of compassion

but had complete confidence in her abilities. He ordered his officers to detain the man, certain they'd find something. "Search him, everywhere."

A stone-faced officer recovered a tiny storage device secured inside the man's belly button with some sticky substance. He handed it to the General and continued his meticulous search. Trauger looked into the mirror. "So, you know what he was planning to do with this?"

"Nope, but he's panicking, big time. You should probably shoot him." Anyone unfamiliar with Dawn might have assumed she was joking, and they would be wrong.

Trauger made a hand gesture that seemed to be orders for the officers to bind the man's arms and legs. They lifted the hog-tied man and carted him away. He understood that the standard military vetting process for engineers was more stringent than for soldiers, which brought a disgusted sneer to his lips. His base security personnel would hear from him.

"The human species would be better without that man in it. Just saying." Dawn pulled back from Ymir's obsessive urge to kill imperfect people. "Maybe cut all their balls off? We don't need them polluting our gene pool."

Trauger ignored her latest descent into homicidal eugenics, he was getting used to it. He left the interrogation room and rejoined Dawn on the other side of the wall. "We'll be checking that last guy and the Russian out more thoroughly." He looked away, uncomfortable with her cruelty. "The others, they're all hard workers. Some people deserve a break."

Dawn made an exaggerated puking convulsion. "Deserve? Who are you to decide that? You take money and purpose from viable strong genetic stock because you feel bad about these people being disgusting?" She removed her hat, letting her hair fall over her shoulders.

"That huge one, you know he gets off on eating more than his fair share, right? He intentionally damages his own body, for pleasure!" Dawn wiggled her fingers in General Trauger's face. "They don't care about anything but their own temporary gratification and getting their next high. They're selfish. Don't reward them. Especially when better people are available."

General Trauger stood expressionless, absorbing Dawn's anger like a boot-camp soldier in a drill line. He was growing accustomed to her tantrums, and he learned not to engage when she got this way. "No matter how I feel, they're all being removed from the project." He opened the hangar door and motioned for her to follow. "You and Alma have the final word on the people we work with."

The hangar was noisy with teams of Dawn-approved engineers poking and prodding at five of the six Kohor ships. Alma kept one for herself. "I cannot believe they built this." Her eye caught Dawn and General Trauger walking toward them. "They are so poor. They live in homes made of sticks and dirt." She ran two fingers across the side of the hull.

Stacey kept close to Alma. No one needed to order her to follow this demigoddess around, she was fascinated with her. "Have you ever heard the term, bomb them back to the Stone Age? According to their data, that's what the Trey did to their world."

"I cannot stand those ugly blue people." Alma's fingers popped up and down as they traveled over wrinkles and pits on the damaged ship's body. She savored the feeling of cold Kohor metal on her fingertips.

Stacey tapped Alma's arm while pointing at a picture on her tablet. "This is what it's supposed to look like, on the outside." Craig worked tirelessly reconstructing the original appearance of this ship from blurry Russian tracking videos and Kohor maintenance data.

Alma rubbed her finger on the image, making it spin and pivot in a virtual three-dimensional box. Wrinkles on the ship smoothed as she played with the computer generated model.

"Please don't do that." General Trauger whispered in a huff, but wanted to yell. "These people don't know about you."

Alma glanced around at the engineers. They were so preoccupied playing with alien technology, they never once looked in her direction. "Then I wish to be alone with this one."

Stacey raised her arm, volunteering for demigoddess-sitting duty. "I can stay with her, Sir."

Dawn made a creepy little smile, nudged Alma with her elbow, and giggled. Stacey turned toward the shipwreck, attempting to hide her blushing face.

Alma whispered into Dawn's ear. "I keep forgetting you are an actual child."

It didn't take long before Alma twisted and coerced her Kohor ship into shape, making it an exact replica of Craig's detailed model. She stepped back to admire her beautiful handiwork, which appeared out of place surrounded by a fleet of large gray military helicopters.

"Hmm. It's not exactly right." Dawn made a swirling motion in the air, highlighting an area near the front of the ship. "That's supposed to be a lot pointier."

Alma pursed her lips in frustration. "Why can she not tell me how to repair it?"

"I guess I'm supposed to do that, but I don't always know how to describe the pictures in my head." Dawn loved that she had a special ability of her own. She loved it more when people, like General Trauger, trusted her with it.

Stacey wedged between them and held a tablet in front of Dawn. "Can you draw? Or, can she draw through you?"

Dawn grabbed the tablet with a head shake and an eye roll. "I don't think you know how this works. Ymir doesn't control us. She can't do anything but talk to us." Playfully tapping on the screen, she spun the tiny three-dimensional ship around. "She doesn't even understand what this tablet is. Human technology scares the hell out of her."

Stacey hadn't worked close with Dawn, so she didn't understand that being annoyed was her normal state of mind. She softened her tone, trying not to anger her further, and asked, "How did she choose you?"

"She doesn't choose specific people." Dawn let out an exasperated breath. "When I was around twelve I got obsessed with healthy food and exercise. We were poor, so we didn't have phones or internet or television. I didn't have a bunch of ugly fat losers telling me I was good enough the way I was, so I tried hard to be better than everyone around me."

No longer disturbed by Dawn's savage disdain for imperfect humans, Alma smiled and shook her head as she endeavored to make her ship pointier. She did feel a twinge of sympathy for Stacey's palpable struggle with Dawn's personality.

Dawn slapped the tablet closed and focused on Stacey. "I started hearing her voice about six years ago and thought I was going crazy. Then she said things I couldn't possibly know. That's when I knew the voice was someone else. She's real, but she didn't choose either of us." Dawn examined Alma's body. "We listened to her and did everything she asked. It was a competition with billions of players, including you."

Stacey swallowed a subtle laugh as Dawn's eyes moved up and down Alma's body. She couldn't tell if Dawn found her attractive or if she was in awe of her. "So, anyone could have been what you are?"

"God no! Hundreds of years of stupid people breeding like animals has really fucked up our DNA. Nature used to kill off the worthless garbage people with diseases, bad weather, natural disasters, and wars." Dawn inspected Stacey's entire body with an approving smile. "The human species is a disgusting mess, but it won't be for long."

Alma's eyes widened. "What do you mean by that?"

"These people, your Kohor, they're going to kill so many useless humans." Dawn smiled to herself at the thought of humanity cleansed of imperfection. "They're going to do what nature can't do anymore. Human technology makes it too easy for idiots and losers to stay alive, and breed. It's so gross."

Alma turned away with an angry snarl. "Then why is she helping us stop them if she wants so many of us to die?"

"That's easy. The survivors will be the strong and intelligent. They'll breed new generations of awesome humans." She placed her palm against the ship with a disturbing look of arousal. "We'll make them better too. Just imagine all the thoughtless breeding going on in those giant spaceships."

Stacey grappled with the contradictions emanating from this attractive young woman, sensual one moment, terrifying the next. It was obvious there were at least two different people inside that beautiful head. "I would like to be better, like you. Is it too late?"

"You're hot and smart. You'll be fine, and Alma will make sure you're around for a very long time. The human species needs women like you to make lots of smart babies with strong, masculine men."

"How am I supposed to keep anyone around for a very long time? I have no desire to be a bodyguard for pretty people." Alma was trying to talk with Dawn and make repairs to her ship.

Dawn walked behind Alma and wrapped her arms around her belly, giving her a strong hug. She spoke with her mouth buried in one of Alma's long braids. "Do you remember that chair you were moving in that hangar? I'll bet you can make that exact chair right now, even if something completely destroyed the original one a long time ago."

Alma stopped playing with her ship as her face grew several shades more pale than normal. "Guð minn góður, what are you saying?"

"I'm surprised she hasn't made it super clear to you yet. She probably did, you just don't want to listen." Dawn moved behind Stacey and placed her hands on the sides of her shoulders. "You get to save the high quality humans, like this one. You know, the ones that care about themselves. The ones that make our entire species better. Let the useless eaters die and save the useful ones."

Stacey may have understood what Dawn was saying better than Alma did. She stepped closer with a gaze reflecting the same strange worship Dawn displayed for General Trauger. "Do you remember everything you've ever moved? Can you move me, please?" She wanted to be live forever, or at least for as long as Alma existed.

Alma despised being equated with a modern deity, but the ability to return people from death destroyed her argument she was a typical human with some interesting magic tricks.

The magnetic energy binding Stacey's particles released their grip, allowing them to fall apart. She didn't feel herself splintering into a swirl of subatomic dust, and in the blink of an eye, her life dissipated with a near undetectable radioactive puff.

On the other side of the hangar, Alma scooped up trillions of particles from the air, floor, and walls. She bound them together, creating new atoms. From those atoms she built the molecules needed to craft a perfect copy of the young engineer.

Stacey's head whipped back and forth as she scanned her change of location, then made her way across the giant room to rejoin them. "Thank you." At that moment she experienced something new, a kind of awakening. "Does this mean, if you choose, I'll live forever?" She understood this wasn't automatic, that Alma was the key to her eternal existence.

Dawn rolled her eyes, unable to hide her festering anger over Alma destroying and recreating her the first time, without permission. "Uh, Alma just killed you, so, you already died, once."

Alma wanted to earn Dawn's forgiveness but feared

she would make matters worse, so she puckered her lips and said nothing.

Dawn wrapped an arm around Alma's lower back and leaned against her shoulder. "Don't worry, I'll get over it."

Unlike Dawn, Stacey was a born scientist and engineer. She didn't view her destruction and reconstruction as an affront to some God. Alma's power over their physical universe excited her. Being an integral part of these two demigoddess's lives became her singular obsession.

General Trauger burst through the side door, interrupting Stacey's moment of spiritual enlightenment. He was delighted to view Alma's progress. "That looks fantastic!" His arms stretched out to the Kohor ship as if, from his perspective, he was holding it in his hands. "Are you already done?"

Alma's voice expressed disappointment. "I worked on the outside and some inside walls and floors. I do not know how to repair the more complicated things like the controls."

Trauger reassured her. "Craig has a team to help with that. Those people get all worked up about this stuff. They're annoying but I love them."

"Where are they? They need to help me finish it." She wanted to see this beautiful machine flying in the sky with Raven at its helm.

"They'll be here in a few minutes. Major Halvorson's briefing them on your unique capabilities. They're going to need you to learn some basic engineering, though." He glanced at Stacey with a confident smile. "These people are very intelligent. If they don't get frustrated with you, it means they're afraid of you or in awe of you. Be patient with them."

Dawn pressed her nose against his arm and breathed in his scent. She was disappointed he didn't smell as good as Alma. "I think they should play with the ship without Alma for a little while. Ymir wants you both to visit Cartara."

Alma, confused again and taking it personally, turned to Dawn with narrowed eyes. "Who is Cartara?"

It was easy for Dawn to forget that other people couldn't hear Ymir's words. "It's the Kohor name for that moon you were on."

Chapter 6

Raven

Alma and General Trauger peered down the plateau wall overlooking Raven's village. "You didn't ask if I was ready, or willing." He squinted at the greenish sky, trying to make sense of this moon's mother planet forming a short arc from one side of the world to the other. The curvature of the horizon indicated Cartara was much smaller than Earth.

"Ymir made me feel you were ready. Besides, you are an old soldier. You are always ready." It had been a few months since she last visited Raven's home. Alma fretted over her Kohor family while monitoring a buildup of frustrating holes in space. She assumed these were Trey ships gathering far enough away to feel safe from her influence.

Raven and two young women awaited them at the base of the plateau. Captivated by the site of Alma's large male counterpart, Raven couldn't stop staring at his broad chest. He was the tallest and widest person she had ever seen. His weathered reddish-pink face and intense blue eyes gave her the impression of potentially terrifying rage, which fascinated her.

General Trauger tilted his head toward Alma. "I've spent years hating these people, preparing to kill them. This may take some effort." He flashed a fake smile, as he would for any enemy before engaging.

Raven and the other women knelt in front of them. The voice in her head told her that kneeling was a sign of respect for Alma's people.

General Trauger didn't care for this. "Make them not do that, please."

"They believe we are people called Æsir." Alma shrugged. She sensed Ymir was hiding something about the true identity of these Æsir, who were both feared and respected by the Kohor. "I do not understand what that means, and no, I will not stop them. I do not make people do anything."

Raven stood, never breaking eye contact with General Trauger. "I apologize if we've offended you."

Alma's eyes widened. "When did you learn to speak English? How did you learn to speak English?"

"The voice inside my head taught me the language of the Æsir." Raven motioned to the women beside her. "I have not been able to teach my people, perhaps you could help?"

Alma wanted Ymir to teach Dawn Icelandic. Perhaps Ymir tried, but Dawn refused to learn her native language. "You may already speak better than I do." She followed Raven's gaze up to David's face. "This is United States Air Force General, David Trauger."

His name seemed unnecessarily long. She repeated Alma's words in her head, laboring to remember them. A slight confusion set in as she forgot some.

"Feel free to call me David. I understand you're the Speaker here?" David was uncomfortable looking down on this woman, who had to be shorter than Dawn.

His thunderous voice caught Raven by surprise. "I interpret the words and images in my head for all our people to benefit from. Before Alma, there was little benefit. That voice is much clearer now and more content."

Alma, still stunned over hearing near perfect English flowing from Raven's mouth, felt embarrassed about not knowing her real name. "I have been calling you Raven. What would you like me to call you? What is your name?"

She loved Alma so much she didn't care what she called her. "I don't mind the name you have chosen for me." That voice in her head tried to show her images of an actual raven from Earth, but she couldn't comprehend what a bird was.

Raven moved closer to David and reached out to rub the flag on his right arm. She was mesmerized by it. The embroidered patch looked complicated, far more involved than the beaded patterns the Kohor stitched into their clothing.

David became a popular curiosity for the villagers. Women young and old approached the giant pink Æsir warrior to get a better look. "Are we going to have a problem?" He spoke out above their heads.

Alma laughed at the fearsome soldier worrying about tiny Kohor women. She warned Raven, "Humans do not like being surrounded, or touched." This was the first time David saw her smile, and he enjoyed it, a lot.

With a sweeping hand gesture and some words in an alien language, the women retreated into the village. They could still be seen watching from around buildings and through windows.

Alma and David followed Raven down a wide dirt path dotted with small grass covered homes. David scanned the campfires and simple structures with a frown sullied face. These people weren't the same as the Kohor he'd been monitoring for two years. They were neglected, kept weak and scared. He had seen similar treatment on Earth many times before.

Raven did her best to keep the women a comfortable distance from him as they made their way to a modest house a few hundred meters in. A Kohor family was waiting for them around a pot of boiling vegetables with eager smiles on their faces. Raven's voice reflected rare pride. "We have prepared food for you."

Alma pulled David closer and whispered, "Their food is quite terrible. I expect you to smile and eat it."

Her wonderful scent caught him off guard. "I've been on missions to the worst places on Earth. I've eaten bugs, tree bark, dirt, and rats, a lot of rats. Don't worry about me."

Alma and David took seats on stiff pillows around a large smokey fire-pit. Raven wedged between them. "Are all Æsir men so big?" She appeared a bit friendlier than she did during Alma's last visit.

"I have told you we are not Æsir, and no, David is much larger than a normal human man. He is huge. I am also larger than most human women. We are different sizes depending on our purpose. David leads many soldiers, warriors. Human military leaders love their giant scary men."

Raven wobbled a little closer to him. "I don't think you're scary. We have few men in our village, and they are all the same size as the women."

Guð minn kæri. Like Dawn, Raven flaunted her infatuation with David. "There are very few men on your entire world. Those Trey are horrible monsters."

David picked up on Raven's behavior, but it wasn't quite the same as Dawn's. "There are millions of bigger Kohor men on their way to our world right now." He exaggerated their larger stature but wanted to give Raven something else to think about. The body extracted from the downed scout ship was a few centimeters smaller than the average Kohor villager. "If all goes well, they could be coming home soon."

Raven translated their words to the host family. A young Kohor girl sitting opposite them smiled a huge smile at the thought of more boys in her village. Raven however, disliked this idea. The voice in her head had been showing her images of Kohor brutality wrought upon Alma's people and the Trey in their distant past.

With dinner over, the generous family left them to discuss more serious matters. David couldn't stop looking up at the uncountable bright stars covering the sky. "I'd like to see one of those Trey ships, and their people."

"I squashed one under the ground over there. The living ones are far away. I believe they think I cannot see them, but I see thousands. Many more than before." She regretted dismissing Dawn's warnings about the Trey coming back as a larger and better prepared enemy. "I fear I have made things worse. More keep coming."

"Do they appear in the same area or around a central point in space?" The only reason he could imagine Ymir wanting him on this moon was to help Alma capture one of those ships. Dawn made it clear human technology was far behind where it needed to be, and Pentagon leaders agreed with her.

"You want one of them. I can see it in your eyes." She sensed the obsessive nature of a military mind controlling him. He only cared about humans and protecting them. Alma wished he could love the Kohor as much as she did, but she understood. "How do we do this? Destroying them is not difficult, but capturing them seems harder."

"We're going to need a lot of smart people with a lot of smart ideas." He turned to Raven. "I'd like you to visit our world and talk to some of our leaders."

Alma protested, "She is not ready for that!"

Raven rubbed Alma's arm, letting her know she accepted his request.

Alma capitulated with a sneer. "We will do as you ask. If she is harmed, I will react poorly."

Raven stood awestruck in front of her distant cousins' scout ship. Her attention snapped to the large building surrounding her. The flat gray walls, sharp corners, and hard clean floors were like nothing she could have ever imagined. When she saw the dangling bright lights bolted to the ceiling, her mouth dropped open. "What are those?"

The Kohor vessel was decades ahead of human

technology and Raven's people were centuries behind. "Those are called lights." She pointed toward the ship and guided Raven closer. "Your people made this and other much bigger ships."

Raven approached the smooth black craft and placed both hands against its cold surface. She closed her eyes and daydreamed of a different time for her people. "We have stories about our past. I believed them to be fantasy for so long. When you arrived, the voice in my head showed me the truth. We did this to ourselves."

Alma pursed her lips and spoke with an emotional catch. "No, those horrible blue people did this."

"We invaded their worlds when they appeared to us a long time ago. We were savage, brutal. They were peaceful, at first." The exacting realization that her people's suffering was self-inflicted brought her to tears.

A welcomed distraction lifted their dour mood when Dawn and Stacey barged into the hangar. Dawn made a straight line to Raven, unable to take her eyes off her. "Oh my god, you people are gorgeous! I want to bite your face! Can you hear her?"

"Hear who?" Confused and frightened by the energy pouring from this young woman, Raven froze.

Dawn reached out and stroked the full length of her hair, causing Raven to flinch in disgust. "That voice. Do you hear ours or yours or are they the same?"

"I hear no voice in this place." She tried peering around Dawn's head to watch as the closing door behind her hid Alma's brightly painted world. "Am I not permitted outside?"

Dawn grabbed her hand and dragged her across the hangar where she kicked open the door and pushed

Raven through. Raven stood speechless, soaking in the wonderful colors and shapes in every direction. People of various sizes and skin tones dotted the landscape as unrecognizable smells tickled her nose.

Stacey turned to Alma and David. "She's kind of a lot to handle." She pondered the idea of medicating Dawn, but didn't know if that would harm her connection with Ymir.

Raven couldn't comprehend most of what she was seeing. A Humvee raced passed, prompting her to point. "What do you call that loud thing?" Her focus tipped upward to a large flock of birds. "Are those ravens?" She exhibited the exploding excitement of a child, and Dawn was loving every second of this.

Ymir spoiled their happy moment by showing Dawn images of Raven's tormented history. Her eyes welled with tears, compelling her to wrap her arms around her alien friend.

Dawn regained her effervescence and whispered into Raven's hair, "Just wait until you see a dog." Cartara never hosted animal or insect life, only plants, annelids, and people. Raven's voice tried preparing her for what she'd see on this planet. Earth animals delighted and confused her.

David's growing concern over leaving Raven alone with Dawn pushed him to promote Stacey to babysitter, of both women. "Please keep an eye on them. Show her around the base. Balance Dawn out as much as you possibly can."

Stacey joined them outside in time to see Raven fixating on another Humvee packed with men driving by. "Do you want me to get us one of those to ride in?"

"Absolutely!" Dawn yelled. Her new military friend seemed to have unencumbered access to this entire base. "She needs to pet a dog."

Raven sat wide-eyed in the back of a Humvee. She didn't mind the unyielding seat, deafening engine, or the bumpy roads. The speeds they were traveling at should have terrified her, but she was overjoyed. Earth was marvelous, filled with an endless feast for her eyes, ears, nose, and mouth.

A young soldier chauffeured the women from location to location. At Stacey's request, he was searching for a dog. It didn't take long to find one, they were everywhere, scavenging for food and affection.

Their driver waited in the truck as they jumped out and approached a thin brown dog. His tail swirled and wagged. He wanted people to pay attention to him, so he made his way to the women with his head drooping. Dawn knelt in front of the dog and scratched him behind his ears.

Confused, Raven didn't understand what she was looking at. "What is this?" Raven got down on the ground and mimicked Dawn by touching the soft fur of the excited little creature. He was warm.

"It's a dog. They love people so much that you could beat it every day, and it would still love you." She gestured to its hypnotic wagging behind. "That means he's happy to see us."

She was enchanted by his long strange furry body. He had eyes similar to a person, but didn't appear to be anything like people. "I don't understand what this is for."

Stacey smiled at Raven's sweet innocence. "Humans are a species that evolved over a very long time. There are millions of different living things on this planet that evolved to serve their own purpose."

Raven didn't want to stop touching the dog's soft greasy fur. He pushed his cold nose against her wrist and gave her a quick lick. "For what purpose does this dog serve?"

"Humans probably wouldn't exist without dogs." Stacey knelt with them, hiding her disgust over petting the smelly beast. "When the human species was young and fairly stupid, dogs protected them from predators, other animals that would eat them or their food supplies."

"Eat them?" Raven nervously looked around as she pulled her hand away. "I don't understand what a predator is."

"You're touching one." Dawn giggled as she lifted the dog's jowls, exposing his long sharp teeth. "This little guy likes to eat other animals." She squished her nose into his and rubbed them together. "Don't worry, he wouldn't eat you unless you were dead."

Stacey glared at Dawn as General Trauger's order to counterbalance Dawn's personality replayed in her head. "Earth has evolved a careful equilibrium of power between non-human creatures. Most animals eat other ones. They remove the sick and weak from lesser species, keeping their genetic lines healthy and strong."

Raven was nervous about petting the dog now. "This thing, does it want to eat me?"

"No. Like Dawn said, they lov e us. He'd kill or die for you and protect you at any cost. There are no other animals on Earth like this. They're special. Humans and dogs are dependent on each other, bonded by tens of thousands of years of mutual evolution."

"Come on, I want to show you something I think you'll love." Stacey intertwined her arm with Raven's and dragged her back to their Humvee. She tapped the driver's shoulder and ordered, "Take us to the stables." The happy little dog attempted to chased them until they sped away, causing him to abandon his hopeless pursuit with a drooping tail.

After a short trip, their driver stopped in front of a wooden fence where two horses were hanging their heads over the top rail. They jumped from the vehicle and approached the serene animals.

"Very large dogs?" Raven was obsessed with their giant eyes and weird noses.

Stacey gently stroked the horse's face. "This is a horse. Another animal that had a huge impact on human evolution. Without them, it would have been much harder for humans to spread across this planet. We ride on their backs, and they can pull heavy loads."

Raven fixated on two men racing horses at the opposite end of the stable. "I can imagine how these would be useful." The idea of galloping through grassy fields on one of these creatures excited her. "How do you make these things? Are they predators?" She wanted Alma to bring some to Cartara.

Dawn rested her head against Raven's hair and gave her a gentle nuzzle. "No, they eat plants, like your people. You don't make them, they make themselves. They breed with other horses like people breed with other people." She turned toward Stacey with pleading eyes. "Can we ride them now?"

"Not right now, we have to get Raven back to the hangar. You and I will go riding together, soon." She made an unexpected, but welcomed flirty face.

Raven didn't want to leave the outdoors. Seeing her people's ship again brought back those unpleasant visions of Kohor atrocities. She tried ignoring the scenes of her people slaughtering curious and friendly Trey explorers, but failed.

Dawn sensed Raven's deepening anguish, and draped an arm around her shoulders. "We've all done crappy things we wish we could go back in time to fix. You need to move passed that."

David climbed out from the ship, excited about something. He waved them over, demanding they hurry. "We have a meeting approved with the President." His gamble on trusting Alma was an incredible boost to his military career.

Dawn hugged Raven and whispered into her ear, "The President is the leader of America, this place. He pretty much rules this entire planet. If you like guys, he's beautiful. If you don't like guys, he's still fun to look at."

Alma leaned in to David. "I do not like this person and I fail to understand how so many of your people voted for him." She was distracted by her paranoid scanning of the Oval Office for potential cages. This meeting left her uneasy, as if she were being led into a trap. Ymir and Dawn's approval didn't help, considering they got her killed once before.

David huffed through his nose. "No one likes him, but few people actually hate him. That's why he's the President."

"Well, I like him!" Dawn fidgeted in her chair, excited to meet the President.

Raven ignored their confusing banter. She was scrutinizing the ornate desk, flags, wall coverings, windows, everything. Her home didn't have anything as precise or colorful as the items in this room.

Dawn's doe-eyed stare fixated on Raven's large pupils darting around from object to object. "You're so beautiful." She drew in a deep breath through her hair, and made a slight look of disappointment when Raven didn't smell as good as Alma. "Do you have a name for her?"

Raven didn't appreciate Dawn's aggressive and physical personality. "Who?" No one ever smelled her before, and she didn't care for that at all.

"The voice guiding you and your people. I call ours, Ymir." Dawn rested her chin on Raven's shoulder.

"I call it the voice in my head." She pulled away from Dawn's far-too-close face. "I don't imagine it having a specific sex."

The office door opened, prompting General Trauger to his feet. Dawn and Alma followed his lead and motioned for Raven to stand with them. "He is the leader of this world, or will be the leader of this world." Raven stood, moving closer to Alma and further from Dawn.

President Atkinson smiled and made a downward hand gesture. "Seriously, I read that report about a hundred times." He stopped to stare at Raven. "Wow. I don't need you to pretend I'm important."

Dawn thrust her hand over the desk. "You're the first person I ever voted for." When he shook her hand she could barely contain herself. She looked around at the others and mouthed, "Oh my god!" It appeared as if she was bragging about touching the President.

Alma reached across Raven and pulled down on Dawn's arm, forcing her back into the chair. "I am going to vomit."

President Atkinson sat in his over-sized leather chair

and directed his attention to Alma. "What do you need with me? If that report is true, you don't need me at all."

General Trauger moved to the edge of his chair, trying to appear rigid and tall. "Sir, you lead the greatest nation on Earth..."

"Please stop this." Alma couldn't take any more of his or Dawn's star-struck idiocy. "I have no desire to rule over people on either world. I do not seek power." She tried to hide her disappointment as she gestured to David. "This man will not help me without your approval and I will not force him."

President Atkinson ignored David and focused on Alma. "You are truly an angel sent down from heaven, aren't you. I'll have you know I'm a God-fearing and loving Christian, and I believe, with all my heart, I'm looking at a person resurrected on another world by God himself." He leaned over the desk. "I'll do and approve anything you ask."

Confused by many of his words, Raven fixated on the one he emphasized the strongest. She tipped her head toward Dawn, ensuring she didn't touch her, and asked, "Resurrected?"

Dawn whispered in response, "They killed Alma with a bomb so big it could probably destroy your entire world, and then she came back to life on Cartara. Resurrected."

Raven feared these people more and more with each revelation. Earth, while wonderful and beautiful, was terrifying.

"I am not your new Christ." Alma recoiled at the thought of anyone making her a player in their religious fantasies.

"No, but our Lord has given you mastery over his

fantastic creations. I refuse to question the will of our Lord and Savior. Alma, I know divine intervention when I see it. I'll never run or cower from his will, I am God's servant, your servant, and I want nothing for myself but to receive his glory."

Everyone was aware of this American President's public religious convictions. World medias were obsessed with this during his entire campaign. When Earth's societies spiraled apart with plagues, natural disasters, insurrections, and wars, there was a massive resurgence in religious beliefs around the globe.

Dawn leaned over and exclaimed, "See! This is going to be a lot easier than we thought!"

Alma wanted the President to stop viewing her as some kind of god or demigod, so she pressed him, testing him with an unacceptable request. "I want you to start world war three."

David's mouth fell open.

Raven whispered to herself, "Three?"

President Atkinson pointed at David. "Do you have a plan for this?"

Shaken by Alma's Dawn-like madness, David responded, "I have a better plan that won't make us the bad guys or murder billions of people."

Unable to fathom what she was hearing, Raven asked Dawn, "What does this mean, murder billions?" She understood his words, but hoped she was wrong about their meaning.

Dawn replied, "Killing more people than your moon could hold. It's okay, most humans are useless garbage anyway."

Raven pushed her tiny body against the back of her chair and questioned her voice's desire to work with these crazy dangerous people.

Alma rolled her eyes at President Atkinson, then returned her focus to David. She spoke in a measured tone. "I will help with your idea. I have confidence only in you." Her terrifying lesson made it clear that this world leader cannot be trusted to safeguard humanity.

Chapter 7

New World Order

Alma's hands were shaking. No one bothered to question why she didn't choose to flood her body with the necessary chemicals to calm her rattled nerves. Similar to a birthing mother wanting to deliver her child without medication, she wished she could suppress her anxiety using pure willpower, like David. "Why am I so nervous?"

His instincts compelled him to hold her, but knowing Alma, he kept his arms to himself. "Probably because this is going to go badly. You may have to do a lot of things you don't want to do."

Alma and David stood off-stage, left of the podium

overlooking the United Nations General Assembly. "I feel sick." As a distraction, she revisited memories of Raven when they met in the flowery meadow atop the plateau. That was the first time she had ever been naked in front of anyone. She opened her eyes as President Atkinson sauntered to the podium. He annoyed her.

His level of religious fervor was difficult for her to comprehend since it failed to explain how or why she existed. Atkinson accepted her as proof of God's divine will. She wanted to believe in God, any god would suffice. Her life would be easier if she could blame some omnipotent man for her troubles.

President Atkinson took a moment to survey the packed auditorium before addressing the Assembly. "Madam President, Mr. Secretary General, honored guests and delegates, standing in front of you is a humbled man."

Distant chuckles could be heard echoing through the chamber. He dismissed their relentless hatred of everything American and continued. "This past week marks a fundamental shift in the path of the United States of America and, yes, all humanity."

"A new path, a brighter path, a righteous path lays before us. This path exists without the ambiguity calling into question our purpose in this universe. The veil blinding humankind for millennia has finally lifted." A spiritual energy enveloped his body whenever he spoke of God.

Confusion wafted throughout the convention hall. "During the course of human development, over thousands of years, we've been at war. A secret war. From China to Russia. From Europe to the United States. The sacred duty of protecting humankind from an unknown and misunderstood threat has been carried out, without question, under the clandestine belief that our existence depended upon it."

He balled his hands and lifted them high above his head. "Instead of mindlessly following in the footsteps of our ancestors, The United States of America is turning back from this meandering hopeless path. We are abandoning these costly and devastating wars to embrace a new way, the right way."

A young staff member for the Chinese delegation could be seen fast stepping toward his nation's ambassador. Stiffly bending over, he handed him a message. The ambassador grew angrier with every word he read. He stood, glared at President Atkinson, and exited the auditorium with his delegation.

The Russian ambassador received a similar unsettling message. He dead-stared at Atkinson and rose to his feet with a fist up and thumb peeking between his index and middle fingers. His delegation followed the Chinese out of the building.

Their sudden departure caused whispers and murmurs to spread among the remaining members. Atkinson persisted through their noise. "The United States will no longer be part of this cycle of dog-like obedience to rules crafted by men from a time of great superstition and mythology."

As other representatives left their seats, Alma moved closer to David. "What is happening?"

"I guess you're getting that world war." No longer able to will them away, David's eyes filled with tears. The thought of so many young soldiers who'll die for nothing was more than he could bear. "I trust you're ready."

Atkinson's gestures grew animated as he attempted

to drown out the restless crowd. "Today we are following God. He has chosen our great nation to usher in a new era where humankind need not worry about hunger, disease, or war."

Alma, shocked by his promises, asked, "I did not say those things. David, why is he saying this?"

"He's a politician. They lie about everything, all the time. They lie even when there's nothing to be gained from it."

Her angry eyes focused on President Atkinson. She entertained a desire to merge his lips together, muting his ability to mislead the world. A deep despair distracted her from her fantasies, clouding her mind with fear.

Off the coast of Virginia Beach, a veiled nuclear submarine ascended from the ocean's depths. The Navy had been tracking this particular Russian submarine for over a month.

Various military machines transmitted its coordinates to a young soldier sitting at a terminal in a nearby Air Force base. As instructed, he relayed every word and image to a small tablet Alma carried in her pocket.

Alma chuckled as the tablet vibrated. With her incredible power and their technology, they had no other option but to text her when a war was about to begin. She read the information to herself, *Watch the area around this Russian submarine.* Included in the message was a handy little map pointing at a spot in the Atlantic Ocean. She spent a few seconds locating that area in the real world. There she found the now familiar emptiness of something veiled from her and Ymir.

Atkinson slammed his hand flat against the podium.

"But, these great rewards come at a great cost. We cannot survive under two hundred disparate world governments. To receive the glory of our one true God, we can't do that as a splintered people. We must come together. Unified. With one obedient voice."

The Russian submarine opened to hurl three thermonuclear warheads into the waters above it. Alma, unable to see the hidden submarine, had no problem tracking shock waves radiating from the missile launches.

She solidified the water surrounding each missile, crushing them into tiny heavy balls. Her boastful smile turned to horror as the refined payloads detonated mere meters from the submarine. Concussive forces squashed it, forcing it to the ocean floor. Everyone on board perished. She froze, horrified by what she did.

A single tear rolled down her shaking face. "I have never killed a human before." She wrapped her arms around her body and closed her eyes.

David didn't know what she did, but his military mind had a good idea. "You can't let one missile reach its target."

President Atkinson adopted the cadence of a southern preacher. "I'm asking you to kneel with me and accept this angel from God as our lifeline to eternal salvation." He turned toward a distraught Alma with an extended hand and stepped away from the podium, inviting her to take his place on stage.

Members of the more technologically advanced nations were reluctant to believe their long time friend would betray them. Although they received the same information their counterparts in Russia and China had, they wanted to see where he was going with this.

Alma made her way to the stage, swallowing a wave

of frothy bile burbling from her upset stomach. Her abilities lay in shambles as she concentrated on the UN while thwarting relentless violent attacks from Russian forces. She was overwhelmed and terrified.

She grabbed the podium to steady her shaking legs. Distracted by the wildly unbalanced war, Alma sealed the hall from further escape and took her place in front of every nation on Earth. She looked to David for comfort, which only worsened her anxiety. The mighty old soldier was a broken man, paralyzed by the guilt of sacrificing so many young lives.

Alma removed the chairs and tables from the center of the auditorium and leaned into the microphone. "Please clear away from the middle of the room, please." She was embarrassed by her timid voice echoing around the hall.

There was no need to ask them to move, disappearing furniture was more than enough motivation to send everyone running frightened against the outer walls. World leaders, delegates, press, and visitors stood terror-stricken as a copy of her repaired Kohor ship appeared in front of them. Some prayed. Others were aware of what she was and where that ship came from.

Alma tightened her jaw in an attempt to fend off tears. She looked out over the frantic people. "Please be quiet. You need to calm down."

Cries of "devil" and "Satan" in various languages echoed throughout the chamber.

"I am not what you believe me to be, and I will not harm you." Images of the Russian and Chinese soldiers she slaughtered danced in her head. "That is not entirely true. I have harmed many people today." She buried her chin into her chest wondering if she may be the monster they feared.

Unable to make eye contact with any of them, Alma hated herself as much as they did. "I have no desire to rule over this world or any other. I am here to help."

Germany's ambassador stared her down while stabbing a finger in her direction. In clear English he bellowed, "Bull shit! Do you think we are not aware of what is going on in the seas and skies as we speak?"

Alma ignored him. "You must know that these things the American President has promised are not accurate. There will continue to be hunger and disease. Wars will not cease. I refuse to provide for your needs or cradle you like children, but know this, I will not interfere with your governments. They may continue coddling their people, making them weak and lazy, fat and stupid if they so choose."

Others, emboldened by the German man not being killed, yelled at her in their native languages. Alma raised her voice and pointed at her ship. "You must know that there is a war coming." She swept her arm over the German, Israeli, and British ambassadors. "And these people know even more about this than I do. They have kept it secret from you. They knew about me and kept that secret from you as well."

She glanced back at President Atkinson who was enjoying the show with a pious grin decorating his smug face. Alma sneered. "I have chosen to ally myself with the Americans. We will work together and advance the level of technology on our world. I do not care if you join with them, but I will not tolerate interference. I will help their military protect this nation from you if you insist on attacking."

Great Britain's ambassador stepped to the stage, curious and unafraid. "Tell us who you really are and why you're here. Where do you come from? Please don't insult us with lies."

"I am not an American, I am from Iceland." Her vision blurred as her birth nation's delegates caught her attention. "My name is Alma Ólafsdóttir. I am human, like you." Tears cascaded down her face at the sight of her own frightened people.

Israel's ambassador, angry at being called out in front of the entire world, stood beside his counterpart from Great Britain. "You are lying. You may have been born human, but you are human no longer. The Americans killed you with an atomic weapon and yet, here you stand."

Alma's nostrils flared in frustration. "The source of my abilities comes from a voice. We call her Ymir. There are others like her on other worlds and, yes, I was killed by the Americans. I woke from that death on another planet." She thrust her hand toward the Kohor ship and shouted, "Their home world."

The podium disappeared, leaving nothing between her and the people. "That voice has no real power here. She cannot stop a meteor or cure a person of cancer. She uses me and another as her tools."

Alma tried not to look at the men prostrating themselves near the ship. "She wants us to help America stop a war we will surely lose if fought today. They are called Kohor. Hundreds of millions of them will be here in less than three years. This small ship is decades beyond our technology." She glanced back at the praying men. "No god will stop them from coming."

"But, there is a chance I can mitigate this war by offering to send them back home." Her anger and tension faded, allowing her to breathe a little easier. "I can show them that their home is safe and protected. I can send them home, if they allow me."

At the Air Force base, Dawn, Stacey, and Raven were watching a large television streaming the United Nations conference. Dawn nudged Raven with her elbow. "Are you ready? It's almost time for you to meet our world."

"They seem so angry." Raven's eyes darted around as she stood. Her feelings of awe at seeing a television diminished after witnessing these hostile people showing little regard for Alma's capabilities.

Dawn joined her in front of the television. "They're mostly men. Men are always mad about something."

Alma's demeanor turned serious. "If they do not accept my offer, there will be war. I will follow America's lead and perform as they request." She walked to the platform's edge, knelt, and spoke in a soft upbeat tone. "Until then, the Americans plan to make me into an engineer. I am to help them build things they do not yet have the technology or time to build."

She paused as an uncomfortable looking Raven appeared behind her. "This is Raven. She is a Kohor from the planet Cartara. She is not like the Kohor coming in those big ships." A deafening silence blanketed the auditorium.

Everyone stared at the petrified alien woman. "She is an ancestor of the Kohor who fled their home hundreds of years ago, leaving many behind. The people on her world, Cartara, are kind and gentle." Alma's voice congested as she struggled with her emotions. She turned her head and whispered to Raven, "Talk to them."

Raven stepped toward the crowd while speaking in

a humbled tone. "Your world is so random and beautiful. All of you look different. You are amazing and confusing and wonderful." She used Alma's body as a barrier between herself and the mob.

The Kohor ship seemed ominous sitting there surrounded by so many frightened people. "We are different, them and us. They are angry and paranoid. They are violent. That voice in my head refused to show me what my people were like long ago until Alma came to our world. I am ashamed of what we were, and I am so sorry for anything that may happen to this beautiful Earth."

"They tell me I am of an engineered people. That our Caretaker, our Alma, crafted us. We did not evolve and adapt with a changing environment like you have. Our world was curated specifically for us." Raven noticed a group of Japanese delegates and couldn't help but stare. "Seeing what I see now, I believe we were molded to look like some of you."

Alma interrupted, "They have been here before. Thousands of years ago in China. Not with ships. Something we do not yet understand allowed them to walk from their world into ours. As I am able to do now."

Raven's entire body shivered as she spoke. "When this world and ours connected long ago, our Caretaker wanted it and filled it with Kohor soldiers. They won that war and ruled for many generations. Your world eventually chose a strong Caretaker of its own, who raised an army and killed our people, including our Caretaker, leaving us unprotected. Cartara, our home, never selected a new Caretaker. Over time, we became fearful and distrustful." Her voice choked up, making it difficult to talk.

Alma stood beside Raven and wrapped an arm around her shoulders. "A species called Trey visited them with scientists. They were explorers. The Kohor murdered them and stole their technology. The Trey came back with soldiers and weapons, almost destroying Cartara. They nearly erased the Kohor people from existence."

Raven continued, "That war lasted many generations. Eventually, my ancestors acquired enough technology to move most of our people onto five large ships. I don't know what happened to them or why only three seem to remain."

David joined Alma and Raven on the stage and pointed at the scout ship. "Data in that ship hints at the Kohor destroying several Trey worlds until the Trey people helped them locate Earth in exchange for peace. In their telling of history, humans murdered their protector, leaving them vulnerable to invasion."

"We plan on sending them home or killing them. We're not looking for any non-scientific input from your nation's leaders or your people. We'll accept help from your military, engineers, and scientists, but we are in command. There is no negotiating this."

Alma's eyes panned the auditorium. "I will not be part of your lives. I am with the Americans and Kohor of Cartara. As long as you do not interfere with either of them, I will not interfere with you."

Forsaken by their powerful friend, with China and Russia on their knees, many felt abandoned and betrayed. There was a new world order, and they would have no meaningful role in it.

Raven, Alma, David, President Atkinson, and the Kohor ship disappeared, leaving them to deliberate among themselves. No one uttered a single goodbye as the walls holding the world's representatives hostage evaporated. There wasn't even a parting word from that glib American President.

Chapter 8

The Trey

Months after that disastrous United Nations Assembly, the military, with Alma's assistance, established a large joint Naval Air Force base seven kilometers from Raven's village. To its east laid a sprawling network of homes copied from an average middle class suburban neighborhood in an average American city. If it wasn't for the green sky and giant planet occasionally blocking their view, the residents would feel like they were on Earth.

Alma and David were walking across the nearly complete, Joint Base Cartara when they approached a group of officers heading toward them. The officers made their way to the other side of the street in an effort to avoid her. Alma hated when they did that.

She shook off her dejected feelings and continued speaking to David with wild spirited hands. "I wish you could see this. It is huge. It took me quite a while to realize they are terraforming the planet."

He was amused by seeing an energized Alma, but couldn't shake his annoyance over her keeping a Trey installation in the Yeset solar system hidden from him. "That's the kind of thing we'd like to be kept informed of." The tinge of permanent rage in his voice was difficult for him to subdue. Being yelled at, or yelling at others, was a normal part of his life.

David's intimidating timbre soured her mood, causing her shoulders to droop. "I did not want you to make me stop them."

"Make you? The few orders I've accidentally given you, you've ignored, or flat out refused. I can't make you do anything." The rare glint of cheerfulness draining from her face tugged at his heart, so he tried to lighten the melancholy mood he created. "What's the name of that planet?"

"Fennar." Her downcast tone strangled him.

He managed to fake an upbeat inflection, "Maybe after we make peace with these people, they could take a look at Mars."

"Oh, and Venus as well. It is much closer to being like Earth. They are smart, the Trey. They know so much, and I think they want me to help them go faster, but I do not understand anything about what they are doing." That bounce in her step returned.

They reached their destination, a one-story red-brick building near a grassy airfield. David held open a heavy glass door and waved Alma inside. The potent chemical smells of new carpet and paint slapped them hard in the face as they made their way down a hallway lined with office doors. They entered a large open room at the end where the loud and excited chattering of engineers filled the air.

Raven was there, alone, staring out a window with her hands pressed against the invisible solid wall. Glass fascinated her. A group of men jogging in the distance captured her attention. Raven loved watching the precise organization of American soldiers. It comforted her, like listening to music.

The window overlooked an open field holding twenty-five flat-black war machines humming with anticipation as they awaited orders. They resembled elongated pyramids roughly the size of a commercial jet. In true military fashion, they were given the uninspired designation of, X9 Warships.

Triangle shaped wings attached at the top and bottom of the fuselage met at a point several meters out. Between each set of upper and lower wings rested two cone-shaped turrets cradling menacing weapons affixed to pivoting joints. Near the ship's rear, a small gray American flag adorned their bodies.

Raven pushed her nose onto the glass as her hands traveled around the hard clear material. "They look strange." Not evolving on Earth, or at all, Kohor people never developed the fear of animals that made humans view these ships with respect and awe. To a human, these beasts exuded power and danger.

"They are beautiful." Alma loved them like they were her children. Months of building machines that build other machines gave birth to a manufacturing facility decades ahead of normal human technology. They worked together as a team, and now it was time to release their creations into the wild.

Raven sensed a bubbling energy from the crowd as the warships lifted off the ground and disappeared in the Cartaran sky. The entire room roared with clapping and cheering. She had seen Trey ships throughout her life, so she didn't understand their enthusiasm. It was becoming apparent to her that these giants from Earth were not the mythical Æsir.

In the center of the room, Alma gathered enough superfluous matter to build a model of Cartara. A solid human-sized replica of Raven's home world floated in front of the scientists, engineers, and soldiers. It rotated on its axis as twenty-five intricate little black ships revealed themselves escaping her gravity.

The American fleet approached a lone Trey space station, traveling at speeds beyond anything human technology was capable of a few months earlier. They maintained a flawless distance from each other and an unwavering symmetry of movement. Everything about them was beautifully orchestrated by thinking machines.

Fifty thousand kilometers from the Trey station, a menagerie of sensors on board every ship sprang alive. These noisy warships emitted so many random wavelengths of energy they overwhelmed Trey monitoring systems.

To the Trey, they looked like one fast moving giant blob of brilliant light, and it was heading toward them. In response, a door slid open underneath the station and pushed out a pack of shiny warships about the same size as the human ships. They raced to investigate the deafening blob.

Military AI pilots fired no weapons in return as thousands of bright beads streamed from the hostile

Trey warships. They danced around the first salvo, dodging and pitching in every direction. Engineers warned the small human crews of the extreme g-forces they may encounter.

Once sensors were able to map their attackers, Alma updated the tiny black Trey orbs to match detailed computer models. Nine Trey ships engaged the American fleet, and they didn't look anything like that ship she buried outside Raven's village.

Turrets resting between each pair of wings on the twenty-five warships targeted a single enemy vessel. One hundred bursts of invisible light radiated from the fleet to their unfortunate prey. Surprising everyone, including the AI, their lasers shredded the Trey ship into fiery pieces.

David analyzed the lopsided battle playing out in the middle of the room. "What the hell?" In less than ten minutes, each Trey ship met a similar fate. He placed a hand on Alma's shoulder and asked, "Were you able to get anything?"

Uncomfortable with physical contact, she twisted away from his touch. "No, I warned you they are easy to kill. Tell them not to attack one ship at a time like that."

He pulled his hand back with an apologetic expression. "I can't. The whole point of using AI is for them to learn on their own. We should have told them we wanted an enemy ship intact before sending them up."

Their fleet moved closer to the Trey space station. One separated from the pack, lined up its target and launched a small stealth missile. They made a hasty getaway as their weapon detonated, creating a substantial nuclear explosion that expanded to engulf the entire base. Their target laid lifeless and adrift.

The room fell quiet as Alma's theater played out. Within thirty minutes the same scenario left another Trey station a rudderless husk. Alma cracked the stunned silence. "The Trey are terrible fighters."

Raven walked to a floating space station and plucked it from the air. She squinted with puckered lips and shook it as hard as she could. "Are there Trey in these?"

"They are only avatars." Alma scolded her with her eyes as the ship disintegrated and reappeared in deep orbit of the Cartara model.

The remaining large black orbs moved away from the American fleet, retreating in the direction where they first appeared.

Panic rippled through Alma's body. *They are going to take the terraformers.* In an instant, the American ships found themselves orbiting Fennar. Her display updated to show a bright white world with a cluster of tiny black orbs floating nearby the human ships.

Every X9 warship fell dormant and unresponsive. "Are they confused? Did I confuse them by moving them to Fennar?" Alma looked around for someone to answer her. David's red-faced glare caught her eye.

He could barely contain his boiling rage. "You removed our ships from an active combat theater."

She shrank away from his incensed stare. "The terraformers," she uttered before returning her focus to the display of Fennar, but continued to feel his burning eyes.

Without warning, several high-yield nuclear warheads detonated above the terraforming stations on Fennar, leaving the Trey installations on the planet's surface in ruins. Alma jumped to match

David's glare. "Why?!"

Her display splintered into subatomic dust as she and David stood angry, facing each other. Not wanting to lose his temper in front of their teams, he left the room to cool off in an office.

Alma looked around at the engineers' expressions of absolute terror. She slinked away and followed David to the office. Inside, she slammed the door. "You did not need to do that!"

Raven, not understanding what was happening, followed close behind. When Alma slammed the door in her face, she remained in the hallway and listened to their conversation through the thick metal door.

David concentrated on his breathing. "You took my ships. You can do anything you want. I get it. You're acting just like the others."

She was seeing a new side of him, a side his enemies probably see. It made her a little nervous knowing this military leader, who had an intimate understanding of her capabilities, was courageous enough to chastise her. "I only wanted to protect them."

He fought an incredible desire to throttle her. "Kill me, bring me back, kill me again. I don't care. I'll never tolerate what you did." David's face contorted as he stretched out his aching jaw.

Alma hadn't seen him this angry before. Something about him, about those ships, told her the military had a backup plan in case she became a problem. Fear compelled her to sit. "I do not want a fight with you. You did not trust me. You knew I would not control myself, and they were ready for me."

He leaned over the desk, their faces so close they could feel each other's breath. "Do whatever you want.

It's not like we can stop you. Please try to remember they're just soldiers following my orders."

"Guð minn, I am not going to hurt anyone." A frustrated tear spilled from her left eye. "I made a mistake."

"You do understand that your mistakes are far more serious than a normal person's, right?" David reclined back in his chair. He hadn't been this furious with anyone in quite a while, and he was already exhausted.

"Why did you need to kill all those unarmed scientists? I would have put our ships back had you demanded." Her voice cracked from the oppressive feeling of so many innocent lives snuffed out by the machines she helped create.

He didn't want to say it, but she left him no choice. "You don't get it. Alma, you killed them. The AI saw you as a threat and probably determined the installations on Fennar were why you attacked them." Every word from his mouth tasted like acid, he hated saying this to her. "They made the decision to remove your reason for interfering with their orders."

Alma scanned Fennar's orbit and its surrounding space. David wasn't lying. The AI viewed her as a threat and chose to hide themselves after destroying the Trey facilities on the planet. Her voice was a barely audible whisper. "I killed them."

"Actions have consequences." His empathy for her tempered his wrath. No matter how hard he fought to stay angry, he succumbed to his compassion for Alma's unique situation.

Alma had no desire to continue fighting with him since she was losing, so she changed the conversation. "They are all going to the same place and completely disappearing. The Trey ships. I do not know how they are doing this."

David was growing tired with playing the irate General. "Alma... I don't work for you, and I'll never serve you or Ymir."

Raven's voice was warning her things were getting bad. She fidgeted with the door handle until she figured out how it worked, then burst into the office. "I need to help." She wrapped her arms around Alma's head and glared at General Trauger. "You are an old man. She is a child with enormous strength. You need to be patient with her."

"She's older than I am!" He tried to corral his simmering fury.

Fearless, Raven countered, "For an immortal person, she is only a baby."

David's anger returned, but now toward both women. "We lived as humans on the same planet for the same amount of time during the same period of time. Her maturity level needs to reflect that."

The voice in Raven's head guided her through some of Alma's life in Iceland. "She lived afraid, in isolation. She didn't know what was happening to her mind and body and feared her abilities. She did not have the diverse existence you had. You have lived a hundred experiences for every one of hers."

Alma looked around the room trying to distract herself from crying. "I will be better, get better."

He fought against his own unwanted emotions, and whispered, "I just don't trust you."

"I do not trust you either." She couldn't stop thinking of those ships turning on her. There were no warnings from Ymir or Cartara's voice and no hint of the missiles over Fennar. The silence, stealth, and logic of American military technology terrified her. "Are you going to imprison me again?"

The heavy weight of her words smothered his will to continue fighting. "I would not allow that. Not from the Trey, not from humans, but I don't think we should work so close together anymore. Maybe we can make some kind of mutual protection deal where you run this solar system."

She tipped her head against Raven's chest in frustration. "This is not acceptable. I do not want to be separated from you or my home."

Raven sensed his distress and tried helping one more time. "She needs you to tell her what to do. Like one of your soldiers."

Not wanting to give her orders but wishing for this fight to end, he struggled with what to say or do next. "The Trey ships, is there something near where they're disappearing?"

Alma wiped her face on Raven's sleeve. "There are many large rocks spread out over a wide area."

"We have some things to work out, you and me. When these Trey ships are all gone, I'd like you to move our fleet into that area. It'll save us about nine hours. Please."

She made a teary-eyed little smile. "Yes, I will, but I can no longer see our ships."

"I'll send orders for them to stand down, if they still see me as their superior." He was only half-joking about that. "Just so you know, I fight with our engineers every day. Loud, screaming fights."

"You do not fear them. It is different between us."

"I think you're strong enough to hear this. At least I hope you are. I'm much more afraid of their AI than I am of you. I fear those things will turn against us like a bad science-fiction movie and decide we're a problem that needs to be fixed. Every day I grit my teeth, waiting for those soulless things to realize they're better than us."

Alma couldn't tell if he was exaggerating to make her feel better. She hoped he was. The idea of intelligent invisible machines working together to exterminate humanity was nothing short of horrifying.

Raven wished to silence his disturbing words. "I don't know what AI is, but I have heard more than enough from humans. You are much too frightening for me as of late." That was the first time she referred to them as anything other than Æsir.

Alma, Raven, and David could hear their teams hushing one another as they walked down the corridor into the main room. An engineer rushed over to welcome them back. "Well, the world didn't turn to ash, so I guess you two made up?" They continued past him, ignoring his woeful attempt at humor.

A detailed miniature version of a deep wide asteroid field sparkled in the center of the room. Tiny models of Trey ships were making their way to an unknown destination inside the cluster.

Alma apologized, "They look the same because I cannot see them. They are probably different looking."

Military personnel and scientists speculated on what was happening as each ship vanished, one after the other. Still hovering over them, the engineer asked, "Are they disappearing, like completely gone?"

"They are completely gone. There is no ship after they disappear. It is as if I am doing this." Her first thought was that there was a Trey version of herself somewhere in the Yeset solar system.

Alma wiped glistening beads of sweat from her forehead while imagining a battle with someone like her, and losing. The possibility of these people dying because she started a war triggered a panic attack. A debilitating fear strangled her. Unable to answer any more questions, she spun on her heels and stiff-walked out of the room.

David followed her back to the office and turned on the lights. He found her sitting in the corner of a sofa with her legs pulled to her chest and her arms wrapped around them. She didn't look up at him.

He had seen many soldiers spiral during the first hours of battle. Those experiences taught him not to acknowledge her breakdown. "We all know your abilities are probably recreatable with the right technology. Our people understand most of the science behind what makes you so strong. The Trey probably do too. You told me they're smart."

Alma's trembling eyes peered over her knees. "I cannot fight someone like me. I will lose. I will fail to protect us and the Kohor, and we will all die."

David unclipped a walkie-talkie from his belt and radioed for Craig, now Lead Engineer on Cartara. "Major Halvorson, I need you in office A4." Without saying another word, he sat beside her, wanting to cradle her in his arms, but knew better.

Craig entered the office to witness Alma distraught and curled into a ball on the couch. *This can't be good.*

David glanced up at him. "Tell her about the huge problem you have with replicating her core abilities."

Shock paralyzed Craig for a moment. Digging into the science of Alma and Dawn was a classified project. "Well, beside the technology not existing, if it did, it would require an enormous energy source just to move a chair."

The most powerful being in the known universe, pouting like a frightened little girl, troubled him. "To do the stuff you can do, as fast as you can do it, as big as you can do it, as far as you can do it? That kind of power doesn't exist except maybe at the poles of a supermassive singularity. A huge black hole."

David patted her on the boot and gently gripped her lower leg. "See, you're impossible to reproduce." He nodded toward Craig. "If the Trey could do one thing, like destroy and recreate one ship, couldn't they do this with less energy?"

Craig thought hard for several seconds. "We can't imagine anything besides a singularity being strong enough. If this is what they're doing, it's likely they encode, destroy, and transmit the ship data somewhere else to be recreated by another machine with its own power source."

They could almost hear the math grinding away inside Craig's head. "Whatever they're using is probably a complex computer system rather than a person, like Alma. It would be limited in scope, and I highly doubt they'd be able to send and receive at the same time."

Alma didn't mind David's comforting hand on her leg. "This is probably why they disappear one at a time. There isn't another Alma out there looking for a fight. Can you see them, black holes?"

Craig wanted to interrogate Alma on the physics of quantum singularities, but managed to control himself. Instead, he pulled a chair in front of her and stated, "You should look for energy radiating from the poles of something unnaturally dense and small, like an entire planet the size of an orange."

Alma sat up facing David. "There is something, but it is not like what he said. There is a big rock near where they disappear, maybe a small moon. It does not feel right, but I do not see energy coming from it."

Craig was so excited he wanted to run from the room and get his team. "If they're capturing and using its energy, you may not see that, but yes, that thing would be incredibly massive."

"I cannot see what is inside. Whatever it is, it is masked from me." She was happy to feel useful and relieved to learn there wasn't an ugly blue Alma somewhere out there itching for a fight.

When the Trey fleets were gone, the twenty-five American warships appeared in distant orbit of an unprotected lumpy micro-moon. Eager engineers went to work deciphering what that moon was and how it functioned.

Chapter 9

Æsir

"I wonder what happened to my apartment. I just kind of abandoned it." Dawn chuckled while opening a box labeled, Dawn-Bedroom-Shirts. The military's packing skills were quite thorough. She wandered around her government issued home with an arm full of clothes and yelled into the air, "I only see one closet."

Stacey was busy inspecting the cabinets in their modest kitchen, trying to locate the perfect spot for coffee mugs. "Is this really a problem? How many khaki shirts could you possibly own?" Thinking of how great her life had become since meeting Alma and

Dawn brought a satisfied grin to her face.

Tired of unpacking, they relaxed together on their new couch to watch television. Stacey was listening to Dawn as she corrected dubious reporting from a popular national news anchor when an unfamiliar alarm interrupted them. Stacey asked, "Is that our doorbell?"

The comforting warmth of Ymir's strange and intense love for David cascaded over Dawn's body. "It's Trauger."

He stood outside in the cooling dusk air, waiting for them to let him inside. Stacey swung open the door to see him holding a comically large potted plant. She displayed a laughing smile as she struggled to take his generous housewarming gift. "Thank you, Sir! There's water in the fridge if you want any."

Seeing boxes scattered everywhere, David mumbled, *they were supposed to put all of this away.* After looking around their home, he walked into the living-room where he found Dawn tucked into her sofa under a fuzzy blanket. "I'd like to talk with you. In private. Please."

Dawn admonished him with her eyes. "Stacey has the military's highest clearance. I think she can stay. Besides, I just tell her what we talk about anyway."

David let out a disapproving huff as he dropped into a deep soft chair next to her.

His red puffy eyes and exaggerated forehead wrinkles caused Dawn to scrunch her nose. She wiggled her fingers in front of him. "You look like crap. Alma can make you look and feel a lot better. You should ask her to fix you up."

"Yeah, she's the one wearing me out." He forced a half-hearted laugh. "I'm in a kind of abusive relationship with her at the moment, but that's not why I'm here." His vacant expression made it apparent he wasn't getting enough sleep.

David fidgeted in the love-seat. "Ever since I set foot on Cartara, I haven't been able to stop thinking about Ymir and Raven's voices. When I'm over there, I feel like a huge burden is lifted, a feeling of intense relief. I don't understand why. I've asked around and others feel it too. There's a darkness here I didn't notice until I spent time on Cartara. Is this from Ymir?"

Stacey sat on the floor between them, prompting Dawn to nudge her with her foot. "I doubt it. We all kind of hear everyone's voices. Maybe there's too many messed up people here. This planet is way overdue for an asteroid or super volcano. I have my fingers crossed the Kohor will clean us up a bit."

"I thought you could, possibly, ask Ymir? Please?" He sounded anxious, abnormal for such an unexcitable man.

Dawn's facial expressions fluctuated as she and Ymir discussed David's torment. "There is something, another voice. Not as strong as Ymir but stronger than normal people." She paused. "Æsir?"

David's appearance changed in an instant. His eyes widened as adrenaline pumped through his veins. "Where the hell did you hear that word? From Alma?"

"No, it's what Ymir calls them. They've been here for thousands of years." She shrugged.

"Here? On Earth?!" David's face colored a much darker hue of red than his ordinary pinkish-white. An uncomfortable heat flooded his ears, reminding him of the frequent warnings regarding his blood pressure from teams of doctors who monitor his health every few hours each day.

"I don't know. Probably." Dawn was growing bored with his questions and exhibited a creepy little smile. "Just so you know, Stacey is cool with you and me making a baby together. I know you're married, so we don't have to do it the fun way. Alma can mix our stuff up in me."

David ignored Dawn's disturbing request and Stacey's flushing cheeks. "What are the Æsir doing here? Does Ymir know?"

Dawn tipped her head and concentrated on the Æsir feelings. "They're messing with us. You know how Ymir talks to everyone like she talks to me and Alma, with emotions? They're doing it too, but the Æsir voice is quiet. I mean, it's stronger than yours but way quieter than Ymir's."

"What are they saying? Can you hear their words or decipher these feelings?"

She furrowed her nose and dulled Ymir's powerful voice to focus on the Æsir. "Basically, they're telling us that being happy, popular, and content is more important than anything. That seems weird. Ymir doesn't think the Æsir can hear our thoughts like she can."

A subtle panic tainted his words. "Are they from the same place as Ymir?"

"Nope. They're like us but way more advanced. I mean way, way, way more advanced." Her expression blanked. "Now I see why Ymir doesn't talk about them. We'd lose a war with them in about five seconds."

Her revelations cranked his heart rate up to a dangerous level. "I need to know where they are. Do you think Ymir can help Stacey figure out how to track that voice? Would she be willing to help?"

Dawn's eyes brightened at the thought of being

useful to the military again. "Of course we want to help. I'll bet that's worth at least one baby. Right?"

"No. I need you two, three, to find a way to measure that voice. I have to know where it is and what it's doing here." There was an uncharacteristic urgency to his request.

"Can I go inside yet?" Dawn circled a huge quantum electron microscope occupying the center of an otherwise empty bright white room. She found a small keypad on the side and couldn't resist playing with it. An audible groan escaped her mouth upon realizing it was locked.

Stacey focused on her console. "It's ready now. Go ahead and lay down on the table." The thought of peering into Dawn's beautiful disturbed mind was a dream come true.

Dawn stood in front of her in nothing but a crinkly baby-blue gown and socks. She teased Stacey, "Do I have to wear this or can I get on the table naked?"

"Be my guest. I don't know why you're wearing that thing in the first place. I'm only scanning your head."

Dawn peeled the paper gown from her body and dropped it, piece-by-piece to the floor. Stacey glanced up from her screen and let out a long calming breath while delighting in Dawn's seductive show. "Okay, you can lay down now."

The cold metal table enhanced Dawn's mischievous mood. To her dismay, Stacey's focused enthusiasm for playing inside Dawn's head subdued her baser cravings. She tapped a small button on her screen and the table slid into the QEM's bore.

A map of every atom comprising Dawn's brain would have taken much longer to build had Ymir not pointed them in the general direction of her amygdala. She rolled a trackball under each hand, searching for something Dawn described as a tiny vibrating bubble.

Stacey lost herself in the computer generated landscape of Dawn's mind. "Oh! Crap!" She forgot Dawn's head was still in the machine. The table slid out of the QEM revealing Dawn had fallen asleep, so she covered her with a lab coat and returned to work.

After an hour of zipping around inside virtual Dawn, desperation set in. *I wish you could tell me exactly where to look.*

As if Ymir heard her prayer, a microscopic mass caught her eye. Magnification revealed it to be a protein blob two nanometers in diameter protecting a winding worm-like lattice of molecular chemical bonds. She tipped her head to the ceiling and whispered again, *thank you.*

Stacey gazed down on Dawn's peaceful sleeping face, then shook her awake. "Time to go, get your clothes on. I need to be alone."

Dawn had experienced this version of Stacey many times before, and didn't care much for it. "Fine, but you will come home tonight."

With her tempting distraction gone, Stacey focused her attention on their new discovery. She placed her own head in the QEM, where an AI helper found a similar mass inside her brain, but her lattice held different chemical bonds. She needed more people.

The military supplied an unlimited stream of young soldiers for her to play with. Their excitement echoed throughout the hall as they queued outside her lab. Stacey swung open the door to address her subjects.

"This will take less than five minutes each, and you won't feel a thing."

She left the door open, allowing the nervous women and men to see for themselves there was nothing to worry about. One by one they climbed onto the table for their scan, which was faster now that the AI knew where to look.

By the end of the day Stacey compiled a comprehensive database of more than one hundred brain masses she named, the Vogt Mass. A handful of volunteers were missing, or held much smaller, Vogt Masses, prompting her to dig through their medical histories. She discovered they had diagnoses of psychopathy. Something interesting she would have to circle back to later.

Stacey needed more data, so she enticed Dawn back to her lab with certain promises she didn't mind fulfilling. Dawn laid on the table, fully clothed this time. While it slid into the QEM, Stacey instructed, "Okay, this isn't going to be fast, but you can't fall asleep. Concentrate on Ymir, ask her how her day is going."

"She doesn't have days."

"Don't talk, or move. I need you to ask Ymir something." The AI recorded thousands of frames during Dawn's secret conversation and compiled them into a useful video. A triumphant smile stretched across her face as the video revealed a faint vibration. "Now shut Ymir out and concentrate on the Æsir voice." She didn't understand the mechanism Dawn employed when muting voices, but it proved essential to her tests.

With Dawn's suppression of Ymir, the AI jumped from one large rung to another looking for the same tell-tail vibrations. It didn't take long to find, that rung was thicker than most of the others. Stacey examined Dawn's body laying on the table. "There's no way you know how completely awesome you are."

"Well, I think I'm pretty damn awesome, so…" Dawn wiggled on the table, dancing to music playing inside her head.

Stacey searched her database of Vogt Masses, locating the Ymir and Æsir rungs in every healthy sample, but their molecular compositions were different. The effort needed to decode the disparate information would be next to impossible, but that wasn't what she was tasked to do.

"Alright. I need you to move around the room like you have to pee or something." The table glided out, allowing Dawn to sit up.

"I do need to pee." She wandered to one of the walls and walked the perimeter while running her hand across the pock-marked, but smooth painted concrete. "Like this?"

"Perfect." It wasn't difficult training an AI to locate and follow a moving person, but teaching one to track and monitor that person's Vogt Mass was a bit trickier. *This would be simpler if I could just cut one out of somebody.* With General Trauger's intense agitation over that Æsir voice, she chose not to ask him for a human sacrifice.

The particles inside each atom of every molecule in the Æsir rung spun with an almost unperceivable wobble. Stacey calculated rays emanating from the heaviest point of their weighted imbalance to its entangled sister particle. "It's working."

Once the pieces coalesced, it wasn't long before they created a functional prototype. Dawn's face beamed with pride as she caressed their ugly digital child. "She's kind of sexy, and we made her together."

Dawn summoned Alma to the lab, and much to David's surprise, Stacey called him instead of Alma moving him against his will. Alma was making noticeable efforts to respect his military authority.

In the center of their small air-conditioned warehouse, a large metal frame holding exposed wires and fans rested on an ankle-high platform. Attached at the top and sides of the box were flat rectangular detectors pointing up at an angle.

Stacey walked to the machine and gestured toward a monitor on a nearby desk. The display showed four green blobs, each resting above a long number presented in an eye squinting tiny font. They read, seven hundred and thirty-seven, with a fluctuating decimal value.

Dawn pointed at the screen and said, "That's in millions of kilometers."

Alma narrowed her eyes at the detectors and turned her head in the direction they were aimed. "It is pointing at nothing but empty space."

Stacey joined them at the computer. "They're not antenna. They don't need to point at the source to work. They're actually looking inside us. These smaller numbers below are an estimated difference between vectors of rays calculated from the particle oscillations in our Æsir rungs." No one in the room understood anything she said. "It's not triangulating an actual signal, this is more of a quantum entanglement detector, of sorts. It's saying the target is coming from somewhere around Jupiter."

David's voice echoed his agitation. "Is it able to pinpoint them yet?"

"Probably within a few hundred thousand kilometers, Sir. The Æsir entanglement follows the planet, so it's orbiting Jupiter or inside it somewhere. I'm working on the sensitivity, and I'm confident I can get that down below two thousand kilometers or better." Stacey was proud of the fat little baby Ymir, Dawn, and she created.

David couldn't stop watching the updating numbers. "I'm extremely impressed with this, Captain."

His face soured somewhat as his mind filled with images of a more advanced species sitting out there monitoring them and whispering horrible things into everyone's ears. He feared what they'd do after realizing their human subjects were staring back at them.

David's concern caught Alma's attention. "Is there something wrong? Did you not tell me something?" The accusation in her voice was evident.

"No. It's just that I'm afraid of them and I don't really know why. I don't like this feeling." The man who yells at her without fear and warred with an unknown alien species was admitting he was afraid of something he couldn't see. This didn't help Alma's anxiety.

Dawn spun around in her chair so fast, she had to steady herself from falling off. "That's their stupid voice. They want you to be afraid of them. Remember, they talk like Ymir, in feelings." It was a simple matter for her to discern whether a voice came from Ymir or not, but to the rest of humanity, they are a jumbled mess.

"For them to give me these feelings, they have to know I'm thinking about them. I thought you told me they can't hear us?" He was trying, and failing, to keep paranoia from sounding in his tone.

"I told you Ymir thinks they can't hear us." She shook her head. "She's not infallible."

A large team of physicists under Stacey's command stood surrounding tall tables with tablets in their hands. They were plotting three-dimensional data models of digital information pouring in from her new machine, which she named, the Moser Array.

This was the first time most of these people worked with Alma, so Jupiter appearing in the center of the room was an awesome sight to behold. One man uttered, "God, you're absolutely amazing."

Alma wasn't sure if he was talking about the big planet or her. Since leaving her Icelandic farm, she endured constant comments regarding her abilities and her appearance. The adoration was quite annoying. "Is your machine telling us where that voice is coming from?" She was growing tired of the time engineers and scientists need to form conclusions.

Some members of Stacey's team gathered around Jupiter to compare notes. Stacey sat off to the side monitoring the health of her Moser Array and neglecting Dawn, who was getting a little bored.

Dawn weaved her way to Jupiter, forcing herself between two focused scientists. She thrust her hand inside the world, and wiggled her fingers in the clouds, causing them to swirl in beautiful patterns. She looked at Alma. "Very detailed. Nice."

Alma laughed at Dawn's childish antics. "I did that for you. I knew you could not keep your hands out of it."

She plunged her arm deeper into the atmosphere. "It's wet in the middle."

Alma joined Dawn in front of Jupiter and laid her cheek on Dawn's hair. "I have missed you. Raven is not so funny like you."

Dawn ran her arm through the colorful storm bands. She pushed in so deep that part of her shoulder sank into the clouds where she found a small solid mass in the center. "I thought it was a gas world. There's a ball in here."

A young astrophysicist desperately wanted to sound impressive, so he offered his unsolicited knowledge. "The gravity of Jupiter is so intense that gasses and other matter compress under pressure into liquids, and near the core, solids." He was overjoyed for the opportunity to stand beside this perfect redhead.

Dawn squinted and sneered. With her free arm she pointed to Stacey sitting at a computer near the edge of the room. "Your boss is my girlfriend. I'm just putting that out there."

Disappointed, he stepped away with a wide gait. "Sorry."

General Trauger interrupted the chattering group of scientists, and pushed them for an update. "We're not asking for perfection. If you have a large area for Alma to start looking, show it to her now." Like Alma, he was also growing tired of how slow engineers worked.

An astrophysicist made her way to Jupiter and gently nudged Dawn to the side. She circled her index finger through the clouds in the Southern Hemisphere. "We're pretty sure it's somewhere in here, under the clouds. We'll keep trying to make that area smaller, Sir."

David recognized the frustration on Alma's face as

she searched for something without a description. "Dawn said they're thousands of years more advanced than us. Maybe change the way you search, I don't know."

The woman returned and reached in front of Dawn, this time poking a smaller spot in the clouds with a pen. "It's somewhere deep down inside, Sir. Close to the core." Dawn sniffed her hair and made a creepy sideways nod of approval.

David rested his hand on Alma's shoulder. "Dawn said it's wet inside. If there's an ocean of some kind, look on the surface of that."

"I believe I found it." Jupiter disappeared, replaced by a shimmering liquid ball of make believe hydrogen. A tiny silver bump floated on its surface. "It is large and hard. I cannot see inside, but it feels heavy. Like that Trey moon, but different."

Stacey shooed her scientists away from the display and joined Alma, Dawn, and David in front of the shiny blob. "How big is it?"

"About twelve kilometers the long way. I have never felt anything like this before." She tried to copy the alien trespasser, and failed. "I cannot move or copy it, but it is not like the human and Trey veils. I can feel that it actually exists."

"Can you make it bigger and get rid of the hydrogen?" Stacey's heart pounded at the sight of another alien device in the Sol solar system.

A car sized rippled silver egg with a flat bottom filled the area that once held Jupiter. "I do not know if there are people inside. It is also making no vibrations that I can feel."

After dismissing Stacey's team from the room, David stood in front of the Æsir egg. "I'm starting to hate this universe. It's getting crowded."

Stacey reached out and caressed the smooth egg with her fingertips. "You're probably going to hate it more, very soon, Sir. It stopped talking. I think it knows we tried to move it."

Alma tipped her head back and grunted, "I am sorry, again."

Dawn pushed against Alma's arm and gave her a loving hug. "They knew about you anyway. If anything, we forced them to change their plans and knocked them back a little. It's not like we knew what they were up to before. Nothing's changed."

David nodded, pretending to agree with Dawn. "I know you said it's heavy but what does it feel like to you?"

Alma stared at the egg, contemplating its existence. "Like a locked door."

Chapter 10

Quantum Leap

Craig paced in front of a lecture hall filled with high ranking military members from every service branch, including Alma and General Trauger. "That Trey moon isn't a moon at all. It's a Dyson Sphere surrounding a quantum singularity, a black hole with an event horizon about forty kilometers in diameter."

Alma created a three-dimensional model of the sphere at center stage for Craig to use as a visual aid. He pointed toward its top and bottom. "There are two control stations acting as collectors for ionized particles jetting out from the singularity's poles. These are also the same machines responsible for sending and receiving Trey ships."

Craig's mouth could barely keep up to his adrenaline fueled mind. "Here's the best part. The sphere is an active mesh, collecting raw materials like small asteroids and dust. It feeds the singularity, so it maintains a specific mass. Everything about this technology is mind-blowing!"

David interrupted from his seat in the audience. "There were no Trey inside either facility. It's a completely automated system with virtually no security, making it easy for our teams, and Alma to investigate. We assume they intended to protect it with ships and didn't anticipate evacuating the entire solar system."

Navy Fleet Admiral Ander Falk cleared his throat to silence David. He scowled at Craig. "So, the Trey just happened to find a black hole in the Yeset solar system, and somehow built this structure around it? Then they abandoned it to an alien military power?"

Craig responded with his normal derisive attitude. "Sir, we don't think they found the singularity. Its small size indicates they manufactured it, and we have no idea how the Trey accomplished this. As for abandoning it, they did. We're in control of it right now."

"Major Halvorson, are you trying to tell us we can use this thing?" The sarcasm in Falk's tone was obvious.

Craig made a slow head shake and corrected himself. "No, Sir, we're in possession of it, not in control. Sorry about that."

Alma's loud confident voice silenced the entire room. "I am to make a copy of their computer core on Earth for engineers to determine how it functions."

Admiral Falk snapped straight and stiff in his chair, his eyes widened. Alma's presence at a military briefing angered him. "You're going to put enemy alien technology in the Sol system? Who's ridiculous idea was this?"

She walked to the front of the auditorium and turned to face Falk with a glower. "This was my idea. You may play Navy in the Yeset System all you like, but I remind you that Americans do not own Cartara. You are here at the pleasure of the Kohor people, and me. Raven and Cartara's voice are not comfortable with Trey technology on their planet."

Falk stood with a finger stabbing in Alma's direction. "So you get to endanger humans, and I assume we have no say in this?"

Alma tried to mask a twinge of apprehension upon seeing this taller man in his medal-clad uniform standing to confront her. She didn't back down. His disregard for the feelings of her Kohor friends enraged her. "As I see it, there are two habitable worlds. Cartara is off limits for Trey machines. Perhaps you should make bigger ships to run your dangerous experiments on, or would you prefer I crush the sphere and be done with it?"

General Trauger jumped to his feet, taking a position between them. He brought an end to their tension filled discourse by explaining, "Admiral, the President and the Department of Defense have approved moving one of these cores to Texas. You're already aware of this, Sir."

Falk sat while maintaining an intense stare locked onto General Trauger's eyes. He outranked David by a considerable degree, but Alma's existence changed many things in his reliable military world, and he

Ascension, The Ymir Trinity

didn't enjoy it at all.

Stacey stood behind a podium in the end-zone of a football field lit by the rising sun, surveying her small army of engineers with smug pride. "Good morning! I'm Captain Martin, and I'll be making your lives a living hell for the next month or two." Some laughed, most didn't.

Her lofty voice had no need for a microphone. "You'll be separated into small teams of about ten. Each team will be tasked with reengineering a subsection of an alien device the United States Navy secured in the Yeset solar system. On your tablets, you'll find your team designations. Do not move to other teams."

Dawn sat on the ground against a chain-link fence fifty meters behind Stacey. She was getting a bit worked up watching her commanding so many people.

Stacey directed her engineers into a large air-conditioned pole shed adjacent to the field and made her way to Dawn with an exaggerated pouty lip. "I'm so sorry. This is going to take a long time, and it's really important work."

Dawn stood, arms crossed, with an unimpressed grimace. "You have to sleep. Don't do it in your lab." Stacey's increasing importance to the military was getting on her nerves. "You sleep at home or invite me to join you."

"I promise." She kissed Dawn's angry little mouth and left her alone on the field.

Inside the building, each team located their workstations and started digging into their assigned section of the Trey computer core. Stacey ambled about the room helping them understand what they were working on and giving them direction when needed.

A couple of weeks into the project, productivity declined, prompting her to task Dawn with assessing her teams mental conditions. Dawn made her way around the room selecting individuals who lacked the confidence or drive required for the project's success. She enjoyed weeding out losers.

Stacey walked the group of under-performers outside and addressed the bewildered engineers in a cold matter-of-fact tone. "I regret to inform you that you are no longer working on this project." Military Police swooped in and escorted them onto a waiting bus where they were taken away.

Her remaining teams finished rewriting the complicated Trey circuitry into human engineering specifications in under two-months. Widespread inefficiencies in the original device made their version smaller, more reliable, and far more powerful.

AI algorithms combed through her finalized schematics to compile a step-by-step manual of Alma friendly components and procedures. Alma stared overwhelmed at the huge set of instructions. "This is more complicated than what I am trained for. I will need you to guide me as if I were a child. Even then, I am not optimistic."

Stacey got a twisted pleasure from watching Alma struggle with something that seemed so obvious to her. "Think of it like painting. When you learn my techniques, you'll be able to reproduce my brushstrokes."

Alma loathed everything about engineering and

engineers. "Why is Dawn not here?"

"I kind of threw myself into this one." Stacey slept little in the past few weeks, which was evident on her gaunt face. "This isn't like the other things we've built. We needed to maintain strict focus, and Dawn is too much of an adorable distraction."

Hours working together turned into days with little progress. Frustrated by tiny details in Stacey's designs, Alma shut down and disappeared on many occasions. To help move things along, Stacey adopted the persona of a kindergarten teacher, stepping her through the project in bite-sized pieces.

After a month of fighting, crying, and celebrating minor victories, they completed a theoretical prototype. "How will you know if this works? I do not believe the military will allow me to create a black hole in our solar system. Many of them are quite angry with me for bringing that Trey thing here."

Stacey gagged at the notion of Ymir's chosen one bowing to the will of ordinary human beings. She pushed aside her strained respect for Alma, grabbed a tablet, and swiped through several screens. "Another team is working on this." She turned it to face Alma. The caption read, "Spherical Toroidal Confinement Particle Fusion Accelerator".

Alma made a disgusted sneer at the confusing title. "Are you saying we can already mimic that Trey moon? How is this possible?"

"It's not. This is more of an ignition system, like the battery and starter motor on an internal combustion engine. There's energy all around us, everywhere. Our particle accelerator just opens the tap. Once the device has access to that power, it can keep itself running."

Dawn peeked into the lab, pretending she didn't want to interrupt them. "Is this an okay time?"

Stacey waved her over to show off their creation. "Look at this beautiful thing. With what we've built, the United States military will be much more than a curious anomaly in this universe." That all-too-common distress on Alma's face caught her eye. "Don't worry. It won't be able to do everything you can do, not even close."

A mild anxiety sullied Alma's voice. "This entire project feels wrong to me, but I can admit it is incredible you can do this."

Dawn leaned her head against Alma and nuzzled her shoulder. "Ymir is happy with this. Trust her."

A beautiful new Navy warship, fifty times larger than her X9 sisters, sat on a sun-baked tarmac awaiting her cue to perform. Inside her belly rested Stacey's latest creation, the Hallberg Reactor. It was wrapped within the military's spaghetti-like particle accelerator.

Military leaders and politicians funneled into bleachers near the runway to witness her maiden flight. General Trauger stood at a podium overlooking the newest addition to their warship family where he addressed the same people who enjoyed slowing down his projects. "I'm not going to play around with the usual ass kissing pomp you're all too content with." Half-hearted laughter trickled from the audience.

"This is the Q9 warship, a space capable craft utilizing our new Hallberg Reactor. It will enable the ship to travel great distances in seconds." He paused, expecting a reaction he didn't get. "The Q9 will rise above the ground and appear at different locations in a three-dimensional grid over the airport."

A faint but audible whine filled the air as her particle accelerator reached capacity. Swirling tiny quantum vortices formed at cross-sections in the clump of tangled tubes and dissipated into high energy collapses. Utilizing that energy, the Hallberg Reactor sprang to life.

Faster than the human eye could perceive, the machine Stacey and Alma built memorized every atom comprising its mother and her contents. It bound to matter at the target location, ripped the atoms into their base particles, and recombined the subatomic structures into a perfect copy of itself. The copy then dismantled its original. This process lasted less than one one-hundredth of a second.

The ship popped into random positions above the airport, prompting several audience members to their feet, clapping and cheering.

A Congress member shouted over the excited crowd. "How does this compare to Alma?" Everyone fell quiet.

"It doesn't. She can move light years away. She can alter incredible amounts of matter simultaneously. We don't have the technology or power to replicate her full capabilities, and likely never will."

The man continued, "How far can it go in one jump?"

"First, it's not jumping. It's being copied and destroyed in a fraction of a second." David searched for the ship's specifications on his tablet, and mechanically read aloud, "It can move thirty-eight billion kilometers at a time. It takes approximately eighty seconds before the Hallberg Reactor can move it again. The amount of energy used to move one meter is the same needed to move one billion kilometers."

The ship settled to Earth at its original resting place. David's tone turned serious as he spoke into the microphone. "We're planning on sending thirty Q9s to the Trey solar system, Daneln. It's our hope this show of force will end the conflict between our people, convincing them to negotiate with us. That's where some of you take over."

With confident piercing eyes, a middle-aged man wearing an expensive business suit called out. "Alma will replicate them, right?"

"Of course." David's suspicious mind knew this person wasn't a regular government employee.

The man pushed further, "Just to save time, not because we can't make them?"

David stepped away from the podium and raised his voice. "We ask Alma to help speed things along. Anything, everything we ask of her can be done by us, but it would take a much longer time to do it."

"I'm not questioning our abilities. I'm just trying to understand a few things. We should talk, one-on-one." He didn't seem to be asking, more like requiring.

With the main show over, a small team of military personnel escorted their audience to the ship, allowing them on board to wander around. David and the well-dressed man walked back to an empty building behind the bleachers.

Inside an unused office, David threw his tablet on a dust covered desk. "Alright, who exactly are you?"

"My name is Carl Fremont. I'm an operations officer with the DIA." He pulled a chair away from the desk, dusted off the seat, and sat.

David joined him at the opposite side of the desk. His annoyed tone set the mood. "What do you want?"

Fremont continued in a calm and controlled voice. "That ship, it's impressive, and the Hallberg Reactor, wow."

"Just get to the point." David was growing tired of people talking in cryptic sentences, pretending to be smart.

Fremont pursed his lips while trying to present himself as friendly. "It's literally perfect. It's as if we had some outside help."

"It's based on a Trey device, and you know that. This isn't a secret. Are you talking about Ymir? I don't think she helped at all." He disliked it when people talked around a subject. It was frustrating and a waste of everyone's time.

"I'm not talking about the Trey or whatever that thing in Ms. Branagan's head is." Fremont unzipped a leather binder and removed a thin stack of papers. He placed them on the desk and slid the stack toward David. "There is no way in hell this person hasn't made it on your radar."

David didn't bother looking at the intelligence report. He already knew who it was about. "Damn it."

"The Pentagon fears that your faith in this person is a potential national security liability. For now, we're going to let you deal with this. We trust you'll do what needs to be done." Mr. Fremont pushed back his chair and walked away, leaving General Trauger alone behind the desk with that stack of papers staring him in the face.

Dawn and Stacey sat side-by-side at a computer terminal, viewing data pouring in from her Hallberg Reactor. Dawn focused on a tiny live-streaming video of military and political leaders touring the new Q9 warship. "They have no idea what they're looking at. Oh, Trauger's coming, and he's pissed about something."

Stacey spun around as he entered the room. "I need to talk to you, alone." His finger pointed in the direction of an open office door.

Dawn taunted her with a singsongy tune. "You're in trouble."

David closed the door behind them, pushing it shut tight. He sat at the desk and struggled with how to start their conversation. After glaring into her eyes for an uncomfortably long time, he blurted, "You're Æsir."

She countered his glare with a mocking smile. "And? I'm impressed you figured this out so fast. It was that reactor. I knew I should have slowed down on that thing."

His mouth dropped open. Stunned by her brazen candor, his mind raced with conspiracies centering around the technologies she helped develop.

"I won't lie to you. Ask me anything. You know, it's kind of funny. In the entire known universe, which isn't much, there are only two sapient species, Æsir, and human. We look so similar. That can't be a coincidence."

He spoke through clenched teeth, "You look exactly like us." David scanned every centimeter of her face for any signs she wasn't human.

She displayed a guilty smirk and pointed toward her own head. "Well, not quite. I sort of stole this person."

"What?! You murdered a human?" Stacey's cavalier

attitude made him want to punch her in her stolen mouth.

"Technically, no. Over time, I reordered her neurons and built a few neural pathways to match mine. Took me years. After she became me, I killed my original self. So, this is the same person, with my memories and intelligence." A pompous grin thinned her lips. "And, with my help, we'll save billions of humans. It's a fair trade you'd make yourself."

"No, no I wouldn't. What are your people doing on Earth?" His blood-red face was showing the hallmarks of enormous stress as a nagging pain radiated down his left arm.

Stacey struggled to pull her chair closer. "You've ordered people into battle, some of whom surely died. I know at least one guy who did. You've probably killed people yourself. So, yes, yes you would."

She could smell his souring sweat as his rising blood pressure pushed him to the brink of a heart attack. "I started out wanting to help with the Kohor, but then we killed Alma and made her into a Guardian. Now you really need me."

"Why would Alma mean we need you? What's a Guardian?" It was obvious they needed her. That reactor wouldn't exist without her. Stacey's brilliance was far beyond anyone he had known or read about. It had been clear for some time she wasn't who she appeared to be.

"With our fusion bombs and our pretty new ships, and that wonderful AI, we'll easily beat the Kohor. But now we've attracted the Æsir. They'll slaughter us in minutes and burn this world and Cartara. They'll probably kill off the Trey for building that tech we captured."

"They don't allow nature to make sapient species like us. They don't really like any animals besides worms. We were a fun curiosity for a while, but Alma's existence changed that. Now we're a big problem. They only tolerate Æsir Caretakers and Protectors."

David looked confused, prompting her to explain further. "Caretakers are like Alma was before we nuked her. She could see only this planet. Protectors see an entire solar system. Guardians, what Alma is now, control multiple solar systems. Guardians are virtually unkillable."

He pulled his squeaky chair toward the desk with enough force to push air from his mouth. "Aren't your people thousands of years more advanced than us?"

"They're about one hundred years ahead of us and that was before we made the reactor. They've stagnated for centuries. Their Guardian only cares about expansion, getting control of new solar systems. We just need a few more toys, and then they shouldn't be a serious threat any longer."

"You're admitting you're a traitor to your own people? That sure as hell won't make me trust you."

"Right, because Americans hate traitors? Britons, Nazis, Chinese, Russians, we embrace them with open arms and wonderful gifts, and awesome jobs. We love them when they're useful." A mischievous askew smile adorned her face. "And you know I'm very useful."

David's voice assumed an urgent cadence. "What about Dawn, are you just using her to get to Alma? Why hasn't Ymir warned them about you?"

"I'm in love with Dawn, and Alma in a weird way, and you, and this planet, and humans in general. I don't know much about Ymir, but I know what they are, and this strange relationship Dawn has with him, her, it, whatever, is not normal."

Stacey made an abrupt subject change. "Do you really want a hot war with the Trey fifty trillion kilometers from Alma's protection? I know everything about them. All their planets, their Caretaker, Shan. I'll bet you didn't know they already have a war going on in their own solar system right now." She pulled her chair closer and lowered her voice. "The Trey are at war with an ugly race called Stuulla."

"You said there are only two species. How do you explain the Kohor and the Trey, and the Stuulla?" David's growing interest fueled her excitement.

Stacey talked as fast as her mouth would allow. "There are two Anthropic sapient species. The Kohor, Trey, and Stuulla are all Æsir. They were created to colonize new solar systems. The Æsir alter their genetic structure to work best with the worlds they're inhabiting. It takes hundreds or thousands of generations before they gain the trust of their world's Jötunn, what Ymir is."

David devoured her every word. She continued, "The goal is to get the Jötunn to choose a Caretaker, and eventually make him a Protector. Once they become Protectors, the Æsir Guardian absorbs the entire system into his empire."

Dawn knocked on the door, bringing a sudden halt to their conversation. "All good in there?" She enjoyed taking advantage of the fact that people forget Ymir tells her everything.

Like a strung out junkie after hearing a distant police siren, David whispered, "Does she know?"

"Probably not, I don't completely understand the Jötnar. They hide or gloss over things that complicate the connection they have with their Speakers." She opened the door with a cute little smile and motioned for Dawn to come in.

David didn't waste any time pretending to be gentle about Dawn's girlfriend. "Stacey is Æsir."

Dawn was unfazed by his revelation. "Biologically, how would that work? Would your babies be Æsir human hybrids? Can you even mate with humans?"

Her flippant attitude caught him by surprise. "You already knew about her and didn't bother to tell anyone? Can we trust her?"

"Hell if I know. According to Ymir, they're in a kind of war with the Æsir." Ymir filled Dawn's mind with confusing images of Æsir experiments attempting to poke at the Jötnar in their own universe. She shook her head at Stacey. "You know they don't like it when you try to touch them."

David puffed out his cheeks with a dramatic exhale. "Can you get Alma here? I need a way to talk to our people on Cartara without going through Ymir."

Stacey lifted her hand high above her head like a little school girl. "I can help with that, Sir. Just saying."

Without warning, Alma appeared standing beside David, staring at Stacey the Æsir. "Dawn, did you and Ymir hide this from me? Why would you do this?"

"Kohor, Trey, Jötunn, Æsir, Icelander, American, who cares? No, I didn't know but I kind of suspected something. Honestly, I thought she was an avatar of Ymir. That would have been so hot."

Alma fell back into a cushioned chair as it materialized behind her. "I am tired of everything changing every time I turn around."

David nodded in exhausted agreement.

Chapter 11

Shan

Thirty Q9 warships accompanied by sixty smaller X9s waited for approval to make the twenty-seven-hour journey from Cartara to the Trey system, Daneln. Navy Fleet Admiral Ander Falk stood tall and proud on the bridge of his new flagship as his massive armada developed around him.

Granted permission to proceed, Admiral Falk shouted his first order as the Commander of humanity's only military space fleet. "Initiate jump protocols." Under the control of AI, they disappeared from Cartara's orbit.

Falk walked away from his bridge while listening in

on a sailor talking with a friend. "Watch that star. Five more seconds." After the five seconds passed, he exclaimed, "Boom! Gone." They experienced no sensations during these jumps.

The Admiral sat alone in his stateroom swiping through screens of telemetry and performing distance math in his head to fritter away time. By his calculations there were seven jumps remaining before they exited the Yeset system. His heart pounded at the thought of them being on their own, without...her.

Eleven hours in, one of the diplomatic team members, Ambassador Simon Holt, stood in his doorway. Uninvited, he walked inside and sat down. "It feels good, doesn't it?"

Falk glanced up at his unwanted visitor. "What feels good?"

Holt responded, "Alma can't see or hear us, and that psychopath she's always with, I don't miss that creepy little girl at all."

With no expression, besides a hint of annoyance, Falk asked, "Do you need something, Holt?"

Holt leaned over Falks desk. "We should talk about the plans they made. From a diplomatic perspective this is a declaration of war with two species we know little to nothing about. A two front war? Three if you count the Kohor. We need to rethink this approach."

The Admiral stared at Holt for a moment before responding. "We're already at war with the Trey. They tried to kill Alma, attacked our ships without warning, and they've been slaughtering innocent Kohor citizens for centuries."

Holt had a quick response prepared. "Alma is a frightening thing to experience. They were probably terrified of her."

Falk stabbed a finger in Holt's direction. "All the Trey in the Yeset system were scientists, engineers, and a small military contingent. According to Alma, they're an extremely intelligent species. So, intelligent poorly armed people launched an attack against a military of unknown strength and size who have a literal god backing them up, because they were scared?" He reopened his tablet. "We'll call on you when you're needed. You're excused."

Over the following hours his ship grew quiet. Most of the sailors gathered in the game room to fight in simulated wars against grotesquely exaggerated aliens. Falk could hear the heavy sounds of boots in the hallways as some of his sailors spent their time jogging around his large ship.

Only a handful of crew members bothered sleeping during the next fourteen hours. Those who did were jarred awake after their latest jump. When the armada materialized deep inside Daneln's bow wave, every ship shuddered, lurching hard to starboard.

Admiral Falk rushed to the bridge where his Executive Officer waved him over. "This says we're caught in some kind of sheer." He motioned the Admiral closer and whispered, "Every ship is reporting serious injuries. Sir, three ships are missing. There are no signs of them anywhere."

Falk exhaled through a tight-lipped frown. "Keep me updated if anything changes." He paused to look out at the stars before returning to his stateroom where he sat thinking of his next move. *This is stupid.* He opened communications with his remaining ships. "I'm restarting the jump protocols."

Holt loomed silent in his doorway, watching him and listening to every word. He waited for Falk to finish ordering the resumption of their mission, then interjected. "Leaving people behind? That can't be a good sign."

"We'll send a buoy back with the location and data. Another team will figure out what happened. We're not equipped or allocated for search and rescue, and we're definitely not here for scientific studies." He grumbled under his breath, "Why do I keep leaving that door open?"

Holt's tone reeked of sarcasm. "Well, it's not like any of us can die permanently, right?" He turned to leave while muttering loud enough for the Admiral to hear. "Trusting that abomination to bring us back from death is already making us reckless."

The last handful of jumps passed without further incident. Now numbering eighty-seven, the automatic sequences stopped, leaving them inside Daneln's heliosphere. Humans and machines worked together to map their final jumps.

Some orbited the Trey home world of Seleen, while the others found themselves orbiting the Trey's outermost inhabitable planet, Moele. According to Stacey's data, Moele was the host of a war between the Trey and an ugly people she called, Stuulla.

"I do not understand why this feels so grim." Alma spoke to David at one end of an empty airfield on Joint Base Cartara. At the other end, a Navy Honor Guard and a small band were readying for the return of their fallen sisters and brothers.

She caught herself glancing at him in his crisp blue formal Air Force attire. Her burgeoning and somewhat unwanted feelings made her act awkward whenever he was around. *What is wrong with me? I am becoming like Dawn.*

He inquisitively watched the twitching muscles of her face acting out her internal struggle. "Is this the first time you're doing this after people actually died?"

"What? Uh, yes." She wished Dawn were here to say something horrible, somehow making her feel better about this entire situation.

David startled her out of her thoughts by shouting into the air, signaling it was time to welcome home their lost family members. While the band prepared their instruments, he leaned over and said, "Alma, whenever you're ready."

She lowered her head and swallowed hard against her jumbled emotions, then materialized the three lost ships, without a sound, in the center of the airfield.

Commander Tao of the resurrected Q9 warship read a far-too-casual note from his AI. It informed him his life had been reset. The crews of each ship fell silent as the bleak reality rolled through their ranks. They all died.

Admiral Falk's flagship, and twenty-nine others, appeared in deep orbit of Seleen. Human stealth technology augmented with stolen Kohor and Trey know-how rendered his ships virtually undetectable.

Similar to the Kohor generation ships nearing Sol, Trey communication encryption was rudimentary, requiring little effort to decipher. Falk's fleet laid in hiding as they absorbed and decrypted information flowing from the Trey home world and her satellites.

A gentle sweeping tone resonated throughout Raven's cabin. She jumped from her bed to face the door, which had no discernible handles. She puzzled over her options while running her eyes around the rectangular frame, looking for anything that could make it open.

That tone sounded again. She placed her hands against the wall-door and was about to push before it slid open to reveal Admiral Falk staring down at her. "I'm sorry. I didn't know how to operate this door."

He tried maintaining his expressionless facade, but couldn't stop a breathy chuckle from escaping. "We're orbiting Seleen. It's time for you to earn your keep." He motioned for her to follow. "Were you trapped in your room this entire trip?"

Raven grabbed her camouflaged Navy jacket and struggled to put it on over a t-shirt she believed was far too tight. "I mostly slept." She left out the part where she cried herself to sleep under the crushing silence of losing her voice and not having Alma to comfort her.

The commotion on the busy command bridge couldn't pull Raven's eyes off of Seleen displayed across multiple screens along a wide curved wall. She had never seen a world from orbit before, and paused to stare at it. Falk put his fingertips on her back and led her to a crew chair.

A young man scrambled to hand her a pair of headphones. Raven was growing irritated with humans feeling the need to help her as if she were incompetent. "I have been trained for this, I know how to perform my tasks without your assistance." She snatched them from him and placed them over her ears.

Raven translated streams of decrypted Trey communications into English while teaching an eager AI how to speak their language. She made for entertaining background noise as Admiral Falk was already bored. He amused himself by watching her random expressions as she spied on her lifelong enemy.

Commander Kathryn Pruitt's fleet appeared in distant orbit of the Trey world, Moele. Her sedate tone kept the young bridge crew calm. "Airman, scan for any communications and nearby ships."

They initiated passive scans of the planet, listening for any data emanating from Trey or Stuulla technology. Encrypted Trey signals radiated from the world but no ships or satellites orbited her.

"Sir, there's something huge about a million kilometers from the planet. It's as big as Atlanta, and it's loud." His wavering voice broke into a nervous high-pitched squeak.

"Jump us to three hundred thousand kilometers from that ship. Let's see if it's what we're looking for." The small blue world disappeared, replaced by an AI enhanced image of a smooth bulbous dark-green vessel twenty-five kilometers long. "Damn, that thing is not pretty to look at, but it's impressive." What they found matched Stacey's detailed descriptions of a Stuulla generation ship.

Pruitt's shoulders slumped. She expected to land in the middle of a raging battle, allowing her fleet to side with the Trey. "Make just our squadron visible."

Her flagship and two X9 warships unveiled in a

failed attempt at getting a response from either the Stuulla or the Trey. "Start active scans of that thing. Maybe that'll wake them up." The Stuulla reacted to their benign particle bombardments, but not in the way she had hoped. Both parties exchanged harmless sensor barrages, assessing each other's capabilities.

After fifteen minutes of back-and-forth scanning, a single-file stream of four hundred small fighters poured out from the massive ship's port side. Pruitt's eyes popped open as an excited smile brightened her face. "Well, here we go! Hide us and jump the entire fleet to the other side of their ship."

To everyone's surprise, the little fighters arced over their mother toward the fleet's new location. She chuckled, *I guess we don't need to hide anymore.* "Assume a defensive configuration."

The Stuulla ships opened fire as Pruitt's fleet moved to form a large sphere in front of them. Similar to Trey weapons, strings of bright beads flowed from their enemy, filling the dark sky with thousands of tiny points of light. AI controlled laser turrets had no difficulty targeting and destroying these slow and predictable weapons.

"Maneuver into an offensive configuration and target their lead ship." She assumed the Stuulla fighters would be as easy to destroy as the Trey ships were during General Trauger's initial encounter with them.

Hundreds of lines of invisible photons emanated from half her fleet, focused on a single enemy vessel. It continued its approach as if nothing happened. Pruitt sat back in her chair looking over statistics streaming across a large screen at the front of her bridge.

The Commander sensed her crew's fraying nerves

as the Stuulla fleet closed in on their position. She curled her upper lip and drew in a deep breath. "Commander Erling, would you please nuke them."

An audible sigh of relief escaped the mouths of several anxious crew members as Erling passed her order on to the ship's military AI. Intelligent machines assessed their situation and goals to calculate the spread and yields needed to halt the enemy's advance.

Three small nuclear warheads materialized within and around the advancing Stuulla armada, detonating in a dazzling display of eye-scorching energy. The radioactive spheres expanded to envelop the enemy fighters then dissipated, leaving behind four hundred lifeless shells.

Frantic Trey communications flooded in from every planet and ship in the solar system. Raven, overwhelmed and frustrated, scolded her AI student. "Please silence yourself. You are making this unnecessarily difficult." She couldn't keep up with the panic filled chatter.

Falk amused himself by watching Raven struggle to translate a deluge of incoming messages to the ship's AI. He laughed as she reprimanded the emotionless machine for getting a translation wrong. It was kind of cute. "I'm guessing we made an impact around Moele?"

A small group of well-dressed diplomats entered the hectic bridge in response to an urgent call from Admiral Falk. "We got their attention. It's about time for you to smooth things over." Falk couldn't wipe the smug grin from his face.

Ambassador Holt pushed through his team. "Exactly how did we get their attention?"

"Commander Pruitt nuked the Stuulla." Holt's displeased reaction turned Falk's smirk into full-blown laughter.

Holt rebuked him with a patronizing tone. "Nuclear weapons may bring a forced peace, but they don't make for trusting friendships."

Falk taunted Holt's team with upturned palms. "Making friends is your job, not ours."

A nervous officer interrupted them, "Sir, seventeen Trey ships incoming!"

Raven focused her eavesdropping on the inbound ships. "They are warning each other about you. Your large bombs terrify them." Although she feared her giant human allies, she was happy to be with them at this moment.

Falk's voice remained steady. "Put a nuke far enough out that they can see it, but it won't hurt them."

It was a minor challenge convincing their AI to target empty space. They had evolved a somewhat bloodthirsty personality over the past year. He called in his Rapid AI Team to help it understand why it needed to target nothing.

After some gentle coaxing, a small nuclear detonation illuminated the Trey fleet eighty kilometers off their port side, halting their approach. "Raven, ask them to talk with us."

Raven relayed Falk's request and squished her body against the back of her chair, waiting for their response. That response came rather quick. "They want us to move closer to Seleen, where their Caretaker has influence."

Falk spun around to face his diplomats with a huge grin. "Well, what do you think?"

They huddled together to discuss their options. Upon their failure to reach a unanimous consensus, Holt asked, "What's the worst that could happen? Alma resurrects us on Cartara?" The condescension was evident in his sanctimonious tone.

Falk understood Holt was acting childish, but didn't want to withhold information from his crew. "They could imprison us and keep us alive for eternity. There's a rumor Alma can't bring us back if we're alive somewhere."

Holt didn't appreciate his candor. "I can't make that kind of decision for all these people."

Falk rolled his eyes at Holt's unearned self-importance. "I'm only asking for your opinion. We don't take orders from you. I'll make the final decision."

Holt hesitated. "I don't see how we can progress without showing we're willing to trust them."

Falk pivoted on one foot and shouted, "Unveil this squadron only, and move us into near orbit of Seleen."

Their flagship and her two support ships set a course for the planet with the Trey fleet flanking them. When the ship entered orbit of Seleen, five pinkish-blue unarmed men appeared on the bridge. Instincts compelled Raven to cringe at the site of her abusers. They looked her over before turning their attention to Falk, who stood a full head taller than them.

The Petty Officer made his way to Raven and tapped her on the shoulder. "They're probably going to need you."

Nervous, she walked to the center of the room, joining Admiral Falk at his side. Raven addressed their guests in their native language. "I will act as your interpreter." She was unable to make eye contact with them.

Her voice signaled a submissive tone as she introduced the two most prominent Americans. "This is United States Navy Fleet Admiral Ander Falk and this is United States Ambassador Simon Holt." Holt's title was much longer, but she forgot the rest. It was something about aliens.

One of the Trey men reached out to touch Raven's face, causing Raven to flinch. Falk assumed an aggressive posture, grabbed his arm, and forced it away.

Raven stepped back, half-hiding behind the Admiral. Four American service members snapped their hands to their side-arms. None of the Trey reacted to the situation at all.

Falk turned to his team of diplomats and spoke in a bemused tone, "This doesn't seem to be going well."

Hundreds of low yield thermonuclear detonations saturated Pruitt's fleet, decimating over half her armada. "Erling! Nuke that ship! Use the biggest bombs we have. Tell the AI to go wild."

Warheads materialized around the Stuulla generation ship, blanketing the green monster in fire, but the Stuulla assault continued. She was unwilling to accept any more losses, and issued the command to retreat. "Fall back two hundred and fifty thousand kilometers." *Damn it.* Pruitt grimaced as she read the failure log of her counter-attack. "That thing's shields and hull must be a kilometer thick."

It was a stalemate. The Stuulla couldn't launch ships and the humans couldn't harm their base. Out of desperation, Pruitt skimmed the transcripts of Alma's debriefing after her initial encounter with the Trey. She wanted to know how Alma worked through the Trey shields.

Morale in tatters, her crew sat quiet at their stations, waiting for orders from their faltering leader. It was difficult to watch friends and family perish in a nuclear holocaust, and Alma's promise to bring them back from the dead garnered universal skepticism and fear.

Pruitt assembled her Rapid AI Team and thrust a tablet in front of the Executive Officer with a single paragraph highlighted. "Can we do this?"

He grabbed the tablet from her and read far more than she selected. "If we made several of them work together, the reactors could create the spears but not the dust. It's only capable of applying inertia to large masses and only in one direction."

She slapped his back, ignoring his concerns. "So, that's a yes?"

"No. We don't have enough reactors or enough power. This describes a sustained onslaught of fine tipped spears weaving in and out of shielded Trey ships. Alma did this after saturating them with microscopic dust to test their shields for weaknesses."

He stood to face her. As with most engineers, he studied every bit of information about Alma. "We can't do a billionth of what she can do, and she did this in less than a second, according to that Kohor woman."

Pruitt made a disapproving frown. "We don't need dust. We can use our lasers to find holes. We just have to make some new friends who'll let us install them on a few thousand of their ships, and we won't need spears. Good old-fashioned dog fighting missiles should work fine."

Falk and his Trey visitors stepped back from each other. Raven, trying to ensure the Trey weren't too upset, attempted to explain his behavior. "Humans don't appreciate being touched." She forced herself to look into his eyes. "They would like to know your names."

The man who tried to touch her smiled, letting her know he wasn't offended. "They can call me Shan."

Raven moved out from behind the Admiral, but remained glued to his side. "His name is Shan."

Holt stepped closer to Raven. "Shan? Is this the Caretaker of Seleen?"

She translated his question and Shan's response. "This is Caretaker Shan of Seleen."

Holt could barely contain his excitement about meeting the Trey version of Alma. "They clearly want to trust us. This is huge. He knows we could imprison him on this ship. This is a great show of trust."

Admiral Falk nodded. "Good, that means you won't need me any longer, and Holt, don't let them touch her." He left Holt and Shan to discuss matters without a military shadow hovering over them.

Caretaker Shan and Ambassador Holt, with Raven's assistance, developed a cordial rapport. Shan couldn't stop staring at her during her translations. A helpful docile Kohor who wasn't trying to murder him gave him much-needed hope, so he sent his soldiers away as a show of good will.

Holt explained how mutually beneficial an alliance between the Trey and humans could be, endeavoring not to portray humans as some kind of white knights swooping in to rescue them. Raven helped by embellishing Holt's words with extraordinary anecdotes of human creativity and their endless bouts of convenient luck.

Excited, holt yelled out the door to Admiral Falk. "He's agreeing to let us help with the Stuulla! Their military is willing to assist with Pruitt's plan!" Nothing in Holt's training prepared him for the relative ease of these negotiations. It occurred to him that humans evolving in relentless conflict may be of great benefit in their expanding universe.

"I guess you people are useful after all." Admiral Falk turned to Raven and asked, "He doesn't think we're Æsir?"

Raven donned a rare look of derision. "None of us believe you are Æsir anymore. Everything about your people is confusing and chaotic. You are far too excitable. All of you."

Human engineers struggled with Raven and her new AI friend while she endeavored to translate their perplexing technical gibberish to Shan. After some initial trial and error, she was able to walk him through the construction and use of American laser weapons. Shan caught on fast.

Trey and human ship Captains played war-games with a prototype vessel, testing her new weaponry. Their eventual success prompted thousands of Trey ships into Seleen's orbit to be fitted for battle.

146

Commander Pruitt welcomed the site of a massive laser-armed Trey armada joining her outside the bubble of Stuulla reach, which was growing. Their warhead yields were increasing as well. "Commander Erling, let me know when our ships are in place."

Bright red and green dots appeared scattered on the main bridge screen. They moved toward their marks on a simulated three-dimensional sphere surrounding an AI representation of the Stuulla generation ship. "Sir, all Trey ships are in position. Just waiting on us humans."

"Eager little guys, aren't they." Trey willingness to allow the Navy control over their fleets came as a pleasant surprise. She prepared herself for many heated arguments and tough negotiations.

Pruitt stood at the front of her bridge, waiting for the final American warship to find its place. With both fleets in position, she drew in an excited breath and shouted, "Initiate shield penetration tests!"

A spectacular array of laser weapons pummeled their target in a series of calculated patterns. When a beam of light broke through to kiss the Stuulla ship's ugly green skin, an AI recorded that breach in search of a predictable exploit.

The Stuulla attempted to counter the assault by varying their shield energy and intensity, but sapient creatures cannot escape their natural instincts for consistency and repetition. The original purpose of the first rudimentary AI was to take advantage of this weakness, which proved far easier than anyone anticipated.

It wasn't long before reliable patterns emerged. "Sir, we have a green light from the penetration tests. Should I tell them to stop?"

Pruitt's entire body shuddered with adrenaline. "Yes. Commander Erling, weapons free."

One hundred and twenty veiled missiles appeared at specific locations around the Stuulla shield, waiting for their perfect moment to strike. A warhead readied for its opening, ignited its rocket, and propelled itself through the porous Stuulla barrier.

The missile stopped a meter before it touched her hull. Its nose-cone popped open and pushed out a small shaped-charge, sticking it against the ship. Missile after missile breached the shield to attach their payloads.

One hundred and twenty nuclear warheads detonated. The intense heat burned through her skin, filling her outer corridors with radioactive fire and wind. Another pack of missiles made their way into her open wounds. Burrowing deep inside her body, they erupted, tearing further into the armored beast. This sequence repeated until she could no longer sustain life.

Shan's mind flooded with a calming sense of relief and contentedness. His gentle tone reflected a waning anxiety as he spoke to Raven with a subdued voice. "Seleen's Jötunn is warming me with feelings of solace. Plaguing us for so long, the Stuulla have become a normal part of our lives. A loss we will not grieve."

Raven displayed a sweet tight smile in return. "They are creative, these humans. Their world is full of useless things to entertain their eyes and ears. Their minds are so active they don't have enough in their lives to keep them occupied, so they intentionally manufacture chaos." She glanced at Admiral Falk celebrating the news from Commander Pruitt. "War is one of many forms of entertainment to them."

"Will they allow the Trey to continue?" His Jötunn made him want to trust the humans, but he was reluctant. He did however, trust Raven.

"Guardian Alma is beautiful and kind." Raven sensed Shan had tired of leading his people. He wished to surrender his world to the humans, to Alma. "They will protect and nurture your people."

An exhausted expression of defeat tainted his face. "I have failed to safeguard the Trey and our worlds on many occasions." He glanced at Falk, ensuring he couldn't see him, then reached out to touch her hand. "Guardian Alma is strong?"

Raven placed her other hand on his. "Alma is the strongest person I could ever imagine. Her cooperation with human military leaders only serves to amplify her power. Your people and humans will learn so much from each other. I know my people have." She chose not to describe how unpredictable and terrifying humans could be.

Chapter 12

Victory Day

The military government on Cartara declared the day of Admiral Falk's return from Daneln, Victory Day. Not only did they make an ally of the Trey, they defeated an advanced space-faring alien enemy. This celebration marked humanity's first true battle outside the protective bubble of a planet and without the direct assistance of an omnipotent demigoddess.

Alma stood in front of the noisy officers' club, wanting to go inside, but didn't want to darken their festive mood with her unwelcome presence. The boisterous sounds of young women and men acting silly for each other's attention compelled her to enter.

Everyone lowered their voices, including the drunken officers. She was in the middle of turning to leave when David, sitting by himself in a booth on the opposite side of the bar, caught her eye. She ignored the whispers and derisive glances to weave through the revelers like any normal human would.

They cleared a wide path, making sure not to touch her. She hated everything about this. When she reached David's booth, Alma breathed out and relaxed her tense body with a single shiver.

Unaware of her standing over him, he swiped at pages on a tablet as she motioned to a group of people surrounding Admiral Falk and Commander Pruitt. "Why are you not drinking with your friends?" She hoped he wasn't here with them.

Before he could answer, she sat across from him at the table. He closed his tablet and smiled. "I'm not the social type. I'm just here to honor them. They did a great job." David sensed the countless uncomfortable stares cast in their direction. "They don't care much for me either."

Alma looked around the bar, but not at anyone's eyes. "They all seem to hate me. I do not understand this." She lived the majority of her life in rural seclusion, so she was used to being alone, but feeling alone when surrounded by hundreds of people crushed her heart.

David chuckled in an oafish attempt to play down her concerns. "Well, you don't see me surrounded by adoring fans either." He nodded toward a drunk couple kissing. "I'm married. I hang out with two actual goddesses, and the terrifying one can hear our deepest secrets. Plus, there's an Æsir in our exclusive little club, wearing a human skin suit."

Alma blurted out a weird rumbling laugh. "Oh, do not forget about our tiny motherly landlord." She tapped the side of his glass with the back of her fingernail. "How many of these have you had?" She preferred this version of David more than the serious Air Force General one. His trademark scowl was nowhere to be seen.

The enchanting sound of her laughter caught him off guard. "Just two. If I have one more I'll probably start singing, or crying, and no one wants that." He was enjoying their conversation until that annoying voice inside his head ordered him to stand down.

Unable to ignore his sudden mood swing, Alma thumped her palm against the table. "That. That, right there. We are getting along, and then you flip a switch. What did I say?" Dawn suggested many times what his real problem with her was, but she had a difficult time believing anything she said.

David spun his cup in his hand and avoided eye contact with her. The alcohol was melting his hardened personality. "I really like being around you. It's more than your looks. You make me feel important, like I matter. Then I remember who I am. A married old man. An old soldier with rules and responsibilities."

Her lips trembled. It felt wrong letting him ramble when tipsy, but she wanted to peer over the barrier he constructed between them. "I like being around you as well. Besides Dawn and Raven, you are the only person I trust. Honestly, I trust you more than Dawn. She is not completely right in the head."

Distracted by the loud chanting of a drunken group of officers, Alma and David turned to see what the commotion was about. An ocean of people were surrounding Admiral Falk who held a shot glass in each hand. A female officer stood in front of him holding two more. He slammed both shots, grabbed the two she had and gulped them down as well. Falk threw his hands into the air, made victory signs, and screamed at the top of his lungs. The entire bar erupted in applause.

David had a slight slur to his voice. "He's two years older than me, and he gets more out of life in one day than I do in a month. Just ignore me. I usually disappear for a while when I get like this."

Alma tightened her mouth, trying not to laugh at him. Introspective David was quite different from normal David.

He lifted his cup and inspected its emptiness. "Before you and Dawn showed up, my life was pretty much over." His hopeless stare brought tears to Alma's eyes. "I wanted children."

She reached across the table and squeezed his hand. He was startled by her initiating physical contact. "I wish I knew you and your wife before she grew too old to have children. I would have repaired what was wrong with her, so you could be a father. You should be a father."

Alma tensed as she struggled to control her own swirling emotions. "I have liked you since the first day when you imprisoned me in that office." The soothing warmth of his weathered skin surprised her. Different feelings, personal feelings she hadn't experienced in decades made her entire body flush. "I do not mind that you like me."

His military training begged him to pull his hand away, but he didn't. "You, coming along when you did, you saved my life." With his other hand, he patted the top of hers. "It's noisy in here. Do you want to go for a walk?"

They left the club and continued walking until they were far enough away to have a quiet conversation. Stopping near a rail fence separating the sidewalk from the road, David looked to Cartara's mother planet, Bondi. She reflected no light as she covered a quarter of the sky with an inky blackness. A faint outline of brilliant gold radiated a small arc on her eastern horizon. The Yeset star was somewhere behind her.

Alma followed his eyes upward, but failed to understand the appeal of that gas giant. Able to see everything, all the time, dampened those feelings of awe so many humans on Cartara had. She was jealous of them. Even Raven's childlike wonder when she visits Earth left her with the impression she was missing out on something special.

"I can't imagine ever getting used to seeing that." The vision of Bondi against the night's sky was a comforting sight for him. It reminded him he wasn't anywhere near his loveless wife and their marriage of duty. He made a pathetic smile. "I try hard to avoid looking at you, unless you make me mad."

Alma bashfully glanced around. "Then you have had to look at me a lot of times." She moved in closer, deciding to be less subtle about her intentions. "I have never been with anyone."

His eyes widened. Not only was he shocked by her bold revelation but also for what he hoped she was insinuating. "What about Dawn? Everyone kind of assumed you two were a thing until Stacey showed up." She pulled away, forcing his mind to scream at him for ruining what could have been an incredible night.

Alma never understood why everyone thought she and Dawn had a physical relationship. She shook off her mild irritation and pushed her body back up against his arm. "She is a child. An insane child and I do not like women that way." She closed her eyes, breathing in deep then out. "I did not like men either, until you."

The realization this may be happening made him nervous, and it showed in his sweaty palms, which Alma pretended not to notice. He couldn't imagine living over sixty years without human contact. "You could take your pick of any human or Kohor. Male or female." He struggled to understand why she'd choose to be with him when younger and stronger people were available.

"When I was a teen, I started having my abilities." Her eyes watered. "I terrified myself. I was so afraid I would hurt someone that I hid from people on our family farm."

She paused to compose herself. "My father was unaware. I hid it well, but he knew something was wrong with me. He worried about me. A few years after he died, those horrible feelings started. Like Dawn, all I could see was repulsive and defective people everywhere."

David pointed toward a group of young soldiers loud-talking in a circle with beers in hand. "You should have joined a military. Armies tend to vet out most of the physically inferior people." He regretted his words. She wanted a listening ear, not his worthless insights.

"Young strong people are pleasant to look at, but they have not been around long enough. You cannot know what terrible things are lurking in their genetics." She forced a single laugh through her nose.

"You are an old man, and you look better than most of them. Your genetics are good."

Alma wondered how long she had to continue flirting until he figured her out. She questioned whether she was doing this right since she never tried to attract anyone before. "I could give you hundreds of children, perhaps thousands. We can spread our beautiful genetics across this entire universe."

David squeezed her hand and gestured down the street. "My house is just a few blocks from here." He struggled to think of simple things he could ask to test her, to ensure he didn't make a fool of himself.

Alma pulled in tight around his arm as they made their way to his home, an encouraging signal. "Please stop me if you think I'm pushing you." In his head those words sounded idiotic. He told a woman who could decimate armies with a single thought that she shouldn't be afraid to speak up.

They didn't utter another word during their short walk to his house. He imagined several worsening scenarios for the night. His mind kept focusing on how easy it would be for him to ruin everything by saying something inappropriate. He was also concerned he may have read too much into her actions. Maybe she only wanted to talk. He decided he'd be okay with that.

She was also pondering her next steps, worried her lack of experience could make this night somehow unpleasant for him. Embarrassing visions of her being boring or clumsy dominated her thoughts. The stress was overwhelming. Alma was clueless about how human male minds functioned.

When they reached his tiny military supplied home, he opened the door. "Sorry, it's not fancy." Alma stepped inside and spun around. She wanted him to kiss her the way they kiss in movies, but instead of kissing, his gruff confidence collapsed into a pool of spineless insecurity. "I'd like to kiss you if that's okay."

Alma looked at him with a chastising expression. "This is going to be a long and awkward night if you intend on asking my permission about everything." She trusted him and wanted him to take complete control of their evening. "Do things. I will let you know if I do not like something."

He followed her inside with a gentle nudge, and slammed the door behind them. With his arms wrapped tight around her waist, he leaned in to kiss her. Each kiss grew more passionate and forceful than the one before it. Her head was spinning.

Alma's usual aroma of candied cinnamon sweetness transformed into a soothing eucalyptus scent. "God you smell incredible." Her fragrance flooded him with a euphoria he had never experienced before. He wondered if this perfume was intentional or some strange demigoddess quirk. Besotted by her mind-altering bouquet, he lifted her from the floor and carried his precious cargo into his bedroom.

Daybreak left her wide awake alongside David's sound asleep body. Unable to restrain herself from making a few changes, Alma flattened a couple well-earned wrinkles and darkened some of his gray hairs. She nuzzled her shoulder into his armpit and whispered, "I will keep you forever."

Chapter 13

Sacrifice

"I hid for so long, and now I am in the middle of everything. A centerpiece." Alma, General Trauger, and Admiral Falk were the only people on the bridge of Falk's flagship. "Dawn is quite excited about this. I know I should trust her, but I do not. Not about this. She and Ymir seem too eager."

Like Alma, David didn't care for any of this either. "The Pentagon is very eager as well. What I don't understand is why would he do this? Why give up everything?"

Alma daydreamed about her Icelandic seclusion. "That I understand completely." She looked out at the uncountable stars with quivering eyes emphasizing her profound anguish. "It is too much at times. When I think I am in control, something bigger, usually worse, happens. It seems so endless." She rested her head against his arm.

Admiral Falk turned away from their unsettling show of affection. Witnessing this lionized military General trying to console their anxious demigoddess was unpleasant to watch. "We have contingencies if they try to capture you. I'll nuke every planet in their solar system, one by one, if they attempt anything." Dawn and Alma believe she would return to either Earth or Cartara if she died. If she didn't come back, many, including Falk, wouldn't shed a tear over her absence.

Outside the Yeset system, Alma's abilities, and composure, faded. The stress of Ymir's silence heightened her human senses, churning her stomach. "I am not feeling well. I need to lie down." David draped his arm around her shoulders and walked her to their room, leaving Falk alone with his ship.

Together on their bed, Alma nestled into David, resting her face on his chest. She listened to the rhythm of his breathing and heartbeat steadying as he fell asleep. "You are a good substitute for Ymir." She snuggled in as close as she could.

Resurrecting sailors killed by nature and Stuulla shattered the icy barrier she built and fortified for decades. The vast number of human deaths during that brief war traumatized her. David's strong character when faced with difficult times soothed her in ways Ymir and Dawn couldn't, or wouldn't.

She ran her fingers over the lines on his forehead, pretending to flatten them using her now powerless mind. Although he held personal issues with her repairing his body, he understood she had no desire to lay next to a wrinkly old man, so he tolerated her meddling.

Frustrated, her active brain couldn't suffer doing nothing for long. "David, wake up." she shook him until his eyes popped open. "I need you to entertain me."

David chuckled at Alma's inability to be a regular human for a few hours. "Alright, alright." He looked into her beautiful face as an agonizing twinge of marital guilt washed over him.

Alma had seen that look many times, but chose not to acknowledge it.

He panned the room, but couldn't find any cards or games. "We can play a guessing game. I'll say something shockingly mean, you guess if I heard it from Dawn or Raven."

"To be fair, Raven does not understand when she is being mean. Dawn, however, seems to draw energy from her cruelty." A suggestive little smile brightened her face as she pushed him against the bed and straddled his hips. "I believe I have a more fun game we can play."

Stacey awoke to the pleasing melody of Dawn's hushed voice flowing from their living-room. It sounded as if Dawn was having a secret conversation with someone.

She tiptoed down their short hallway to spy on them from around a corner. Their house was dark, but she could make out Dawn's silhouette roaming the room, gesturing as she talked. A second silhouette caught her eye. It was taller and wider than Dawn. Now close enough to see who she was talking to, Stacey yelled, "What the fuck is that?!"

A swirling column of dust swept the floor to form the dappled shape of a large man, then ambled about the room like a drunken ghost. Stacey turned on the lights, which yielded no reaction from it. "Seriously, what the hell is this?"

"I don't know. Kind of thought you'd know something." Dawn mirrored the ghost's uncoordinated dance, but her rendition was more graceful, sensual.

The ghost noticed Dawn no longer paying it any attention. Stumbling around, it knocked over several nick-knacks from a small shelf above their television. It was difficult to determine if this crude bumbling was unintentional.

Dawn snickered at the dorky poltergeist. "He's kind of clumsy."

A wave of goosebumps rippled across Stacey's arms and neck. She was horrified that Dawn found this thing amusing. A faint buzzing sound emanated from it, prompting her to ask, "Is it talking to you?"

Dawn reached out and wiggled her fingers inside its poorly articulated hand. "He vibrates the air. He's quiet, but you can make out most of his words."

"Does it speak English? Could this be Alma playing with you?"

"Alma is too far away, we can't feel her at all. I don't like it when I can't feel her. He does talk kind of like her though, like he just learned English or something." She continued wiggling her fingers in his dust.

Stacey yanked down on her arm. "Don't touch it. What's Ymir saying about this thing?"

Dawn bit her lower lip with a mischievous smile as a

little giggle escaped her mouth. "She's saying, don't touch him."

Stacey thought of calling the Military Police. "What's it saying to you?"

Again, reaching out to the ghost, Dawn waved her fingers in his swirling dusty chest. "He wants us to help him. He says he's in danger. In case you didn't notice, he's not from around here. I think he's from a different solar system or universe or something."

Unable to calm herself enough to study this thing alone, Stacey rushed to the kitchen counter and grabbed her phone. The two people she wanted were out of reach, so she settled for one of her engineering team leads. "I need you at my house, now. Get everyone. Go to the lab and gather every bit of equipment you can carry. Make sure you bring the Entangled Particle Scanner."

The inquisitive scientist side of Stacey overpowered her unease. She spun a chair away from the dining-room table and sat to observe them. This thing appeared far too comfortable around her girlfriend.

Over an hour passed before her team pounded on their front door. It felt like minutes. Stacey hurried them inside and helped them unload their gear on the dining table. She motioned toward Dawn's ghost. "It keeps asking for help. I want to know where this is coming from." She snapped her fingers to break her teams focus. "Hey! Hey! Start setting up."

Dawn pretended to hold the ghost's hands and danced with him to music playing only in her head. "Where are you from?" Her dancing partner lifted one arm and stretched it up at an angle.

Stacey hurried to the monster and grimaced while mingling her arm in its dust to match its upward pointing gesture. With her other arm she waved to one of her team members. "Bring a tripod and laser pointer."

The young man nervously unfolded a tripod to the right of her arm, secured a laser pointer to it and adjusted the dot to mimic her finger's direction. He pushed her aside, replacing her arm with the laser.

Stacey grabbed a tablet from the equipment pile and secured it to the tripod where she aligned it to the laser. An augmented reality app displayed a starry sky, mimicking what they would see if the ceiling wasn't blocking their view. She compiled a large list of nearby stars, then reduced that list to the nearest ten. Only a few had known planets in their orbits.

Distracted by a low hum emanating from what appeared to be an upside-down pyramid made of smooth metal rods and plates, Dawn turned to face the team as they assembled various pieces of monitoring equipment. "When did you guys get here? What is that thing? You're not going to hurt him, are you?" She stood between her new friend and Stacey's engineers.

"It won't hurt whatever that thing is. We call this our, `Where in the Worlds is Alma Ólafsdóttir`, device. You know, like that old kids show." She smiled at Dawn's unamused stare.

With their device assembled and ready, Stacey focused its attention on Dawn's ghost. The tablet showed a three-dimensional representation of several million atoms comprising a section of the dusty creature. It mapped the spin of entangled particles within each atom and located a subatomic hint of quarks spinning heavy to one side.

The machine plotted rays from the weighted wobble of entangled particles to their sister particles trillions of kilometers away. They appeared to be anchored in one of the star systems she cataloged.

Her team's astrophysicist calculated the positions of every celestial body intersecting the plotted rays. "Only one planet is on that path. It's orbiting Proxima Centauri, Proxima B."

While the scientists and engineers engaged in speculative babble, Dawn lifted two ornamental ball-shaped candles from a table. She held them inside the dusty man's head where human eyes would be. "Hold these here." She let go and the candles remained suspended in his swirling face. "There, that's much less creepy looking." They dropped to the floor. "Oh."

"All of this is extremely creepy." Stacey muttered as she searched her phone for whoever was in charge of the Military Police at the Air Force base.

On their approach to Seleen, Alma, David, and Ander regrouped on the bridge. Falk wondered if he should accept General Trauger as his superior given that the most powerful human ever couldn't keep her hands off him. "Captain Martin was vague about what happens next."

Caretaker Shan appeared at the front of the bridge when their ship entered orbit of his world. He faced Alma with surprised eyes and exclaimed, "You are more beautiful than Raven described." David already disliked him.

She shrugged in frustration. "Ymir does not teach me languages from other people. Why do they teach everyone English? Why not speak Icelandic?"

Shan walked to Alma and examined her entire body.

"You are adapting to support a child. This has not happened before. Curious how the Jötnar will react to this." He motioned toward her abdomen with both hands.

Alma impishly shied away from David's wide eyes. "I wanted to tell you, but I did not know how you would respond. Things have been very good between us."

David's mouth dropped open, then turned up into a proud smile.

Falk shook his head and exhaled with an exasperated huff before addressing their guest. "Caretaker Shan, as you know, this is Alma and this is United States Air Force General David Trauger. This process is new to us. How do we proceed?" He was hoping Alma's pregnancy wouldn't affect Shan's decision.

Shan squinted at David, trying to memorize another long human name. "The transfer is a simple matter. You will join me on Seleen." He gestured to Alma. "With your permission I will take you there."

David assumed the posture of a territorial animal and stepped between them. "I'll be joining you."

Falk rolled his eyes as David succumbed to futile jealousy. His first thought was to drag the General away and lock him up, but his escalating angst concerning Alma forced him to censor himself whenever she was present.

Shan smiled at her and narrowed his eyes at David, choosing not to react to his needless grandstanding. "We will all go."

Alma, David, and Shan found themselves in a deep arid canyon somewhere on the surface of Seleen. Alma spoke through clenched teeth. "Will this hurt me?" She huddled close to David and tangled her arm around his.

She was vulnerable, and David knew he couldn't protect her if the need arose. He squared up to Shan anyway, making it clear he was willing to die trying.

Shan didn't care for David. Something about this giant man and his angry looking mouth made him uneasy. "I will perform a small change in your brain. There are no nerves at that location, so you will feel nothing."

David moved between Alma and Shan. "That isn't very reassuring. What, exactly, are you going to do to her?"

Alma was surprised to see David confronting another demigod, a male this time. There was a nagging feeling in the depths of her brain telling her he didn't fear her because she was a woman. She smiled at being wrong about that.

Shan stepped back from David's aggressive posture. "There is a cluster in all of our brains connecting us with the Jötnar and with each other. It is unique in every intelligent being. This is why you cannot duplicate a life and have the two remain connected."

Alma's eyes sprang open. "What if I do copy someone? What happens to them?" The horrible deaths of several thinking military machines after she replicated them came to mind. She murdered a lot of them before engineers found a workaround to that issue. She was glad she never made copies of Stacey or Dawn, even though the military would have loved an army of Staceys.

Shan's face contorted as he searched his thoughts for the correct human words. "Without a distinct connection to the Jötnar a person becomes dýr."

Alma didn't understand why the Jötnar kept mixing

in some of her Icelandic language when teaching everyone English. She turned to David. "An animal."

"A tiny part of me will be copied into that cluster in your brain. It will enable your mind to connect with this world's Jötunn." The concern on David's face made him seem somewhat less terrifying. "When this is done, you will end my life. You will not be harmed. At this time, Seleen's Jötunn will choose to accept you, or not."

David wrapped an arm around the mother of his child. "What effect will this have on our baby?" He fought a flood of paternal feelings he hadn't experienced before. When he learned his wife couldn't bear him children, he silenced an instinctive part of his mind. That part woke up screaming inside his head.

"This is unprecedented. I don't know what, if anything, will happen to your child."

Alma couldn't shake off something Shan mentioned. "I will end your life? Killing in defense haunts my every minute. Killing for gain? This is a thing I will not do."

"We cannot exist together once this is done. We would both be irreparably harmed." Shan turned to David. "There is no doubt your child would be harmed as well."

David nodded, conveying to Alma and Shan he would do what's required.

Her hands were shaking. "Okay, I, I guess I am ready then." David held her while trying, and failing, to hide his own unease. She pulled his hand to her belly. "I hope you are not angry with me."

He fought against tears of both panic and incredible joy, barely able to speak. "Absolutely not."

Alma looked around with huge trembling eyes. "There should be candles or people chanting or something. At least some people." She was heartbroken standing in front of a man about to sacrifice his life and none of his friends were here to comfort him. "This seems so impersonal, so cold."

"I will create anything you need to make this less— cold?" Already envisioning her as this system's Guardian, he wanted to please her.

David hugged her to his chest, pressing her tear soaked face against his shirt. "We don't need things, but we do celebrate our fallen heroes. Humans have done this for thousands of years. We'll celebrate your sacrifice."

The notion of being a hero to the same people who defeated the Stuulla and his own military filled him with a warmth he hadn't experienced in generations.

Alma's crying grew more intense, curling her body in agony. The only thing keeping her from falling was David. "Let's just get this over with." He lowered himself to the ground, holding her, but now in his lap.

Shan knelt beside them, and stated, "It is done." Hoping David wouldn't mind, he reached out and caressed her cheek. "You are beautiful in every possible way." He then turned to David and tried to mimic his cold expression. "I have lost my link to Seleen's Jötunn." He compelled David's attention to his own service weapon, using only his eyes. "I assumed this was to be Alma's responsibility."

David covered Alma's ear with his left hand and pushed her tight against his chest as he unstrapped his side-arm. With a shaking hand, he raised the weapon to Shan's forehead. He didn't hesitate, and probably couldn't have done it if he did.

She flinched hard at the sound of the single gunshot. They sat together on the ground near Shan's lifeless body for thirty minutes, crying. David couldn't stop staring at him laying motionless in the dirt with blood running across his forehead. Alma couldn't bear to look.

Alma was curious if David had executed someone before, but decided she didn't want to hear the answer. "We are taking his body back. I need to make this special. Why do I not feel anything yet?" The thought of Shan sacrificing himself for nothing was unbearable.

Without warning, her body flooded with powerful vitriolic emotions from a new voice, Seleen's voice, but it was more than one planet. It was the entire Daneln system. Visions of eleven worlds, six teaming with sapient life, filled her mind.

She struggled to manage this Jötunn's oppressive darkness. "There are no people on this planet. Where is everyone?!" Seleen's passionate feelings overwhelmed her, wrapping her in a crushing rage. "He was completely alone. He had no friends in his life." She moved to Shan's body, lifted his cold hand from the dirt, and held it close to her chest.

Her expression changed from tear filled depression to anger. "David, I will need you to help me."

"Anything." He preferred this brooding confident version of Alma more than the childlike vulnerable one.

"They want me to kill them all. All the Trey."

David harbored no love for the Trey people, but held less for the Jötnar. "I won't help with that. Xenophobic genocide wouldn't sit well with the Pentagon."

"No, I need you to help me ignore them, these horrible urges." She laid her exhausted body against his, begging him to stroke her hair.

Chapter 14

Destroyer of Worlds

General of the Air Force, Hanna Shaw, paced in front of a warehouse filled with excited military personnel. Her strong authoritarian voice carried. "Tomorrow, we'll be celebrating with our new Kohor friends on that ship, but first, we have to convince them we aren't their enemy."

Shaw paused to flash an uncomfortable glance at Alma, who stood along a back wall with Dawn and Raven standing to either side of her. Shaw looked away. "For almost three thousand years, from generation to generation, these people were taught to hate us. Our number one priority is to show them we are not the monsters they believe us to be."

General Shaw made a quick upward nod to Alma and walked from center stage. The trio weaved through an assortment of desks and uniformed soldiers until they reached the middle of the room. A detailed three-dimensional replica depicting the Neptune theater of operations materialized in front of the crowd.

Dawn bobbed up and down on her tiptoes, looking around the light-blue planet. "Where is it?"

Alma responded in a brusque tone. "I cannot see it yet. I am waiting for the Navy to finish their scans."

Raven pushed against Alma's arm. She was excited and terrified to see her people. "I hope they choose not to fight." The American military's glee filled celebrations after setting fire to millions of Stuulla adults and children continued to haunt her.

A Navy stealth squadron made its final pass over the massive generation ship, allowing Alma to update her display. Emerging in the center of the warehouse near Neptune, a giant brown flattened-oval Goliath took shape. Covering her top and sides, thousands of cylindrical buildings of varying heights and widths protruded outward like short spikes.

Their ship was larger than Dallas plus its suburbs. Dawn's eyes lit up. "Wow! It looks like a giant puffer fish! Put a Q9 next to it to compare sizes."

"Look closer. There is a small fleet in front of it, but our ships are tiny in comparison." Alma wasn't the least bit concerned about the Kohor ship until she visualized it. She increased the size of the Navy ships and yelled over Neptune to General Shaw, "General, it is no longer at scale. I would need a much larger display for them to be visible."

In a first attempt to mollify their visitors, the Navy detonated a thermonuclear warhead, illuminating the Kohor vessel's bow. She didn't change speed or trajectory, but several thousand tiny ships dropped from underneath to respond.

Mesmerized by a Q9 warship floating in front of her face, Raven fought an intense desire to pluck it from the air. Her juvenile obsession with toy spaceships grew more pronounced after spending weeks on a real one in Daneln.

Alma recognized her rare wide-eyed look. "I will make you your own little spaceships." She lifted Raven's hand and placed three small toys, replicas of an American and Trey warship along with a Kohor scout ship, in her palm. Raven clenched them in her hands as an intoxicating wave of satisfaction flooded her body.

Dawn whispered behind Alma's back, "You're getting weirder every time I see you." Raven presented a dismissive sneer and clutched her new toys tight against her chest.

Alma held out a closed fist and gave Raven a gentle nudge. She dropped a small version of the Kohor generation ship into her cupped hands. To her delight, a Kohor fighter fell right after it, making her haul of toy ships, five.

Raven's response to her simple gifts brought a wave of tears to her eyes. Her strong and distorted emotions prompted Dawn to chide her. "Haven't got a handle on those new hormones yet, huh?" She giggled at Alma's blushing face.

"I do not want to control them. I fear that my child will be affected if I start changing things inside me." Alma stroked her slight belly bulge while daydreaming of holding her baby. "I must do this right by nature."

Events near Neptune intensified as the Navy fleet moved to engage a swarm of enemy fighters. Their little single-pilot vessels were fast, much faster than the lumbering Navy warships. In an effort to avoid a fight, they jumped to the other side of the Kohor mother ship. One thousand additional fighters detached from the bottom.

Jump after jump they coiled around their mother, encasing her in a loose ball of her own confused fighters. The Navy was toying with them, hoping they'd grow tired of this and choose to talk instead of fight.

Their entertaining game of Marco Polo ended when the mother ship trained tens of thousands of powerful laser turrets on their location. Tearing through their shields, the lasers carved into each ship's hull in a matter of seconds. Alma had to bring them back from the dead.

This is ridiculous. She wanted to remove their ships from the combat theater but didn't wish for another, Alma verses the United States military, situation. She stood tall to speak over her giant animated display. "General Shaw, this is unproductive."

Shaw flinched at the sound of Alma's voice. Every moment that passed, she expected this frightening demigoddess to take command. "They're making poor decisions because they know you'll just keep bringing them back."

Alma grabbed Dawn by the shoulders, crouched down, and looked into her eyes. "I am going to talk to the General, you are not to tease or bully Raven. I will send you home if you cannot restrain yourself."

Dawn exaggerated a childish sigh. "Fine, but she's

weird."

Alma joined General Shaw on the other side of Neptune, hoping to make it evident she wouldn't interfere without permission. "I would like you to pull them back, so I may create a large explosion in front of that ship."

Shaw welcomed Alma's self-control. "We will inform the Fleet Commander, when they acknowledge, you may proceed."

On her orders, the fleet jumped eighty-thousand kilometers away. Alma scraped together millions of kilograms of heavy elements and crushed them into a dense ball no larger than her fist. She released the ball and allowed nature to complete the task.

Nine-hundred kilometers off the Kohor ship's bow, a fission explosion bigger than anything humans had ever created illuminated the darkness. The sphere of energy lasted less than a minute before its radiation dissipated into space. Another similar explosion followed.

The tiny short-lived stars grew to twenty times the Kohor ship's widest diameter. General Shaw stepped back and away from Alma as the blood drained from her face. "Good God." The entire room fell silent.

Everyone was aware of Alma's incredible power, but something about witnessing her mastery over nature unfold in front of them gave credence to the tales. "That had to be at least five hundred kilometers wide." The reality of Alma's full strength seared into Shaw's mind. She was capable of destroying all life on Earth, and no one could stop her.

Dawn displayed a beaming grin from ear to ear. "That was awesome!" The look she flashed at Alma held a disturbing mixture of evil pride and arousal.

"What did I do?" Alma's eyes darted around the room from face to face. There was no need for an answer to her question. They were afraid of her, most of them.

"Did I do something wrong?" Shaw's expression of absolute terror broke Alma's heart. When she stepped toward her, Shaw retreated backward.

An officer interrupted them, bringing a welcome break to the tension. "Sir, they've cut their engines."

Shaw drew in a deep shaky breath before forcing herself to stand beside Alma, embarrassed by her unprofessional conduct. "Apparently, you got their attention. You got my attention as well."

"I am only a person." Unable to restrain her overpowering emotions, a tear rolled down her face.

General Shaw muttered, "like hell you are."

A female officer motioned to Shaw with a downward nodding gesture. She was rubbing her own stomach, mimicking Alma. At first, she didn't understand what her officer was trying to convey. Shaw whispered in shock, "Oh my God, you're pregnant."

Alma turned away as she fought another bout of annoying tears. She wondered if these feelings were normal for pregnant women or if they were being amplified by Ymir. "You are in command, if you desire that I leave, I will leave."

Shaw swept an arm over the slowing Kohor ship. "We obviously need you." She glanced across the room with a subtle nod at two male soldiers watching them. "Besides, it looks like half my people would treason themselves if I sent you away."

"I do not want that, and I dislike when people see me as some kind of deity." Her eyes darted around the room in an attempt to suppress her tears.

Shaw made an awkward laugh. "Well, at least you sure don't act like one. I'm assuming."

Dawn interrupted their agonizing bonding moment, hopping and waving her hands. "Someone should look at that egg on Jupiter." She pointed at Raven. "Ymir says it's talking with her people now."

"It is always two things. Why is it always two things?" Alma's nerves morphed into fear laden frustration.

"We'll deal with this, you and your engineers need to address our Jupiter issue." Shaw patted Alma's shoulder. "We'll win. We always win."

Alma, Dawn, Raven, and a team of men sat around a small circular table trying to ignore the onset of a battle between the human fleet and the Kohor. "I cannot crush it and I cannot see, feel, or stop the signals coming from it." She looked to Dawn. "Is Ymir ever going to be useful to me anymore?"

Dawn shrugged. "Maybe, she says you should try to annoy it."

Raven made a tight-lipped smile as a little giggle escaped her mouth. "Have Dawn spend some time with it." Everyone laughed, except Dawn.

An engineer offered some old fashion American psyops advice. "I know you can't play music in Jupiter, but constant random sharp vibrations may work."

"I will try anything." Alma fluctuated downward pressure on the Æsir outpost, varying the intensity from extreme to mild. "How long should I do this?"

"You're doing that, and you're keeping the big display going?" The way he looked at her was different from the obsessive and lovelorn stares most engineers showed. To her, this felt more like religious worship.

Her Neptune display clouded with a half a million

tiny black dots appearing in a giant cube formation in front of the Kohor ship. Each dot represented a pilotless AI drone.

One million Kohor fighters dropped from their mother to engage the AI cube. As both sides converged, thousands of laser turrets on the mother ship targeted her enemies. Navy drones swarmed and shredded Kohor fighters as they were being shredded by powerful lasers.

Distracted by an increasing commotion near Neptune, Alma's team abandoned her and gathered to watch the busy exhibition. She shook her head. "Men cannot seem to resist fighting and war."

"Well, I guess I'm kind of a dude then. I'm going to watch." Dawn joined the engineers around the exciting space battle.

Alma and Raven followed her to the display. Raven tangled her arm with Alma's, wincing at every destroyed Kohor fighter. "Please put an end to this."

She leaned over and pressed her cheek against the top of Raven's head. Alma whispered into her hair, "I am so sorry. You know I do not interfere with the American military."

Hundreds of X9 warships materialized behind and to either side of the Kohor mother-ship. They formed flights of three, with each group concentrating their efforts on destroying one laser turret at a time. The drones helped by spreading themselves out in an attempt to draw enemy fire.

Her engineer moved in closer, but made sure not to disrespect Alma with his touch. "Couldn't you end this faster?"

She repeated what she said to Raven, "I do not interfere with the American military." She was somewhat concerned about her growing comfort with human worshipers.

He leaned in to whisper, making it clear others in the room wouldn't approve. "No matter what you decide to do, a lot of us have your back."

Alma's enthusiastic disciple was goading her into crossing a line she wasn't willing to cross. "I need them more than they need me. They can fight outside solar systems. They are much more powerful than I am permitted to explain, and I certainly do not want these Kohor, the Æsir, and Humans as enemies."

"I suppose Gods seem to always need their human armies." He appeared to be breathing in some mystical scent emanating from her. Content to bask in her aura, he stood behind her and remained quiet.

Dawn elbowed her. "There are millions of people like him all over this planet. They think you and Ymir are the same thing and me and Raven are supposed to be some kind of lesser gods."

Alma's eyes widened. She had no idea humans were coalescing around her as their savior. "I trust you discourage this?"

"Hell no. Those people are crazy. They think killing me will get your attention, and you'll pick one of them to replace me. Do you know how many times they've tried to murder me?"

"What?! If you are harmed, I will respond poorly."

"Don't worry, the Secret Service is good at their jobs. They don't even question when I say Ymir doesn't trust someone. They just scoop them up and take them away. It's too bad they don't kill them, though."

Alma wrapped her arms around Dawn and squeezed as she looked down at Raven. "Are people threatening you as well?"

Raven rubbed Dawn's back in a clumsy attempt at comforting her. "They have always assumed I am a god of sorts and have treated me with great respect."

Every gun turret on the generation ship folded into non-hostile positions as the remaining Kohor fighters retreated to the safety of their mother. She floated in space with no propulsion and no outward signs of movement. She was playing dead, or surrendering, or regrouping. No one knew.

The change in room atmosphere forced Alma's attention back on military matters. "Did you kill their ship?" Not being able to see inside it, she didn't know what was happening.

Shaw issued an order for her fleets to hold. Alma barking at her triggered that embarrassing fear again. "We barely scratched their ship, and we have no idea what they're doing."

Alma tipped her head back in what appeared to be the prelude to a tantrum, and shouted, "Guð minn! That thing on Jupiter is doing something. Why does it always have to be two things." She stopped trying to annoy it as fourteen long smooth flat-black ships manifested in close orbit of Jupiter. Alma cried out, startling everyone, "No! Now there are three things." She motioned for Shaw to join her away from prying eyes.

Well, this can't be good, Shaw thought.

Dawn grabbed Raven's arm a little harder than necessary. "They don't know how much they're going to need you."

Alma's hushed voice was barely audible. "Fourteen ships just appeared around Jupiter. They feel much like that egg inside the planet." She dragged Dawn closer. "They are Æsir, and they are not hidden at all. Ask her what I should do."

She wrapped the Æsir ships in a crust of martensite, but their outpost destroyed and recreated its fleet. "I have no power over them." Alma faced Shaw with pleading desperation in her eyes. "Please, I need you to be a military leader."

Shaw tried to muster some semblance of confidence. "Bring Captain Martin here. We're all a team. This isn't something you have to deal with by yourself." She looked to Raven. "I want you to help make that Kohor ship a non-issue. We'll find a way to communicate with them. You find a way to mitigate this standoff. Lie if you have to." Raven made a fear-stiffened nod as Shaw pointed her toward a team of men working at a communications terminal.

When she turned around, Alma was nowhere to be seen. Shaw and Dawn stood together in an uneasy silence for a few minutes before Alma returned with Stacey and David. They saluted while standing rigid at attention.

Shaw made a half serious joke after returning their salute. "You two weren't working on some secret weapon we could use right now, were you?"

Stacey responded, "Well, we may not have a new weapon, Sir, but I do have an idea, and you're not going to like it. None of you are going to like this at all. You need to crush the whole thing." Her tone made it sound as if her vague statement should seem obvious to everyone.

Alma shook her head. "I have tried that, and I have tried covering their ships in various alloys."

"No, not their ships, the entire planet. Jupiter." Stacey snapped back as if her proposal was a trivial undertaking.

Generals Shaw and Trauger simultaneously expressed shock. "What?!"

Stacey moved to the center of their group. Her excitement swept her up into a frenzy of charged energy. "Crush it into a singularity. Their outpost won't be able to come back from that!"

Dawn's voice resonated a rare panic-stricken tone, "Ymir is not okay with this!"

Alma grabbed Stacey's shoulders and spun her around. She stared down into her startled eyes. "It is too big and this seems like a terrible solution. We will run out of planets and moons before long."

Stacey didn't back away from Alma's laughable attempt at intimidation. "That outpost is indestructible with our current technology. It's also not an outpost. It's like the Æsir version of our Hallberg Reactor. Only they're using Jupiter to power it instead of a super collider. The closest Æsir fleet is over five years away without help from that thing. It's five seconds away with it. When we get rid of it, we'll have plenty of time to create better weapons."

David dismissed the unprecedented scope of her plan. "I don't think the Pentagon will authorize making a black hole in our own solar system. Besides, we want at least one of those ships. Sucking them into oblivion won't be very helpful."

Stacey moved around the group, scolding them like a school teacher. "You people need to crack the spine on your middle school physics books. The ships won't get sucked into the singularity. The gravity at distance won't change at all, they'll just be orbiting a much smaller body. Something close to the size of a peanut."

"You are so casual about destroying a planet. Does your Guardian do this regularly? Is this a normal Æsir thing?" Alma was growing concerned with Stacey's constant unbridled overreach, which the United States military seemed willing to indulge.

"The Æsir Guardian hasn't done this to my knowledge, but he could. So can you." Stacey hated being called Æsir, and it showed on her face.

Alma brushed off Stacey's exuberance. "It is too big."

"The Trey, Kohor, and humans can all live without your guiding hand for a few seconds. Let everything go. Once you've crushed it far enough, physics will finish it off."

Alma looked to David for approval. David turned to Shaw, which annoyed her. "No, do not ask her for permission to speak. You tell me what you think. I will not let them rule over me with you as their proxy. Look at me!"

"I trust Stacey on this. I probably shouldn't, but I do." The enormous influence Stacey had gained in military and political realms since being outed as Æsir was staggering. Like his feelings about AI, David feared her true power.

"General Shaw, now I will ask. Will you allow this in our solar system?" The room fell silent as everybody listened to each incredible word spilling from Alma's mouth. Many couldn't comprehend what Stacey was proposing, others couldn't wait for Alma to do it.

Shaw appeared helpless. "This needs to be addressed in a committee."

Stacey admonished the group with a frustrated eye roll, "Okay, but once the Æsir understand what we're planning, we'll be on the wrong end of about a hundred thousand indestructible warships."

Shaw relented. "If you can do it, for what it's worth,

you have my permission." She wagged her finger at Stacey and David. "You two will be with me at our court-martial."

Stacey took Alma's hands and spoke to her in a calm, reassuring voice. "This is nothing to you. Let everything else go, only for a moment."

Unsure of herself, she capitulated. Alma let go of her thoughts and opened her mind to Jupiter. She was a beautiful world, filled with vivid colors and incomprehensible mayhem.

Dawn stood paralyzed, crying from feelings of dread forced upon her by Ymir. This would change everything. Alma wouldn't be the same and their relationship with the Jötnar will be strained, damaged, but she was powerless against her partner's insatiable hatred of her own people.

No one noticed Jupiter's core condensing into a tiny ball. Not even the Æsir detected this unnatural, unprecedented end to the giant world's ancient life. Smaller and smaller, tighter and tighter, Alma squeezed the light from Jupiter's soul.

Clouds stopped circling the globe as gravity seized their winds. Downward, toward the core, faster and faster. Her colors solidified into a murky brown as the celestial monster shrank.

Smaller than Saturn, Jupiter was nearing the point of no return. The outpost noticed its home, its power source, dragging it into an inescapable darkness, but it was too late. The Æsir egg's proximity to Jupiter's intense gravity held time hostage as its shiny body warped and stretched into the void.

Jupiter was collapsing under her own unfathomable weight. Alma refocused her thoughts on the fourteen ships orbiting the vanishing world. As before, she wrapped them in thick martensite coffins for engineers to dissect later. This time they stayed put.

The largest planet in the Sol solar system, squashed down to the size of a pea, left a noticeable hole in the night sky. It was gone and the entirety of humankind gasped in awe at the terrifying strength of their demigoddess. Those who felt comfortable ridiculing her were now aware of her unquestionable omnipotence.

Alma looked around the room at the faces trained on her, some lacked color, others radiated excitement. A cold and detailed announcement from Navy warships near Jupiter shattered the silence as it called out the destruction of an entire world. Dawn sat on the floor at her feet, drained by the raging play-by-play in her brain. Ymir was furious.

Stacey's breathing grew fast and shallow, like a wolf who chased her prey across a great distance. That wolf then stood bloodied and victorious over her kill. "Alma Ólafsdóttir, Destroyer of Worlds."

Chapter 15

Revelations

Commander Kathryn Pruitt stared across her desk at Captain Stacey Martin. "I'm not comfortable with an alien taking such a high level position on my ship."

Stacey scoffed in disbelief. "Don't call me that, and do try to remember this ship wouldn't exist without me. Everything you accomplished in Daneln was because of my contributions. Everything. Without me, you'd still be on a boat in the South China Sea. I made you what you are."

Annoyed by Stacey's justifiable arrogance, Pruitt turned her gaze to her tablet. "This experiment of yours, immortality? So, we're playing the Gods now?"

Stacey donned a derisive smirk. "It's not an experiment anymore. It's a viable and proven technology. You do understand that Alma's abilities aren't some kind of mystical witchcraft, right? All of her magic can be replicated with the right math and incredible amounts of energy."

Pruitt wanted to end this lopsided confrontation, so she motioned to the door and stated, "I'll need you to address me as Commander in front of my crew, please."

Stacey responded with a mocking salute. "Sure thing, Commander."

On the bridge, Stacey assumed the roll of Pruitt's Chief Engineer. Her first assignment was to initiate the time-consuming task of making five separate backup copies of each person on board. She entertained the idea of dragging the process out, but her ego wouldn't allow her to work slow on purpose.

"You have a green light, Commander." Her upper lip furled at the disgusting taste of that word.

Pruitt smiled, knowing how much Stacey hated saying that. "Commander Reis, initiate jump protocols." The large bridge screen transformed from a dusty Texas airstrip into a black canvas dotted with trillions of distant stars.

Stacey deployed a series of buoys containing larger versions of the Hallberg Reactor at specific jump points during their twenty-four-hour trip to Proxima Centauri. These transit lines cut travel time by more than eighty percent and provided ships without Hallberg Reactors a quick route between planets or solar systems.

Along their journey, a few soldiers made laughable

attempts at chatting Stacey up, only to be shooed away. When they failed to make any progress with her, they slept, exercised, and played violent video games to pass time.

Alma strangling an entire planet into a ball no larger than their fingertips was motivation enough to convince the Kohor to abandon their multi-generation mission of revenge against humanity. Raven was excited to hear her cousins' response, but hundreds of generations of separation made it difficult to understand a word they said.

She managed to fumble her way into what she believed to be an agreement allowing a small Marine unit and some envoys to board their ship. "I think I explained that the human soldiers will be armed. I think." Her face scrunched.

General Shaw placed a heavy hand on Raven's shoulder. "You're going with them, so I hope you got this right."

They both turned toward the door when a five-man team of Marines and three diplomats entered. Raven had only seen Air Force and Navy personnel to this point. These men seemed serious, and they were as big as General Trauger. She approached the group with apprehension and looked back at Alma through wide timid eyes.

Alma flashed her a friendly smile. "Stop your worrying, you will be fine." She focused on the Marine team lead. "She will be fine." He didn't acknowledge her unconvincing attempt at intimidation.

Panic set in. "I don't want to do this." Before Raven

could finish her sentence, she found herself staring down an arched corridor at least three kilometers long with hundreds of intersecting hallways. She tried to melt into her group by falling back between two Marines.

The corridor dotted with curious faces peering around every corner, many of them gasping at the giant soldiers. These were not the humans described in stories from their ancestors. They didn't look anything like Kohor, and their size was particularly striking seeing Raven standing in the middle of them.

An older Kohor man stepped out to confront them from a distance. He said a racing stream of words in New Kohor which Raven attempted to translate. "I'm certain he is asking us to follow him." The site of so many male Kohor faces, more in this single corridor than in her entire village, intrigued her.

Two Marines led their team, following behind the old man while tilting their heads to accommodate the low curved ceilings. Raven and her diplomats continued into a large circular room with bench seats configured in broken circles around the middle. The Marines held positions at either side of the two entrances. Their guide turned to face them and patted down at the air with both hands.

Raven stretched out her arms and walked her group back about a meter as a ring in the floor lit bright white. Above the circle a three-dimensional display of Cartara and her mother planet, Bondi, materialized.

Cartara looked terrible, like a smoldering ball of charred wood. Raven's eyes watered at the site of her burning home. She used a formal version of Old Kohor to explain that their world was no longer in the throes of death. "Cartara is beautiful and filled with life. The

Trey repaired the damage and repatriated Kohor prisoners of war." She chose to leave out the hundreds of generations of brutal subjugation and cruel eugenics conditioning programs their people had to endure.

They exchanged stories. She told them about Alma, Earth, and the Trey conflict with her new friends while trying to convey the human military's strange desire to live among disparate peoples. Kohor funneled into the auditorium as Raven portrayed a fast emerging human empire.

His stories, however, did not depict tales of excitement or wonder. He recounted crippling pandemics, mutinous civil wars, and destructive natural phenomena that rendered them helpless and adrift. Worse than that, there was nothing but an empty void between Daneln and Sol.

The gathering Kohor spectators listened to Raven as curiosity muted their apprehension. They begged for more humans to visit their ship, and they wanted to see Alma.

Pruitt's final jump placed them in low orbit of a large desert planet within the Proxima Centauri solar system, Proxima B. The brilliant sphere radiated a blinding bright yellowish-white as nothing but sand reflected light into space. There no clouds or visible water. It appeared lifeless.

"Commander, there's a lot of artificial debris out here." The young man's voice cracked.

Machines went to work scanning their surroundings for any technology that could explain Dawn's living-room apparition. A wide screen at the front of the bridge showed a computer augmented image highlighting several chunks of floating wreckage the AI deemed suspicious.

Pruitt stood, as did most of the bridge crew, and stared at the haunting display. Up to this point, none of them took their trip seriously, but that junk orbiting the planet wasn't natural. It was crafted. It was alien.

Stacey focused her attention on one of the larger items drifting nearby. "Shit." She jumped from her chair and shouted, "Commander! We need to leave orbit, Now!"

Before anyone could react, the crew found themselves standing on the planet's surface. Stacey tipped her head toward the pale blue sky. "Shit!" She slumped her shoulders and whispered one more time, *shit.*

Pruitt weaved through the confused crowd of murmuring soldiers. When she located Stacey, she grabbed her arm and pulled her away from the group. "What the hell just happened?"

"We shouldn't have jumped into orbit." Stacey was disappointed in herself. "Damn it."

Pruitt demanded, "I want you to focus on me and tell me what just happened."

Stacey squinted to block out the intense light. "That debris was an Æsir military fleet. They wouldn't have been here unless this planet had a Caretaker that went rogue or psychotic. Judging by the looks of this place, I'd guess psychotic. It happens. A lot."

"So, what do we do? Kill ourselves, come back to life on Earth, and tell the Pentagon to send a fleet back here to nuke this planet to hell?" Pruitt seemed far too comfortable with this idea.

Stacey rolled her eyes at the Commander's stereotypical military thought process. "The restores recreate us exactly like we were when I backed us up. We wouldn't know about anything that happened here, and then there's the other issue." She quieted her voice. "He could make copies of us no matter where we are. You can't blindly copy people. They kind of go feral after a while when there's two or more of the same person."

"How come you didn't already know about this place? Your people obviously knew about it."

With narrowed eyes, Stacey responded in an angry tone, "I wasn't in the military. Our human military doesn't tell its civilians everything. Do you think the Æsir are any different?" She performed some mental math on the debris in orbit. "There's never been a Caretaker who could destroy an entire Æsir fleet. Alma's a Guardian and she wouldn't be able to do it without help, or a singularity."

Pruitt chided, "You're the smart little Æsir, what do we do now?"

"You know I don't like that, Commander, who lost her ship. I wonder if your superiors will blame me, a Captain in the Air Force, or the Commander of a Navy vessel. As for what we do, we wait. We're at the mercy of this world's Caretaker. At least we can hope it's mercy."

Alma regretted her dismissive attitude toward Raven's concerns. She found herself preoccupied with visions of being imprisoned on the Kohor generation ship and didn't believe the military was capable of making a bomb big enough to destroy it, freeing her through death.

She and Dawn made their way into a packed auditorium where Raven and the diplomats were waiting for her arrival. The first thing that caught Alma's eye was the three-dimensional display in the center of the room. She muttered, "Great, another thing they will no longer require me for."

Dawn smiled at her constant self deprecation. "Come on." She dragged her reluctant demigoddess by the hand into the center of attention.

The Kohor audience stared in awe as she walked by. Raven tried explaining to her new family that Alma didn't enjoy being chosen by the Jötnar. They had trouble believing she had no desire to rule over them, the humans, or the Trey.

One of the diplomats stood to brief her on the situation. "We've explained your offer to give them a home on Cartara. They're quite excited by the idea. Apparently, life on these ships is unpleasant. There's an issue though. When the leadership decided to let us board, they were already on the brink of a civil war. They're fighting with each other right now."

"Do you think I cannot see this?" Alma pushed him aside and made her way to the hologram of Cartara, which she replaced with a current representation of the Kohor world in much higher detail. She waved for Raven to stand beside her and swept her other hand over a green land mass about twice the size of China. "This is where you will live. It is large enough to serve as a home to everyone on all three ships."

She waited for Raven to finish translating. "It is fertile land with plenty of resources. No native Kohor will be displaced. This will be your land to govern as you desire. The current inhabitants of Cartara and I will help you learn to properly work the soil."

Her display changed to an outside view of the generation ship. "I will not permit you to keep these vessels, or any weapons of war. You will not be allowed to continue slaughtering each other."

The entire crew found themselves disarmed of anything Alma assumed to be a weapon. Her anger only grew as they continued fighting with their hands and various tools. She looked to Dawn for advice. "They will not stop fighting each other. I cannot remove their hands. Well, I could, but I will not."

"Just put each group on different sides of this ship. It would take them forever to find each other on this giant thing. You can keep separating them. Maybe they'll give up out of pure frustration."

"I should put them on opposite sides of that continent and build a tall mountain between them."

A member of the diplomatic team interrupted. "There may be systems on this ship that need people watching over them. We should keep the critical crew members until the military can fully take over."

"Why is nothing simple?" Alma turned to Raven with a hand outstretched toward the ship's Captain. "Tell him I have removed the people who were fighting and placed them on Cartara."

As Raven and the ships tenuous Captain discussed what Alma did to his crew, Navy flotillas appeared around the Kohor generation ship. They were filled with teams of soldiers and engineers salivating at the chance to work on this beautiful beast.

Stacey sat on a smooth boulder watching male soldiers, topless and sweating under the hot sun. Commander Kathryn Pruitt stood beside her soaking in her own sweat. "Did you realize all your soldiers are in such fantastic shape?" She looked up. "Oh, yeah, I guess you don't notice guys."

"Don't you have a girlfriend?" Pruitt fantasized about smacking this annoying woman.

Stacey chuckled. "We're poly-amorous, sort of. As long as the other person is General Trauger, or Alma, or both. Dawn's kind of picky about who she likes."

"What's your deal with General Trauger anyway? There's like four of you climbing all over each other trying to get at him." She followed Stacey's eyes to a couple of shirtless soldiers digging a trench with their hands, probably a latrine. "There are much better looking and younger men who'd strangle their mothers just to sniff your feet."

Stacey blurted a laugh so loud they were both taken by surprise. "He's not a bad looking man. It's more than just his looks though. He's extremely focused and dedicated. His intense focus and self-control is very appealing."

She motioned toward one young man digging in the trench. "They're fun to look at, but you have no idea what horrible things are hiding in their DNA. They haven't been around long enough for the math to make reliable predictions."

Pruitt shook her head at Stacey eyeing one of the young men as he stripped down to his underwear. "Can you even have a baby with humans?"

"Not this shit again." Stacey thumped herself on her own shoulder. "This is a real human body."

"Oh yeah, you murdered a teenage girl. I almost

forgot about that."

"You people are like a hungry dog with a bone." She stood to face Pruitt and steadied herself as dehydration made her light-headed. "I added and changed neural pathways in her brain over a very long time. Her knowledge of me became so complete, she became me. The only person I killed was the original me."

Pruitt's mind flooded with a realization stemming from one giant epiphany. "Oh my god, you're a criminal. An Æsir criminal hiding from them in a human body. You're probably like their Einstein but a super villain. I can definitely picture that."

Stacey was a little annoyed by Pruitt's somewhat accurate characterization. "I wasn't a criminal. I was more of an insurrectionist."

"So, you're a terrorist. Great. How hard are they looking for you?" She wondered if their recent problems, including the Kohor and the Jötnar creating Alma, could be tied back to Stacey.

"Try revolutionary, you know, like the people who freed The United States from British rule. We're going to die here so, yeah, the Æsir are terrible people who destroy any hint of natural animal evolution, except worms. They fear everything. They're even trying to attack Jötunheimr, Ymir's universe."

Exhausted, Pruitt rested on the big boulder. Stacey sat in the hot sand under her shadow. "I was working to turn Protectors and Caretakers, trying to get them to fight back. Then I found humans. Humans are fantastic; mental diversity, physical diversity, intense empathy. True explorers. Our curiosity and intelligence make the Æsir look like primates. We just need a little technological boost to catch up."

Pruitt looked down on Stacey, thinking she should probably kill her. "With all your fancy machines, you eventually won't need us at all. That's why you cling to Alma. You want access to her incredible amounts of energy."

"Wrong. It's Dawn who has the real connection to them. I've met a lot of Speakers, none like her. She's special, and I don't know why, yet."

The only thing tempering Pruitt's urge to put a bullet in Stacey's head was the fact she'd resurrect on Earth. "Would your machines need them, the Jötnar, Ymir?"

"Their universe is all around us, we're swimming in it. They don't understand what they have, what it means to us. Except maybe this one. He seems to know more than any of the other Jötnar. He's going to be an issue. This whole solar system needs to be black-holed."

"You think this world's Caretaker is one of them, a Jötunn?" It was clear to her there was more going on in their universe than Stacey bothered to mention during her many military briefings.

"A regular Caretaker would have shown himself by now. This feels different. This guy needs to die because he's on our land. If we don't push back, more will come." Stacey forced herself to yawn in an attempt to water her dried eyes. "If they realize the power they have in our universe, that will be a brief war."

Pruitt inspected her own twitching hand. Dehydration was taking its toll on her muscles. "So, you're trying to start a war between humans and Æsir. You want them to focus their attention on us instead of pissing off the Jötnar."

"I want humans to kill them all. Our naturally

evolved empathy will keep us from pushing the Jötnar too far." Stacey curled into a ball at Pruitt's feet.

Many of the crew buried themselves to their necks in sand in an effort to escape the unrelenting heat. Some had already died, and their bodies placed in the trench. One soldier ended his own life with a loud pop which triggered a series of similar suicides. After a few gunshots, the sounds no longer startled anyone. Several engineers begged for someone to shoot them, and plenty of soldiers volunteered.

It wasn't long before Pruitt and Stacey were the only ones still breathing. She removed her weapon from its holster and admired its simple beauty. "Do you want me to shoot you?"

Stacey's parched lips, cracked and bloodied, tried to form a little smile. "No, I kind of like this feeling, dying. It's interesting to imagine what's happening and what will happen next. I'm guessing stroke followed by heart failure."

Pruitt placed the gun's barrel against her own temple and pulled the trigger. Her body slumped over, falling face-first into the sand. Stacey took her hand and moved in closer.

Her blurry eyes were incapable of focus as she slipped in and out of consciousness. To her surprise, she didn't have a stroke. Instead, her heart gave up and stopped beating.

Each crew member resurrected on their orbiting ship an hour after they died, with every horrible memory intact. Pruitt's miserable death was fresh on her mind as she shouted a panicked order, "Get this ship out of here, Now!" She didn't bother doing a head count.

The Hallberg Reactor seemed to take forever to

charge. "If you see Captain Martin, arrest her and gag her. Don't hesitate. Do not talk to her and do not let her speak." A crew member counted down the final seconds before they could jump away from this nightmare world.

Stacey appeared on the bridge, retching and gasping for breath. Two crew members tackled her to the floor and bound her arms while another filled her mouth with the sleeve of his jacket.

Upon their jump from Proxima B, warnings cascaded across bridge monitors as a warhead materialized inside a crew cabin, already in the process of detonating. Inundated with fiery radioactive bullets, the ship disintegrated into trillions of particles scattering in every direction.

Stacey emerged, standing in a large open room under a cooling tower on the Air Force base. Two days passed since her second death in Proxima Centauri. In front of her stood Alma and four Marines with weapons at the ready.

She noticed several armed soldiers, some of them snipers with rifles trained on her, and raised her hands above her head. "Alma, what's going on?" She had no memory of the mission.

Alma motioned to the long rows of humming machines. "Where is the rest of the crew?"

Stacey's eyes darted around and her breathing shallowed. "I made it bring me back twenty-four hours earlier than anyone else." Her body shook as she knelt, making sure to keep her arms in the air. "I wanted to be available in case there were issues. I want Dawn here."

"No. You and I are going to go someplace private. Will the crew come back without you here?" Alma's furious stare burned into her.

Stacey nodded. "Alma, what happened?"

The dark icy bunker transformed into a beautiful lush green forest. The two of them faced each other among tall trees, under a vivid blue sky. Stacey stood and lowered her arms. "This is Seleen."

"You are so smart. Too smart for the Æsir, and too smart for humans."

"I don't know what I said or did. Please, Alma." Millions of images of past crimes ran through her mind, some of them serious. She searched her memories for something recent they may have discovered, but couldn't recall anything that would make Alma this angry.

Alma displayed a condescending smirk. "I will summarize. That black hole I made, killed at least one Jötunn. You have been creating machines that sap energy from their universe. Machines that will make me obsolete and you into a true god with no tether to a solar system, and you are willing to murder for this. You want to make the entire Proxima Centauri solar system a black hole, killing many Jötnar. You are a terrorist on a level only fantasized about by the most extreme of humans."

Stacey had no idea what could have made her comfortable enough to reveal this to anyone. She hoped there wasn't more. "I'm sorry."

"You destroyed an American warship to hide your confessions to its Commander. You murdered four hundred and thirty-seven humans."

That was it, the line Stacey crossed. Everyone knew

how much Alma feared and respected the military. It was no mystery to her why she destroyed a ship, the AI did it to protect her from something. "Why would I want to black-hole an entire solar system?"

"Dawn's new friend, it is a Jötunn. You fear its presence in our realm as an escalation of hostilities between them and the Æsir." She found it difficult to maintain her anger knowing Stacey had no recollection of their mission, but she put effort into staying mad.

Stacey's mind raced at the thought of a Jötunn able to confront them in their Anthropic universe. "That's not good at all. You really need my help."

"You enjoy telling us that only you can save us from horrible things. After this, it will be another thing. No, I think we are done helping you become a god." She fought her trepidation over her chosen punishment. "You will remain here until I grow too bored with you to continue recreating you, and to ensure you do not get lonely, I will provide you with a friend to play with." She pointed behind Stacey's head.

Stacey spun around. Dread overcame her as the blood drained from her face. She shouted, "Alma, no!" She was looking into a mirror, or what she wished was a mirror. Another Stacey was standing in front of her.

When Alma disappeared, second Stacey cheerfully quipped, "You have to admit, for Alma, this is pretty creative." The original Stacey grabbed a jagged rock, lunged at her clone, and beat her to death. She looked up from her bloody carnage to find a third Stacey towering over her.

Chapter 16

Trespasses

Yeset was setting, blanketing Raven's quiet village in darkness as Alma, Dawn, and David gathered outside her modest home. The Kohor didn't have electricity to light their streets. The military offered all the conveniences of humanity, but Raven declined most of their gifts because Earth's stars dimmed by local lights and atmospheric pollution always made her homesick whenever she visited.

Alma wagged a finger in front of Dawn's nose, trying to circumvent her obnoxious personality. "You will not say anything but compliments. If you do not have a compliment, invent one. If she offers you food, it will be terrible, but eat it and say it is good."

"I'll be nice to her. I really want her to like me." Dawn leaned forward and wrapped her lips around Alma's chastising finger.

Disgusted, Alma ripped her hand away from Dawn's sloppy mouth. "If I understood what was wrong with you, I would repair it."

David chuckled at the two women as he squeezed between them to knock on Raven's door.

Inside her home, Alma and Dawn sat on large woven pillows encircling a humble wooden table in the center of Raven's living-room. There were burning candles everywhere. Alma smiled at the toy spaceships lined up on either side of the table, positioned as if a battle was playing out.

David wandered around her living-room noting a lack of anything personal occupying her shelves or walls, except the spaceships. His heart sank. The brutal Trey occupation robbed the Kohor people of simple pleasures. "I love your home."

Raven handed everyone a clay cup, placed a pitcher of water in the center of the table, and sat in their circle next to Dawn. Feigning sympathy for her loss of Stacey, she reached out and touched Dawn's hand.

Dawn huffed at their uncomfortable stares. "I'm not a child. The Proxima B Caretaker gave me a play-by-play of them dying, which was kind of messed up, but I knew they'd all come back. I'm fine with you asking me about Stacey and him."

It was difficult for David to make direct eye contact with her since he held himself personally responsible for everything that happened between Alma and Stacey. "The only thing the Pentagon wants to know is how he destroyed an entire Æsir military fleet."

"He explained it to me, but I didn't understand. Stacey and I usually worked through the tech stuff together." She looked at Alma. "He wants you to share power in Proxima Centauri, but not with the military. He doesn't want humans or Æsir on his world at all."

Alma rubbed David's arm in an attempt to soothe his rising tension and allay her own bubbling emotions. "The Æsir have been attacking their universe and I killed at least one of them. His lack of trust is understandable. I hope he knows I did not realize the damage I caused."

"He knows, and wants us to help stop the Æsir, and he doesn't want you black-holing things anymore. You have to promise to kill anyone who enters his solar system." Dawn put a finger on the toy Kohor scout ship and slid it closer.

Alma protested. "I would never promise such a thing."

Raven grabbed the spaceship from Dawn and put it back in line with the other ships, then voiced her concern over Alma's reluctance to expand her empire. "I understand the Æsir will destroy every Kohor, human, and Trey world to stop you. The more worlds and stars you govern, the less likely they will destroy our homes."

"Another world without a Speaker, I do not think I can handle that. Seleen is so frustrating. That planet's voice does not like the Trey people at all." Alma sneered in frustration.

Dawn rapped her fingernails on the table in an effort to draw everyone's attention, and blurted, "Seleen has a Speaker. The second we came here I could hear him, his voice. I can hear the one on Proxima B too, inside my head. That planet needs to be renamed." She chose to keep to herself that she also hears Cartara's Jötunn.

Raven's eyes snapped open. She stared at the side of Dawn's irritating face, and refused to join in as the voice in her head welcomed Dawn into her private world, her mental sanctuary.

"Múspellsheimr. It's what he calls his home." Dawn sat beside Alma at a large oval conference table surrounded by high ranking members of every branch in the United States military. President Atkinson held a chair at the table's head. This was the single most exciting moment of her life.

Navy Admiral Ander Falk hadn't met Dawn in person. Distracted by her appearance, he couldn't help but stare. Images in news stories and military reports didn't do her justice. "Does he have a name, like Ymir?"

"His name is Surtr." The thought of so many important men training their eyes on her was something she could become accustomed to. "He's not like Ymir. He feels like most of you people do, like a warrior. Ymir is kind of like Alma, friendly but a little mean sometimes." Alma patted her hand.

David fidgeted in his chair, trying not to seem agitated. The traumatizing interaction with Shan, losing Stacey, and expecting a child, switched his brain into a paranoid and protective mode. Now the military wanted Proxima Centauri.

Alma panned the room filled with old military men, practically salivating. Not over her, or Dawn, they hungered for new conquests, new lands. "He does not want our humans in his system. You should temper your excitement."

President Atkinson smiled his creepy little smile. "Alma, I believe you'll help Surtr trust us. Look around you Alma. These men are eager, excited. There's good reason for this. God is providing us with the tools and desires we need to fulfill his plan. Have faith in his plan, Alma." Several of the men rolled their eyes, as did Alma.

An angry looking man, Marine Corp General Adam Henderson, cleared his throat in a successful attempt to quiet Atkinson. He directed his attention to the out-of-place tiny red haired woman. "You'll be on a human ship with a human crew. Given what Alma just said, why would this be acceptable?"

Dawn analyzed him for a moment. His jaw wasn't square enough, and it bothered her. "Surtr and I are friends. I told him this is the only way Alma can visit him."

Henderson worried about Alma's safety, a rare woman for whom he grew to respect. "You can be captured and imprisoned. This could just be a trick."

Alma's efforts to suppress her anxiety were agitating their child and churning her belly. She pivoted uncomfortable in her chair. "We had the same fear in Daneln, and this Jötunn is no more powerful than Shan was. The same plan will likely work."

"I'm not okay with any of this. Something doesn't feel right." Henderson was more concerned with the possibility of losing Alma and Dawn as valuable military assets than gaining a new world. In his opinion, they hadn't had enough time to grow tired of the huge Daneln system.

Atkinson beamed with spiritual pride. "This is what God wants. They will be protected, just as David and

Alma were on Seleen. General, this is a done deal. We're here only as a formality. God is practically screaming for this to happen. This will happen."

After their meeting, David pulled Admiral Falk aside. "She's literally insane. You know that, right?" He chuckled while watching Alma lumbering behind Dawn who was sort-of chasing Atkinson. "I love her like a daughter, but there are four distinct voices with words and pictures in that head."

Ander smiled. Everything David said only made Dawn seem more interesting. "Does she like guys at all?" He calculated David's warning as a veiled sign of tacit approval.

"If they're physically perfect, maybe." David was warming up to this man. Ander's disdain for his relationship with Alma was no secret, but maybe if he had his own crazy demigoddess they could bond over it. They'd need to. No one was courageous enough to be David's friend anymore.

"I've never been in space before." Dawn circled the bridge of Admiral Falk's Q9, touching every console. "Will we float around?" She tapped some buttons on a complicated panel causing everything on the screen to turn red with blinking words. Her eyes darted back and forth. "Oops."

Ander joined her at the console and swiped the top-left of the display, returning it to normal. He laughed. "No, we won't float around. You can thank the Kohor for that, not the Cartara ones, the generation-ship ones." He wanted to ask her if she was the least bit interested in him, but didn't know if her pain from losing Stacey had enough time to heal. He wasn't even sure she liked men. David's answer was vague regarding that subject.

"Ymir says you like me." She assessed his lithe body. He wasn't ugly or gross, but he was old. Although taller than Alma, he didn't have broad strong shoulders or David's thick chest. "Our children would probably be tall, thin, and hot."

"I'm a fantastic father. I have five kids, and we all actually get along! Plus, when I was your age, I had beautiful blond hair." He missed his youthful thick mane, making Dawn's flawless auburn tresses something of an obsession. "I'm sure you know better than me, but I'd guess our children would be strawberry blonde."

Ander's apparent comfort with Dawn's teasing and his willingness to procreate intrigued her. She assumed that having a soldier partner could help lessen Ymir's anger regarding Jupiter, and his giant warship was an attractive benefit. "Oh, and yes, I like men, women, aliens. Maybe Jötunn. I'd have to see one in real life."

She waved her hands in front of his face, wiggling her fingers. "Alma needs to clean some stuff up here first." He was much older looking than David, especially since Alma made a lot of repairs to him during the months. "I'll talk to her. If Surtr doesn't slaughter us, maybe Trauger can fly this thing back." She struggled to make an awkward wink and turned away to investigate more of his ship.

David sauntered toward Ander. "Are you going to be okay to fly?"

Ander didn't understand why David preferred cold sullen Alma over this beautiful and spirited young woman. "Man, she could mess me up for life."

"You know you'll never be able to hide anything from her. Ever. The Pentagon thinks she knows a lot of things that they're very happy she hasn't talked about with..." David made a single nod in Alma's direction. "...certain people."

"Every time you think you're warning me about her, you just make me want her more." He stretched out his arms and frowned as he examined his weathered hands. "She wants me to look younger. Does Alma do charity work?"

David gave him a friendly smack on the back. "I'll ask."

Ander returned to his duties preparing the ship for their journey. Dawn, Alma, and David sat in front of consoles showing a live image from the bow. "Alma, ready when you are."

Without acknowledging his request, she moved their ship to the edge of her sphere of influence in the Sol solar system, closest to Proxima Centauri, saving them about two hours of travel time.

When they escaped Sol's clutches, Alma's abilities vanished. She plopped down in a chair next to David. "I did not believe I was interfering with our baby. I feel so terrible, and I already need to pee. This is extremely frustrating." She struggled for a moment, got up, and headed for the closest bathroom.

With her out of earshot, David announced, "Pregnancy gives women a glimpse into the normal nightlife of old men." Ander didn't appreciate him reminding Dawn of his age. David pivoted to Dawn and changed subjects. "How does it feel to have some peace and quiet in that head of yours?"

"I still hear them all. I'm bored, how long will this

take?" Dawn twirled in her chair, stood, and wandered the bridge while messing with the ship's consoles again. Unable to make them turn red, she smirked.

Ander was careful not to credit Stacey with the series of buoys Pruitt's doomed mission installed. "Less than three hours. We have a game room and a gym. There's a reading room and a movie theater too."

Dawn made her way around the bridge touching as many important looking items as possible before stopping in front of Ander. "This ship has rooms with beds, right?" With a clumsy smile, she reached out her hand and walked away. He didn't hesitate to follow.

Alma returned in time to witness Dawn taking control of their ship's Commander. With an unattractive groan, she dropped down next to David. He rubbed her back a little too rough, and chuckled. "We men are just like puppies, aren't we."

She leaned in to his touch and laughed at the thought of how much she enjoyed being pet. "We are all like puppies."

The ship's AI plotted a series of jumps placing them in low orbit of Múspellsheimr, similar to Commander Pruitt's ill-fated voyage. Audible warnings alerted its crew to Æsir fleets scattered throughout the solar system. Dawn and Ander rushed to the bridge where he and David huddled at a console to discuss the locations and distances of the Æsir ships.

Alma couldn't help but pry into Dawn's surprising quickie romance. "So, more than two hours? I hope you spent some of that time resting."

"Nope, we didn't sleep for one second." Dawn appeared content as she draped her arm around Alma. "Why didn't you tell me how totally disgusting men are? They'll do anything you want, and let you do anything you want to them. And I mean anything." She smirked as she dreamily lost herself in the two men debating their situation. "They don't even question stuff."

Alma's nose and lips scrunched, repulsed by Dawn's candor. "I do not know what you are hinting at, and I do not want to know." She did want to know, but had no desire to hear it from her.

Ander walked across the bridge to the women and addressed them in a stern tone. "There are hundreds of Æsir warships in this system. Where is Surtr?"

Dawn couldn't keep herself from staring into his pale-blue eyes. "He's evaluating us. You two scare him a little bit." She threw on a naughty grin. "He knows you are a sick and twisted old man."

David pretended not to hear that. The embarrassed smile on Ander's face was disturbing enough. He assumed he'd be troubled by her being with a man, like any normal father would, but Dawn wasn't your average woman. She needed someone outside her head to help anchor her life in this universe.

Given no warning from Surtr or Dawn, they found themselves standing on the planet's blistering surface. They squinted at the bright sky.

Everyone but Dawn stepped back as a crude human shape appeared from the sand in front of them. This sandy avatar was far more solid than the one in Dawn's living-room, but still a miserable representation of a real person. She walked to him and swirled her hand around in his body. "Hi!"

Alma's confidence collapsed as an overwhelming urge to protect their child strangled her. Her first instinct was to hide behind David, which was embarrassing. She fought her fears and moved next to him instead, gripping his hand tight.

Surtr's attempt at speaking was abysmal and difficult to understand. His voice sounded like a combination of humming mosquito wings and an old-time jug band. "Alma." His dusty arm pointed at her. David resisted a natural impulse to jump between them.

She stepped toward Surtr with David in tow. Donning a courageous facade, she stood strong and confident, but her churning stomach was causing their baby to squirm. She wanted to vomit, and pee.

Hidden from everyone, Dawn and Surtr were in constant communication with each other. She labored to keep her new friend calm, but the growing Æsir presence in Proxima Centauri was agitating him.

"He wants us to promise that humans and Æsir will stay out of this system." Dawn focused on David and Ander. Her expression suggested this Jötunn had a willingness to compromise. "He's saying he'll allow one human ship at a time with a small crew."

Unlike her experience with Shan, Alma held nothing but contempt for, and fear of this monster. "No." Her voice was unsteady. She addressed the Jötunn instead of relaying her words through Dawn. "If given this system, I will allow humans and Trey access. I will not permit Jötnar to run amok in our universe. You killed this world. That is unacceptable."

"No Æsir." Surtr was already caving in to Alma's demands.

Alma surrendered no ground and advanced on the avatar. "Trey and human engineers will be brought in to repair the damage you have done." Careful not to allow her big belly inside his dust, she let go of David and stepped closer. "And then humans and their allies will make a home here."

While Alma confronted Surtr, he poured images into Dawn's brain, showing her how he gained influence over the original Æsir Caretaker of this world. Playing with his Æsir puppet, he commanded him to alter the oxygen in the atmosphere into hydrogen, suffocating most of its inhabitants.

Dawn winced at scenes of rising temperatures that cooked any remaining Æsir hiding in protective gear, ships, or buildings. Not wanting to lose his connection with the Anthropic universe, he forced his obedient toy to keep himself alive. Surtr revealed his Æsir pet to Dawn, imprisoned deep in a bunker under the planet.

She spoke to Surtr in silence. *We need to know how to fight them, like you did.*

Visions of a complicated looking Æsir machine flashed behind her eyes as he flooded her body with feelings of dread. Their machine generated a voice similar to that of the outpost on Jupiter, but far more powerful. It was so strong it confused the Jötnar in their own universe, vibrating them with enough force to cause incredible harm.

Dawn's breathing shallowed. Her mind filled with a crudely rendered movie showing Æsir ships approaching Múspellsheimr to investigate the loss of communications with their colony. Surtr and his Caretaker turned the voice weapon against its creators, targeting the orbiting fleet and giving them nightmarish hallucinations. Insanity and misdirection compelled them to attack each other. The Æsir destroyed themselves.

She forced out a stunned whisper, "He has no real power here at all." His singular connection to their universe required an Æsir Caretaker and a machine that mimicked and amplified the Jötnar voice. Unknown to her friends, Dawn made a rare threat. *You will share full control of this world with Alma. No restrictions. If you don't, I'll tell my friends where the Caretaker is. They'll find a way to kill him. Trust me.*

Surtr's avatar collapsed into a dune, leaving the team standing alone under the hot blue sky. Ander was tired of remaining silent. "Did he decide to leave us here to die?"

Dawn took Alma's hand and leaned against her sweaty shoulder. "No, but I don't think he likes me much anymore."

Alma turned toward their partners. "I cannot see the star or other planets in this system, only this world. I do not know how useful this will be." She looked down on Dawn's austere face. "What did you do?"

Dawn drew in a deep breath. "I think I know how to destroy the Æsir fleets. Maybe all of them."

Chapter 17

Changes

*"*You are not unnecessary." Alma squirmed uncomfortable on a pillow in Raven's musty living-room. "Dawn is only one person and most of her focus lies with Ymir and Surtr. The Americans need you here. You keep them updated on the Kohor people. They need to know that Cartara's voice is content." She wrapped her arms around Raven and held her tight.

"Kohor are nothing but an inconvenience to humans." Devastated by Dawn's incredible growing power, Raven fought back tears. "If we all disappeared, they would not grieve, and Dawn can keep them apprised of our voice's mood."

Raven struggled against Alma's affection, but she was too strong. She reflected on herself. "Dawn is irritating and cruel. She makes people feel bad about themselves, but I have heard I am unapproachable. Perhaps I should try to be more available to them. I know they're unhappy with my personality."

"They fear Dawn more than they f..." Alma froze wide-eyed, embarrassed, and scared as she released Raven from their hug. "I will make you a new pillow." Her water broke. It was a gusher, soaking through her pants and into the pillow. "What do I do?"

"Don't concern yourself with my things." Raven carried a puzzled look on her face. "Can you not simply remove the child? It is ready."

Alma's eyes darted around as she shook her head. "No, I must do this right, the way nature intended, the way normal women do it."

Raven stood and reached out her hand. "Very well. We should go to your military hospital."

"I want to do it here. I have seen you do this many times. I want you to deliver my child." Alma struggled to her feet, using Raven's tiny body as leverage. "Treat me as you would any normal woman."

Raven wrapped an arm around Alma and walked her into the curtained sleeping area. "When this is complete, I will be asking you for much more than a new pillow." She maneuvered Alma next to her bed and helped her out of her wet clothes. After she laid down, Raven covered her naked lower half with a blanket.

It didn't take long before a contraction had her gripping the mattress. Alma groaned, "Is this level of pain normal?"

"The majority of human women experience intense pain during childbirth. Your much bragged about evolution has not been kind to the females of your species."

Alma's pain subsided, allowing her to calm her breathing. "Is it too early for me to bring them here?"

Raven lifted Alma's head and pushed a bulky pillow underneath. "I see no reason not to bring him here."

The onset of another contraction distracted Alma from Raven's obvious exclusion of Dawn. She begged through clenched teeth, "How many of these will I have to tolerate?"

"Many more. I will get a wet cloth for your head and maybe something for you to bite down on." Raven exited her sleeping area as David appeared standing beside the bed, facing a wall.

Disoriented, he needed a few seconds to recognize his change of scenery as Raven's home. He spun around to see Alma sweating, beet-red, and terrified.

She spoke with a tired singsongy voice. "Hey. Sorry, I know you do not like when I move you without asking."

"This is more important than anything I was doing." David knelt next to her, took her sweaty hand, and pressed his forehead against her temple.

Raven returned with a damp cloth and a wooden spoon, relieved to see only David. "From what I've witnessed with other couples, you are probably nervous as well." She draped the cloth across Alma's forehead and attempted to place the spoon between her teeth, but Alma refused.

To her dismay, Dawn appeared standing beside the bed, bouncing on the balls of her feet. "We're having a baby! I can't wait for this thing to get out of you. You'll make yourself hot again, right?"

Alma reached out, grabbed Dawn's hand, and squeezed hard. "I am a beautiful pregnant woman." Her grip was so strong, if a contraction happened at that moment, she'd have broken Dawn's fingers.

"You are beautiful. I'm just a very jealous person." Dawn moved behind Raven to get a better view. She chose not to describe the oozing mess Alma was making, and exclaimed, "Are we going to eat the placenta?"

Raven stared appalled at Dawn. "Is that a normal human thing? Why would you want to do this?"

"I heard it's good for you, and it tastes like liver." Dawn giggled at David's uncharacteristic excitement and laser focus on the blanket. "You can cut it up and blend it into strawberry smoothies!"

Alma managed a little laugh. "Whatever Dawn wants I will do it. Sounds terrible though."

Raven wished Dawn would stop talking. She didn't know what a smoothie was, but that didn't matter. It occurred to her that humans eating lesser Earth creatures may be a proxy for cannibalism which, in her mind, was what Dawn was describing. "Please stop. This conversation is troubling for me." She wondered if Kohor people appeared the least bit appetizing to hungry humans.

She tried to erase the mental imagery Dawn painted in her head by focusing on her midwife duties. "It is now time for you to push."

Aided by an intense contraction, the top of their baby's head emerged. "This is more painful than before. How do so many women do this?" When her agony subsided, she stopped pushing, and the baby retreated back inside her body.

Fascinated by what she was seeing, Dawn's cheeks hurt from her constant smiling. "Oops, where are you going?"

"With your next contraction, push with all your strength." Every birth Raven attended for humans and Kohor was clinical, most of them quite boring, but this one affected her in a way she hadn't experienced in a long time.

Alma pushed as hard as she could, forcing her child's head more than halfway out.

Dawn couldn't contain her excitement. "Oh my God!"

Alma's strong hand crushing David's was somehow comforting, connecting him to everything that was happening, but he wanted to see. "I'd love it if Dawn could hold up a mirror."

"Look down," Alma grunted. Dawn bent down and lifted a large mirror resting against her leg. She wobbled it until they could see their emerging baby. "Our child has black hair. Like you!"

Raven ran her fingers around the baby's shoulders, stretching Alma out to help the child escape its mother's protection. "One more big push. The difficult part is nearing its end."

Once the baby was far enough out, Raven pulled it the rest of the way. She flipped their newborn face-down over one hand and gently tapped its back, then lowered it to a towel on the floor. "General, please come here. Dawn will get you a knife."

David's grin spanned ear to ear as he pulled a folded knife from his belt. "I have one."

Raven made a loop in the cord allowing him to sever its physical connection to Alma. She fastened both cut ends with makeshift clips crafted from small twigs, then lifted their child and carried it to its mother. "She is a gigantic baby girl." The enormous size of human babies made most Kohor women quite uncomfortable.

David opened Alma's shirt, allowing their daughter to rest on her mother's bare skin. She looked at him with a blissful tear-soaked smile. "Sunna?"

"I love that name." He climbed into bed with his family and rested his hand on Sunna's tiny head.

"Your eyes are telling me something is wrong. Did they discover another horror for us to fear?" Alma's and David's footsteps echoed through the marble hallway as they made their way to a conference room on the second floor of the Pentagon. He brought her here under the guise of an important meeting with President Atkinson.

David tried masking his disdain for what Dawn and the military had been planning. "I'd rather fight a new monster. Dawn asked me to let the President tell you. Just remember, I had no part in this." He reached out to open one of the massive solid wood doors and guided her inside.

High ranking members of the military waited for them around a well lit, large square table. President Atkinson was on the opposite side of the room, facing the doors. They stood in unison as Alma and David entered. She was bewildered by their professional display.

They took their seats as a serious looking older man in a formal Army uniform quieted the room by clearing his throat. He reminded her of David when they first met, strong, intelligent, and somewhat terrifying. "I'm

Chairman of the Joint Chiefs of Staff, Army General William O'Neil. I'm these people's boss." He motioned around the table, skipping the President.

"The first thing we'd like to do is congratulate you both on the birth of your daughter, Sunna." Several people voiced their congratulations. "Now, how should we refer to you? Do you have a preferred title?"

"Alma. Call me Alma. You have always called me Alma. This is very confusing for me. Why am I here?" She turned to David for answers, but found him staring across the room.

"Alright, Alma. These people represent every branch of the United States Armed Forces. While not unanimous, we came to an overwhelming consensus. By every conceivable measure, you, Alma, are the most powerful person humanity has ever encountered."

He pulled out a tiny Bible and placed it on the table in front of him. "It's been quite difficult for many of us, wrestling with our beliefs and the reality that you represent." He looked at it in the same manner a father would look down on a suffering child.

President Atkinson pivoted around in his chair like a young boy on Christmas Eve waiting for permission to attack the tree. He interrupted the General, who was distracted anyway. "They have all decided it's time to acknowledge you as either a representative of God or God herself."

She didn't appreciate the sound of those words at all. "David, what are they talking about?" He closed his eyes, ignoring her question.

General O'Neil managed to compose himself. "We want you to lead this nation, all of humanity, and the Kohor, and the Trey." He clenched his little Bible. "We'll help make this happen, by force if necessary."

"No. I do not accept this." She shook David's arm. His silence was worrying.

O'Neil flashed a compassionate smile. "We aren't really giving you a choice."

She gripped David's thigh, squeezing as hard as she could, trying to shake him out of his stupor. "I need you to talk to me. Now!"

David responded loud enough for everyone to hear. "This is a military coup. I dedicated my life to this nation, to this uniform." He wanted to say more but couldn't.

O'Neil sympathized with David. "We realize that under your leadership this world will be one unified nation. The entire United States military, as well as many others, are at your disposal. Atkinson will step aside, publicly announcing his commitment to you. You already have tens of millions of followers drooling at the opportunity to prove themselves worthy of you."

With his eyes barely holding back tears, David explained, "This was inevitable, and we both knew it. I just thought it would be a much longer time from now." He looked down at his lap, unable to make eye contact with any of the leaders he worshiped for decades.

Alma's focus darted around the room. "What should I do?"

"You already know the answer." He squeezed her hand as his painful feelings of loss forced out several tears. "You and Dawn have made us greater than anyone could have possibly imagined."

O'Neil tried to convey the inevitability of her situation. "There is no way back from here. A reluctant god is still a god." He felt a twinge of sacrilegious anxiety calling her that. "We understand you wish things were different. They're not." No longer playing with his Bible, O'Neil took a small remote from the table and turned on a projector mounted to the ceiling.

An image of an altered American flag displayed on the room's four walls. its white stripes resembled faded parchment. The field of navy blue held four stars representing the solar systems where Alma maintained influence. It hung vertically, draped from a wooden branch carried by a crow in flight. "This is just a proposal. You obviously can make it anything you want."

Alma stared at the flag in disbelief. "Why is the flag carried by a blackbird? Why not an eagle?"

Atkinson interjected. "Alma, eagles are lone hunters, but humans are intelligent pack animals. We work together to achieve common goals. Like the magnificent crow, we help and watch out for each other. We take care of each other and our friends."

It was obvious the crow was his idea, as he seemed quite proud of it. Alma shrank away from the President's unsettling smile and closed her eyes as a new reality sank in.

"You are making me uncomfortable. Like when men stare at me." Alma sat on Dawn's sofa and unbuttoned her shirt to breastfeed Sunna. Dawn could barely mask her feelings as Alma teased Sunna's lips with her nipple, trying to get her to latch. "Are you looking at her, or my boob?"

She was hypnotized by Alma's motherly beauty. "You know I want a baby. Yeah, this is so cool and sexy in a messed up kind of way, but also creepy since a baby's doing it." Everything about becoming a mother fascinated her.

Dawn rested her head on the clothed half of Alma's chest to get a better view. "Women are amazing." She rubbed Sunna's cheek and breathed in the intoxicating chamomile scent radiating from Alma's body.

Ander being trillions of kilometers away made Dawn wonder out loud. "A long time ago, women stayed home to raise their children together while men went off to war or hunt. I think babies help keep women sane."

The doorbell interrupted their unsettling bonding moment. Dawn hurried to let in their unwanted, but expected guest. She swung open her door to greet their military provided Image Consultant, Lieutenant Katie Pérez. "Whoa. Did not think you'd be hot." She scanned the woman's body from bottom to top. "You're not going to like me much. You'd think the Air Force would know better by now."

Katie managed to work in a kind smile and followed Dawn into the living-room where she shook her head at Alma, sitting topless, with a baby suckling her. She rebuked the future leader of humanity. "All the Abrahamic gods extol the virtues of modesty."

"If feeding my child is offensive, let them be offended." She snarled. "I do not see why you are necessary at all, and you will fail to shame me."

Katie chuckled at Alma's unpleasant personality. "You're fun to look at, but very unlikable." She glanced at Dawn, who was still checking her out. "Both of you are unlikable, but for different reasons."

"So, your job is to make people like us? Cool, I guess." Dawn was in a frisky mood. She hadn't spent any time with Ander since David ordered a military build-up around Múspellsheimr. "I'm hoping this has something to do with us dancing naked under a full moon waving burning smudges. That would be fun."

Katie forced out an apathetic huff at Dawn's childish attempt to shock her. "We want Alma to appear approachable, but you need to be just a little scarier."

"What? I do not believe that is possible." Alma scoffed at the idea of a crueler Dawn. "Perhaps she can eat a live puppy on television?"

"Oh, you could make a realistic looking puppy out of cake or something. I'd play it up for the cameras." She giggled as she pictured the horror on people's faces. "Fill it with raspberry sauce."

"Are you done? I don't want you to look cruel, more like the biblical Destroying Angel, God's avenger. Alma will be presented as a kind and merciful God. You exact punishment on her behalf. When needed, of course." Katie shook off confusing and undesirable images of Dawn dressed in black and carrying a sword. "The goal is to attract worshipers. Either through Alma's benevolence, or fear of Dawn's retribution."

"If having worshipers is so important then why did Ymir not choose a famous person? They already have many drooling morons clinging to their every ridiculous word." Alma's animosity for anything American only grew stronger after partnering with their military.

Dawn snorted. "Just think of all the stupid things a celebrity god would do." She made an exaggerated puking face, pretending to gag on her finger. "They'd destroy our military and prop up mental illness as the genetic model for humanity. The Kohor would have slaughtered us, and we'd deserve it."

Katie tried to ignore Dawn and focused on Alma.

"You're the one who was chosen. I don't know why, and I don't care to know. I'm assuming you'd rather not kill off half this planet's population. Then you'll need to know how to fake a realistic smile and say spiritual things to people you don't know or care about."

Dawn walked a slow circle around their attractive teacher before sitting on the floor at Alma's legs. She looked up through giant green eyes, and asked, "Do you think the Air Force picked her because she's pretty? Like they knew I'd pay more attention just to look at her?"

Alma felt sorry for her frustrated friend, alone for weeks without her partner. "You need to calm down." Dawn quietly disappeared.

Katie froze. "What did you do with her?!" She hadn't witnessed any of Alma's abilities before, so dawn disappearing terrified her.

"She is on the bridge of Admiral Falk's ship. He is her boyfriend. I am sure she will be ready to come back within an hour or two. Likely three." Sunna finished feeding with a loud juicy belch. Alma covered herself and stood chin-to-face with Katie. "Tell me what you require of me."

Chapter 18

Coup D'état

The Oval Office buzzed with excitement. Women and men scrambled to set up cameras, lights, and microphones in front of the President's desk. "Ready for equipment checks!" Katie's powerful voice resonated throughout the room.

Unlike Alma's surprise visit to the United Nations General Assembly, this was curated, flawless. To help keep her anxiety at bay, David sat on a chair beneath the center camera, cradling Sunna in his arms. Alma stood beside them, waiting to be ordered around. "You seem far too calm."

David bobbed his knee to distract Sunna from the

pandemonium. "I've made my peace with this whole thing." He hesitated. "Just letting you know, she signed the papers this morning. My wife."

"Your entire life has been completely destroyed, by me. Your marriage, your country. I wish I viewed change the same as you do."

David reached out to hold Alma's hand. "My life gets better with each transformation. I have a good life."

Katie stomped across the room with an irritated grimace. "What the hell are you two doing? Don't get red puffy eyes right now." She barked at a young woman standing near the office door. "Get her something to clear her eyes."

"I can repair myself. Do not think for a moment I will allow you to put your chemicals into my body." Alma's eyes turned a flawless white as she chastised Katie.

She dismissed Alma's perpetual, but innocuous anger. "Okay, come with me and stand on the X." Katie grabbed her elbow and dragged her in front of the President's desk. She spun her around to face the cameras, and yelled into the air. "Two minutes!"

A young man pushed a teleprompter as close to David and Sunna as possible, allowing Alma to use them for comfort, if needed. She was already staring at him, trying to smile.

He flashed her a gentle grin in return. "You're incredible." She could barely hear him.

Katie snapped her fingers in the air to attract Alma's attention. Angled bright lights illuminated her face. "Five, four, three, two..." A large red light atop the main camera lit. She pointed to Alma and mouthed the words, "We're live".

With a rehearsed look of confidence, Alma spoke to

the world. "Hello, my name is Alma Ólafsdóttir. It is difficult to imagine anyone could not know who I am at this point." David held Sunna facing her mother, bouncing her on his knee.

"I understand there are billions of you who believe I am a hoax. A false flag perpetrated by the United States government to accomplish some perceived psychological sway over the world's population. This broadcast should change many of those minds."

"For decades I have been resisting the inevitable. Hiding on my family farm in Iceland, then hiding behind the protective shield of the American military." Alma needed more than David and Sunna to fight her bubbling emotions. Dawn appeared standing beside them, waving with a cheerful bounce.

She lost herself in Dawn's sanguine eyes and returned to the camera. "I now accept that I have been chosen to lead. Recent and ongoing events have made hiding no longer possible. A few short years ago I warned this world of a threat from a people we call Kohor. I am ashamed to admit, I was misled."

"That threat proved to be part of an insidious plan crafted by a much more advanced species. These creative and powerful people have been living among us for thousands of years, blending in with us, looking like us, speaking half-truths into our ears, corrupting our thoughts. They have been turning humans against one another for millennia."

"Their existence benefits from us fighting and slaughtering each other. To facilitate this, they have been sowing mistrust. Mistrust between races, nations, genders, religions, and more. They need us to constantly war with each other, causing humanitarian disasters that drain us of resources and hinder our technological progress."

She drew in a deep breath. "I am to help push back against this threat. We call our true enemy, the Æsir. Our last confrontation with them resulted in the destruction of an entire planet, Jupiter. That was not my finest moment. I am not proud of that unacceptable display of my abilities. Nor can I reverse the terrible damage I have caused."

"Jupiter was beautiful. I miss her. Unfortunately, I too was swayed by an Æsir voice masquerading as one of us, a human. That voice convinced me Jupiter's destruction was our only option against invasion. It belonged to someone far more intelligent than me, so I trusted it. That voice also held the ear of many military and political leaders in America. I have since silenced it, but there are more."

The teleprompter directed her to darken her mood. "There are so many more of them, that we need your help. As I speak to you, hundreds of American warships are appearing over every major city in every nation. They are not there to harm you. This is nothing more than a show of our capabilities. Of the inevitability you face."

She turned her palms forward and stretched out her arms. "We struggled to find a gentle way of informing you, but we were unsuccessful."

"Today, with the American military supporting me, I am following the path I was chosen to walk. I am taking control of this world." President Atkinson followed his cue, moving into the camera's view to stand behind and to the right of Alma. "President Atkinson is willingly stepping aside."

X9 warships brandishing the new American flag appeared over the most prominent structures in every major city on Earth. Air forces around the globe responded with futile aggression.

"As a precaution, I have removed all weaponized forms of radioactive material from the globe, including from America. We do not want you harming yourselves or destroying your beautiful cities."

A relaxed grin graced Alma's lips as she surrendered herself to Ymir. The flood of powerful emotions warmed her entire body, making her look different, possessed. She shook her head in disagreement with the teleprompter. "My media handlers have conjured a name for our combined singular nation. It is a terrible name. I understand, and do not care, that many of you will disapprove of the name I have chosen. We are all Americans now."

David tipped his head against the chair and mouthed, *I love you.* He understood she did this for him, and probably a little because she was used to calling everyone in the military, Americans.

Katie muttered, "Great, alienate ninety-five percent of the world."

Alma ignored Katie's displeased head shake. "I will not require that you worship me, but I cannot allow you to organize against me." She beckoned Dawn to join her in front of the camera. "This adorable young woman is Dawn. She is my personal advisor."

"Dawn has an incredible gift not even I possess." She wrapped an arm around Dawn's shoulders and gave her a loving squeeze. "Dawn can hear your thoughts and search your memories. She knows what lies within the hearts of every person in all four solar systems."

The thought of billions of people watching her set Dawn's heart racing. Intoxicated by her rapid rise to power, her appearance assumed a villainous facade. Her breathing grew heavy and deliberate as she smiled at the camera.

"I trust her implicitly." Alma glanced at her scary little friend and made a mental note to have David keep tabs on her. "She needs not defer to me. Dawn will ensure that you do not organize against us. She is to decide the proper punishment for those who disobey my simple rules."

Alma waved David over and displayed her family to the world with radiating pride. "This is American Air Force General, David Trauger. He is my partner and my military advisor." She held a finger out in front of Sunna's face, allowing her to grip it. "This is our daughter, Sunna. Before you ask, no, she does not have any superpowers I am aware of."

"Like Dawn, I trust David. He is not required to defer any military decisions to me. He will command the armed forces of our four solar systems and lead our military to victory against the Æsir." Alma reached forward, pinched at Dawn's shirt and pulled her back in line. "It is my sincere hope that David will hide his horrible military secrets from me."

"I will repeat this many more times. No one speaks for me. No priests, no clerics, no Imams, no Popes, no leaders of any kind. Anyone claiming I have given them authority over another will be executed."

Katie's eyes widened. Her plan was to present a kind and benevolent god to the world. She repositioned the teleprompter near the end of Alma's speech and, using only her eyes, begged Alma to change gears.

David nudged her, nodding in Katie's direction. Alma paused, took in a breath and smiled at the camera.

"My military advisor is already advising me. I do not wish you to fear me. My only demands are that you do not harm each other, you do not organize against me, and you do not use my name to subjugate others."

Alma lifted Sunna from David's arms and cradled their daughter. She tried to appear as the humble god Katie wanted her to look like. "You will not need for anything, but this will take time. Until you are self-sufficient, I will provide clean water and healthy food to everyone. If you require shelter, I will endeavor to provide that as well."

Sunna fussed in her embrace. Challenging centuries of pointless shame, Alma unbuttoned her shirt and lowered one panel of her nursing bra. She revealed herself to the world while letting Sunna latch. "This world has changed. If you accept it, your lives will be quite enjoyable. If you fight it, your life will be forfeit."

"Why do I need to drag soldiers along with me? I think I'm good with stabbing people all by myself." Dawn was eager to start her career as enforcer of Alma's three commandments. Her first order of business, inflicting merciless justice on a large Baptist church in Southern Florida.

Katie adjusted Dawn's form-fitting black tunic. "It's all for show. We want the congregation to know that humans are part of Alma's police force."

Dawn was alluring in her black skin-tight uniform. The contrast of her auburn hair resting over her shoulders perfected the look. She protested, "I'm human."

"No, you're a demigoddess. Half human, half

whatever the hell Ymir is. It's how the world perceives you. You need to accept that." She finished messing with Dawn's clothes and stepped back to admire her menacing creation.

Katie's intense empathy begged her to temper Dawn's bloodthirsty exuberance. "You know you don't have to kill him. Just appearing on their stage will scare the crap out of the entire congregation."

"He's all fire and brimstone. Calling Alma Satan, and telling people they're going to hell if they follow her. Then there's that Imam in Detroit promising rewards from Allah based on how many American soldiers his followers kill. These guys, they all need to die. Publicly executed by a cute little girl."

Not wanting herself added to Dawn's murder list, Katie ignored her homicidal rant. Instead, she made a curt smile and opened a project plan on her tablet. "I have some things written down for you to say in Alma's defense."

"Nope. I'll do this with soldiers, but I'm not your puppet and Alma doesn't need anyone to defend her." Dawn's eyes sprang open. She was elated to blurt her latest, Ymir inspired epiphany. "I want them to kill me! Imagine me reappearing over my own dead body! Maybe I should start at a Mosque instead." She wandered around the room as scenes of her dramatic murder played out in her head.

Katie indulged Dawn's suicidal inspiration. "I guess I can coordinate that with the military. Having soldiers with you would probably make them hesitant to try anything, so I guess you're right, you shouldn't bring them the first few times." The defeat in her voice was palpable.

Dawn put a hand on Katie's shoulder and patted her

like a dog. "There we go." Katie's irritating ego met its match. Ymir and Dawn were enjoying their pretty little toy.

Katie was too excited about being part of their inner circle to notice how dangerous and unstable these powerful women could be, but Dawn was so much worse than Alma. She had a bloodlust bordering on psychotic. "How's Admiral Falk taking all this? Your new persona."

"He wants to get me pregnant." Her face contorted as she tried to remember his exact words. She spoke in a comically deep voice, "I'm thinking a baby would help dull your sharp edge a bit."

Katie vomited a little in her mouth at the thought of Dawn as a mother. Obsessed with genetics, she couldn't imagine how Dawn believed her DNA was good for humanity. "I don't think that would be a great idea at all." She regretted saying that.

Dawn wrapped one arm around Katie's fear-stiffened body. "Scared shitless, and you still can't control that nasty little mouth." She pushed her lips inside Katie's ear and whispered, "I'd never hurt you."

Imam Mohamed Nasrallah, speaking in Aramaic, addressed the room with a loud angry voice. "Now we are to assume the Americans are one with God?! No! Alma is of the Jinn and America is her army." His words energized the young male students sitting in radiating semicircles on the floor in front of him.

He clenched his fists and pounded them against the podium. "We are being tested by God. Do we accept the incredible promises of Alma and surrender our faith for her poisoned food and water? Do we bury Islam in the sand as we lay stupid and fat on a beach frantically waving an American flag?"

"Shall we all pray to this sorceress? Do we then worship her bastard child?" He looked around the room and singled out one random man. "Is Alma your God now?" He nervously shook his head.

Dawn's military team set the scene for her first intervention. She appeared without a sound alongside an ornate wooden mimbar containing the impassioned old Imam. In front of her, twenty young men were sitting on the floor, consuming his every word. It took them a moment to realize she was standing beside their teacher.

She stroked the intricate carved wooden frame of the mimbar. "This is pretty." Many of the men looked around at the exits only to find them covered in a thick wall of marble.

Nasrallah's weary red eyes met hers. "You must leave." His spiritual rage dissipated into a strange fear. Not fear for his life or the lives of the men in the room, it was something different. Deep down, he knew his God wouldn't protect anyone from her.

"Or, what?" Dawn chuckled, fantasizing about him pulling out a sword and slicing her head clean off. She pictured him standing victorious over her decapitated body. Then she tapped him on the shoulder from behind.

"I beg you, not in front of them."

Dawn pursed her lips and let out a disappointed huff. She expected someone to have killed her by now. "Yeah, I don't think you get the point of this. I have work to do." She theatrically wrapped her hand around the simple reddish-brown grip of her long knife. An onyx crow's head pommel rested against her wrist as she drew the knife from a scabbard hanging from her hip, never breaking eye contact with the Imam.

She pointed her blade down at an angle in front of the young men while waving it back and forth. "Nothing?" Her excitement at the prospect of being killed faded as it became obvious no one had the courage to try.

Dawn signaled for the Imam to leave the mimbar with her sweeping blade. "Kneel in front of them and I promise not to harm them. Don't do what I say, and I'll start with this guy." She winked at the boy, confusing him into thinking she may be joking.

Nasrallah traversed the short staircase, shuffling his arthritic legs. It took him some time to reach the location Dawn was pointing at. He stood tall and proud before his terrified students.

Dawn moved in closer. With her blade acting as an extension of her arm, she gestured downward. "Kneel."

The frail man stiffly lowered himself to his knees and addressed the room. "Do not be afraid." His once vitriolic tone colored submissive.

Several men wept at the sight of Dawn securing the guard of her blade against their Imam's neck. She wore a creepy smirk as she slid it across his throat, spilling blood down the front of his long tunic. With the bottom of her boot, she pushed his struggling body to the ground as viscous gurgling sounds emanated from the deep furrow.

"Well, that was kind of anti-climactic." Dawn knelt beside him and hovered the tip of her blade above his left eye. She thrust it deep into his brain and made a single twist, putting an end to his feeble thrashing.

"Oh, I like that much better."

She stood triumphant over her slaughter, with her knife dripping blood onto the concrete floor. "You people were very disappointing. I hope the Christians are more fun."

Dawn and the marble barriers evaporated, leaving most of the men staring at the motionless body of their teacher laying in a growing pool of red. The cruel reality of Alma's Destroying Angel scarred their young minds forever.

Military personnel, including Katie, witnessed everything as it happened. Some were horrified, but others found her ruthless justice inspiring. To many of them, Dawn was the focal point for their worship, not Alma.

She reappeared in the center of the staging room, her blade staining the raised tile with blood. Looking around at the shocked faces, it was evident her team had the ability to see her performance. "Apparently, Muslims aren't all crazy people hell-bent on killing Americans. That kind of sucked."

Katie wanted to quit and run away from this psychotic little monster. "We watched you." Her hands were shaking as she fixated on Dawn's bloody sword. "I don't think I can work with you anymore."

Dawn dismissed Katie's concerns with a flip of her hand. "Oh, you'll be fine. Besides, I was pretty clear about how this was going down. It's too bad they didn't kill me. That would have been so awesome."

"I won't be able to watch you do that again. That was beyond sickening. We should get you cleaned up." Her body trembled as she turned and walked away.

Dawn followed behind Katie and swatted at her swaying ponytail. "You should see some of the shit

Ymir's been showing me since I was fifteen. What I did is nothing compared to what other people do to each other, and animals."

Chapter 19

Dangerous Games

Admiral Falk's fleet jumped to within striking distance of a small Æsir flotilla orbiting the tiny Mercury-like planet, Thul, in the Proxima Centauri system. Lieutenant Connolly's excited tone rattled the bridge crew. "Admiral, radioactive particles just appeared all around us. Contact in thirteen seconds."

Military planners warned Falk this would be a suicide mission, but that dust amused him. "I hope they have better weapons than radioactive dust. They're probably testing our shields for weak spots." He brushed off the lieutenant's panicked warning.

Ander enjoyed the menacing appearance of Æsir

warships. Their smooth long black dart-shaped bodies superimposed against a gigantic reddish-orange star appeared ominous. "Gather as much information as you can, and see if the AI can turn that dust into something less cancerous."

There wasn't enough time for the AI to question his ambiguous request. When the first Æsir particle touched their shields, both it and the particles it contacted were destroyed in a spectacular explosion of radiation, launching remnant particles in every direction.

The dust continued its violent assault, stripping away the shields and skin of each vessel. In an instant, Ander's ships disintegrated, leaving nothing but massive amounts of dissipating gamma radiation.

Admiral Falk tapped his finger on the console in frustration while waiting for the backup of his fleet to finish. An alarm sounded, prompting the ship's AI to inform him they had died in combat. He steadied his hand above the keypad. "Huh?" They told him he'd have no memory of events occurring between backups and restores, but this experience left him wanting.

Alma and David appeared on his bridge to welcome him and his crew back. David couldn't help but analyze Ander for any discernible differences. He held suppressed feelings about people returning from their deaths. On a logical level, he understood Alma moving them, and ship jumps employed the same mechanisms, but Ander died, and there he stood, in front of him, not dead.

"I do not like that you can recreate yourselves so easily. It feels wrong in some way I cannot explain." Alma's anxiety over the military growing as powerful as herself was a personal struggle that ravaged her mind. "You have been gone for an hour. At least I can do these things much faster than you, for now."

The dramatic shift from preparing for combat to being briefed on his unceremonious death was disorientating. Ander looked around the bridge and attempted to make light of the situation. "So, no Dawn?"

David laughed out loud. "Business first, rewards later." He displayed the widest grin he had ever shown. "Your reward can't be big enough for what we've already learned. That little test was game changing." He was so eager to tell Ander about the Æsir weapon he couldn't contain himself and shouted, "Antimatter!"

His glee filled enthusiasm over a dust cloud capable of vaporizing an entire fleet of warships in a matter of milliseconds troubled Alma. She never heard the word, antimatter, before. If she bothered reading the report General O'Neil supplied during their insurrection meeting, she would have known antimatter was an obsession of every major human military for decades.

"The containment issues completely disappear when you just materialize it from nothing. I hope you won't mind being killed a few more times. We need you to tease them back here, so Alma can get a closer look at that weapon."

Ander's simultaneous excitement and disappointment was evident in his contorting expressions. This mission sounded fun, but he understood he wouldn't remember any of it. "As long as people sing ballads of my heroic adventures, I'm up for anything."

Dawn tiptoed outside Raven's home trying to sneak a peek into her window. She hoped to catch her being her genuine self. Able to experience the thoughts and feelings of every normal sapient creature in four solar systems, over ten billion people, she couldn't hear Raven. It was an intriguing feeling, making her something of an obsession.

Through her home's thick mud walls Dawn could hear her chastising someone in her native language. She peered around a small window frame to see Raven sitting on a big pillow, screaming at her phone. She threw it against another pillow and slumped with her head in her hands.

Dawn jumped back to the front door and knocked on it irritatingly fast and hard. It took Raven a long minute to open it. "Where is Alma?" Seeing only Dawn made her uneasy.

"She's playing with my boyfriend." Dawn chuckled at her unintended innuendo. "Oh, not, not like that. She's getting him killed, over and over and over. I think that war is finally starting, but it's tough for me to tell, and I don't think we're winning."

Raven stood staring, not knowing what to do or say. Dawn pushed past her and walked into the living-room. "You can have a bigger nicer house. Just ask. They'll give us anything we want." The toy spaceships on her center table were in a different arrangement, making Dawn imagine Raven playing with them.

She followed Dawn inside and asked, "What do you need from me?"

Dawn pointed at Raven's phone resting on a pillow. "When did they make phones work here? Can we call each other from different planets now?" She picked it up and tried opening it, but was thwarted by a biometric lock screen. Flashing the phone in front of Raven's annoyed face, it unlocked. Dawn laughed. "You got that mad over a game?"

"It is a frustrating thing, making all those different shapes fit together. They keep falling faster." Raven's cheeks flushed. She had seen many human soldiers playing these games and assumed her level of agitation was normal.

Dawn giggled and tossed the phone onto a nearby pillow. "You know there's no winning, right? It's a top score thing. The game doesn't have an end." She looked around Raven's lonely little home. "You're supposed to compete against friends for the highest score. There's a link in the corner to add them."

Raven's tone turned bitter. "Did our voice tell you to come here?" Being forced to share Cartara's voice with Dawn stirred unproductive feelings of jealousy, an emotion she hadn't experienced until meeting humans.

"No. She doesn't tell me anything about you. She doesn't talk about you at all. You're a cute little mystery." Dawn selected a squishy looking pillow and took a seat. "You should really get some chairs. Big old humans won't be able to stand up from these things."

"I only experience Kohor feelings, so all humans have been a mystery to me. I do hear things about you from the soldiers though. Disturbing things. How did you get here, and why are you here?"

Dawn laid down and spread her body across multiple pillows. "You know it doesn't take a full day to get here in a spaceship, but I had Alma do it. She's way faster. It's weird, I hear everyone, everywhere. Kohor, Trey, humans, but not you. I wonder why."

Overwhelmed by her own people's increasing population, Raven sympathized with her. "I cannot imagine the weight of that burden. Of all those feelings." She sat next to Dawn, who scooted closer and laid her head in Raven's lap.

"There's a lot of dark shit in people's brains. Humans are the worst. I like your people, they're so calm. Well, not the new ones. It's difficult to swallow so much bad all the time."

Raven stroked the length of Dawn's long hair. "I remind you I've seen bad in person. I was forced to watch my entire family slaughtered, tortured. Friends beaten and killed. The Trey are a nightmare I cannot forget, or forgive." A frustrated teardrop rolled down her cheek. "Thinking of Alma working with them on a planet in my solar system feels like a fire smoldering inside my head."

Dawn cuddled up against Raven's stomach. "I forget about that sometimes. I feel sorry for you. I had to beg Ymir and the Seleen voice to stop showing me Stacey. It's a lot harder when you care about the person. Thankfully, I don't care about many people. Alma, Trauger, Ander, you, and Stacey. I miss her so much."

Their similar agonizing lives bound them to each other in a way no one else could comprehend. "We are alike when it comes to these things. A person grows numb to it all, but you always seem so much happier than me."

"I'm broken. It's the reason I haven't let Ander get me pregnant yet. I'm afraid of myself." Dawn dabbed her eyes on Raven's dress and sniffled. This was the first time she confessed self-doubt to anyone. "Making another monster, like me, I don't think that's a great idea. I do want a baby though."

Raven made a failed attempt at humor. "We are all afraid of you. I am quite content not being able to hear the troubling things that must clutter your thoughts." She regretted her words, but Dawn didn't mind as long as she continued touching her hair.

The realization that someone could appreciate her lifetime of mental anguish allowed Raven to lower her guard. This crazy dangerous human understood her. "I have my own wrong, selfish thoughts. More so lately." Her breathing intensified as she ran her hand down Dawn's arm, interlacing their fingers. "Some of these thoughts don't make sense." She leaned over and whispered into Dawn's ear. "No one has ever gently touched me."

Dawn's eyes snapped wide open. She didn't want to say anything stupid or heartless that could ruin this moment, so she remained silent. Raven moved her face in close, prompting Dawn to turn her head and kiss her. Raven didn't pull away.

A crippling urge to be as perfect as possible spun Dawn into a mild dread. The thought of being Raven's only paramour was more than a little intimidating. She imagined many men felt this way when they were with a woman for their first time.

The kissing went on for quite a while. Raven was hungry, and devoured Dawn's lips. However, in Dawn's mind, this had gone on long enough. She reached around Raven's neck and pulled on the string securing her dress.

"Ahem!" Startled awake, they looked up to see Alma hovering over them. A disgusted expression puckered her face. "Stand and put your clothing on." She turned away as Dawn nonchalantly stood proud in front of her.

With a sly smile, Dawn asked, "How long were you watching us?"

Raven slipped into her dress and sat in silence.

Dawn gathered her clothes, moving as slow as possible while trying to get Alma to look at her.

"Long enough to worry about what this will do to Admiral Falk. He is fearless and intelligent, our bravest ship Commander." Alma glanced over Dawn's naked body. Unswayed by her beauty, she remained angry.

Raven grew agitated or excited, no one could tell with her, and blurted, "Her name is Eir."

"Yeah, I like that." Dawn found Cartara's voice choosing a name for herself intriguing. She questioned if Ymir picked her own name, but for undisclosed reasons, made her think she selected it.

Alma watched Dawn's exaggerated performance as she dressed and tried to see her the way Raven did. In her personal encounters with women, she couldn't recall any who didn't desire both genders, or only other females. Since she had no attraction to anyone but David, she was feeling a little excluded. "What are you two talking about?"

Raven dragged her eyes away from Dawn and answered, "The voice in our heads, she wants to be called Eir."

Alma had a growing suspicion of the Jötnar's true intentions for some time. They appeared to be much more complicated and nuanced than most understood. A creepy realization ran a shiver up her body. *Did Ymir and Eir use my friends as sexual avatars?* She shuddered off that unwanted image. "Ask them why they desire to ruin the greatest Commander our military has."

Dawn pulled her shirt over her head, not bothering with a bra, and brushed off Alma's concerns. "Ander will be fine with this. He jokes about it all the time."

Alma shook her head. "Male fantasies are quite often not what they would want or tolerate as a reality."

Ander and his crew died, again, but his latest game of cat-and-mouse proved fruitful. He managed to annoy a small Æsir fleet into Múspellsheimr orbit before being annihilated. Alma, feeling the human ships and crews disintegrate into a radioactive puff, hunched over and began to retch.

David was too excited about capturing and reverse-engineering that dust to properly comfort her, so he patted her on the back. "How is this any different from when you or ship jumps do it?"

She paused to recover from her convulsions. "I remind you that Ymir and Surtr amplify my feelings here, and this feels different. There is nothing left for me to manipulate. It is as if a piece of our universe was erased."

Never bothering to learn basic physics or chemistry, she couldn't comprehend what made antiparticles so special. To her, they appeared identical to normal particles. "I can reproduce this dust with little difficulty. It is nothing more than parts of atoms and parts of the parts of atoms." She surrounded the enemy fleet in a loose shell of their own weapon.

Alma's face drained of color as her antiparticles interacted with the Æsir trespassers, obliterating several of them in a massive release of energy. Her eyes widened in horror. "I cannot accept this to be normal in nature. Why would you or anyone want this?!"

Three Æsir warships disintegrated in a fiery tumult of gamma radiation as two managed to jump outside Alma's sphere of influence, but not far enough to escape Surtr.

The bridge Watch Officer screamed in a panic. "Alma!" Addressing the ruler of four solar systems by her first name left him feeling uncomfortable. "The last two enemy ships are firing on each other."

A detailed, albeit confusing scene unfolded on the screen at the front of the bridge. Both Æsir ships deactivated their shields and launched what appeared to be all of their close combat weapons against each other. Neither vessel lasted long. "Why are they doing this?"

David couldn't hide his excited smirk. "It's Surtr. He's making them attack each other."

Alma suspected Dawn and David were keeping dark secrets regarding Surtr from her, but likely for good reason. She exhaled with a slight head shake. "No. Do not tell me about it."

Ander's reward awaited him in his stateroom. After a quick wrestling match with Dawn, which he lost on purpose, he reached into his nightstand for a condom.

She climbed on top of him and pinned his arms. "Let's make a baby."

Ander stared into her eyes, shocked and delighted. "I kind of assumed you changed your mind about that." She hadn't mentioned wanting a baby in quite some time.

Dawn grabbed the condom between her teeth, flipped her head, and spit it onto the floor. "I don't think we'll be needing that." She rolled off and laid flat on the bed with her arms and legs extended in a submissive and uncharacteristic display. "Now you use your teeth."

Ander afforded Dawn the freedom to lash out, to work through the traumas battering her mind. He was different from her other partners. The things he was willing to let her do would send normal men scurrying for the door. She was a violent lover, and this didn't bother him at all.

Dawn was the only woman who could bring him to absolute exhaustion. She dug her fingernails into his skin and sliced him from shoulders to buttocks. He never escaped these playful torture sessions unscathed.

Ander collapsed sweating and breathless beside her after enduring four hours of pleasurable brutality. He made a breathy laugh while looking at the bloody sheets. "I'm done. I need some water, and maybe a transfusion."

She stamped her blood soaked hands on her stomach and chest, making dark red prints in artistic and disturbing patterns. *Yep, I definitely like guys.* She'd never consider scarring Raven's beautiful body the way she did Ander's. "I think we need to talk."

Ander didn't care for that terrifying statement at all. He rolled toward her with the bedsheet sticking to the open gashes running down his back. "Sure."

His humbled tone made her eyes water. "I cheated on you yesterday." She couldn't look at him, instead she focused on the ceiling, concentrating on a tiny box she failed to notice during their many cathartic escapades in Ander's bed. "I didn't plan it. Alma caught us, and now she's really pissed at me."

Ander closed his eyes as his mind replayed everything he did to ruin his previous relationships. In each case his mistakes were obvious. This time, he had no idea how he drove another woman away. Dawn was special, different. If he lost her, it would destroy him.

"We were just talking and then Raven got really, weird. I thought she hated me." Dawn cuddled against his chest. "Having her like me is a big deal. I can't promise to stop doing things with her."

A rejuvenating flood of relief washed over Ander's face. "What? Raven? I assumed you two were doing it anyway." He scoured her forehead for a spot not covered in his blood and gave her a little kiss. "Yeah, I don't have a problem with that. Unless you're leaving me for her."

Dawn repeatedly fast-kissed his mouth and asked, "You're not mad?"

"I assumed you and her hooked up all the time. You're mean to each other like a regular couple." He wrapped his arms around her, hugging her tight. This torturous roller coaster ride of emotions sucked any remaining energy from him.

A mischievous smile stretched across Dawn's face. She pushed him over and climbed on top. Too aggressive for most men, she dug her nails deep into his chest. The site of fresh blood seeping out from under her fingertips reinvigorated them both.

Chapter 20

Necessary Evils

Æsir warships captivated Admiral Falk's imagination. These shadowy, elongated darts pointed in the same direction within each group while remaining precisely spaced apart. He respected this enemy, they were agile, and quick to counter his chaotic maneuvers.

Ander found himself excited by the prospect of killing some of them. "Let's see if this stuff works. Target them all." They jumped into the middle of an Æsir armada where both sides enveloped each other's ships in tailor-made clouds of antiparticles. Ander's warships disintegrated into nothing, but the Æsir vessels, stripped of their shields and skins, left haunting skeletal corpses.

Commander Pruitt was experiencing similar successes, although her fleet managed to avoid being vaporized. AI drones materialized near an Æsir ship, deployed an antiparticle cloud, then suicided themselves in a massive thermonuclear explosion. Her method was slower, but more sympathetic of her nervous crew.

Alma and David stood in a command center on Archytas Station, an enormous Trey research ship orbiting Múspellsheimr. A hologram depicting the Proxima Centauri solar system filled the large chamber, with a bright orange star hugging the ceiling and planets orbiting below it. Nothing was to scale.

Blue and green pyramids created only of light, Ander's and Pruitt's fleets, appeared close to or within clusters of yellow pyramids representing Æsir ships. Yellow pyramids were in every direction they looked.

Unimpressed by this simplistic display, Alma made a conceited chuckle. David's boyish excitement amused her.

He pointed at a group of yellow pyramids disappearing one by one near a pack of green. "Looks like your antiparticles are working perfectly."

Alma's tight lips turned down as her eyes drooped. "Helping Craig replicate this weapon was humiliating. It is unfortunate he lacks a willingness to engage with someone below his level of intelligence. We could accomplish so much if he was more understanding and possessed a desire to educate." She was talking and watching blue pyramids intermingling with a large cluster of yellow.

David laughed through his nose as a green pyramid

disappeared halfway inside an oblivious communications officer's head. "He's terrified of Dawn, and he hated Stacey. I'm guessing his issues run a little deeper than simply being a condescending asshole."

He pointed to a clump of green pyramids near a pack of vanishing yellow. "We haven't figured out why they don't retreat and regroup. I'm starting to think they're all like Ander and don't care if they die."

"This is troubling, them not fearing death. It makes me believe they are being restored somewhere nearby." Alma leaned her body against his as a group of blue pyramids disappeared and resurrected in deep orbit of Múspellsheimr, then jumped into another cluster of yellow. "We may be learning, but so are they."

Dawn sneaked up behind them and wriggled her head between their arms. "We're all here, almost. Surtr's having some issues getting his avatar working on this confusing ship." Alma's scent wasn't as pleasant today, reminiscent of fresh cut grass.

She swatted at a small group of yellow pyramids floating around her head, and huffed when her hand passed through them. "Hmm. Raven wouldn't like this at all." She stood on her tiptoes with her mouth opened wide, pantomiming eating one.

Alma, Dawn, and David appeared in the conference room where Craig was sitting alone, fidgeting in his chair. He jumped up, knocked his chair over, and saluted. "Sir." He wouldn't know what to say if Alma entered without the General.

They sat at the opposite end of the table from Craig. David grumbled, "We're still waiting on Surtr."

Craig righted his chair and perched stiff on its edge.

He tapped his finger on the table, nervous about seeing his first Jötunn. "Are there things I shouldn't say?" The idea of meeting a creature from another universe worried him. "Do I shake his hand? Does he even have hands to shake?"

Dawn couldn't wait for everyone to see Surtr's new body. "Say whatever. I think he's way more human looking now, and you can actually understand his words! Mostly." Surtr showed while Dawn was talking. He stood wide and tall at the end of the conference room table next to her. He never bothered trying to mimic sitting.

David cleared his throat to silence Dawn and opened the meeting. "We're here to discuss Surtr's Æsir Voice Machine. He's successfully used it to disorientate some of their ships, convincing the crews they were each other's enemy. Alma and I saw this in action. It was impressive." He pointed at Surtr, not knowing if the avatar could see him. "Care to elaborate?"

Unknown to anyone in the room, Dawn explained complex human questions and actions to Surtr, making him appear more informed than he was. His booming voice startled everyone. It was still gravelly, but clearer than before. "Æsir used as a weapon in my home."

In Dawn's head, she prodded him to offer additional information.

Surtr continued, "It shakes us, tearing Inguz from Kenanz."

Dawn shrugged her shoulders in response to David's bewildered stare.

Surtr lifted a modeled hand and pointed one thick finger in Alma's direction. "Alma and Æsir have relinquished many to Laguz." She turned away as it was obvious he was referring to her killing the Jötunn bound to Jupiter.

Seeing Alma upset tugged at David's heart. "Let's get back on track here. Dawn and Surtr are going to explain how he uses this machine."

Surtr didn't understand why it was now acceptable to tell them after Dawn threatened him to keep it a secret for so long. He was also confused by Dawn's reasons for keeping his machine hidden from humans in the first place. In a non-anthropic way, he was proud of how he bested his enemies.

"You won't like it." Dawn was playing her standard cute little girl act, which had grown tiresome over the years. She met Alma's annoyed gaze. "Fine. The machine can only be used by an Æsir. Surtr has one he keeps alive, barely, and forces him to operate it like a puppet. He was the original Caretaker of this world. It's the only reason we're able to sit on this ship, around this planet."

David leaned back in his chair, ignoring Alma's look of disgust. "Yeah, I'm completely okay with this. We've counted over one hundred thousand Æsir ships waiting outside our own solar system. I would eat their babies alive with a giant stupid grin on my face if it meant saving our home."

For no defensible reason, Dawn decided to pile on. "You should ask him what we're planning to do in case you get captured. I dare you." She ignored David's burning stare.

"You claim I am your leader but both of you do as you please." Alma puffed out her cheeks and closed her eyes tight. "I know. I told you to hide things from me. Do what you need to do and keep me out of this." She disappeared without giving them a chance to respond.

David stared angry at Dawn and uttered only one word, "Why?"

Dawn exaggerated an eye role and sarcastically said, "Sorry. She's crying in your room."

He sneered at her, shook his head, and left the conference room.

Surtr spoke inside Dawn's mind, questioning if they could continue trusting Alma. *Of course we can trust her. She just doesn't like knowing about the terrible things we have to do to keep us safe.* She wrapped her hand around his mostly-solid, cold fingers.

Craig had no idea Dawn and Surtr were talking to each other, making their silence feel heavy and awkward. "General Trauger said something about a project?"

Their surroundings changed from smooth walls to gray pockmarked concrete. Still seated at the conference room table, they appeared to be in a bunker where the humid air carried an unpleasant moldy aroma. Dawn stood beside Surtr and motioned toward a hallway with poor lighting. "Let's go for a little walk." Craig didn't want to go. "You know I'll just force you. Come on."

Craig tagged along as they made their way down the corridor. He asked in a timid, fear-filled voice, "Where are we going?"

"We're deep under the planet." She walked alongside Surtr, never looking back as she talked. "This is where he keeps the Æsir Voice Machine protected from everyone." Dawn didn't react as they passed through a veil surrounding Surtr's residence.

Bright lights illuminated the large cavern as they entered. On the far side of the room, a man sat motionless, facing the wall. Craig's breathing grew rapid, an anxiety attack was building.

Dawn pointed at the odd-looking thin man balanced tall and stiff on a backless chair. She carried a rare expression of sympathy on her face. "That's Draugr. He's the only one who can operate the machine. You don't talk to him or touch him. Leave him alone. Well, I guess you'll need to scan his brain, but that's it."

Surtr compelled Draugr to rotate his chair. Blinking at regular intervals, he held the vacant look of a lobotomized man.

Craig struggled for the courage to speak. "Nope. I'm not participating in this at all. Tell General Trauger I'm out." He spun around to find his escape covered by a wall of pitted stone.

"You can leave when we have our own version of this machine. One that doesn't need an Æsir zombie running it." She walked to within a meter of him and wiggled her fingers in his face. "We're going to lose this war. Did you know that? Without this weapon, the beautiful human species will disappear, forever."

Dawn's merciless personality was legendary, and now she was holding him prisoner. His voice cracked as he begged, "What if I fail?"

She moved in closer. "Then you'll be the last living human in this entire universe."

Chapter 21

Godless

The Officers Club on Archytas Station was empty, except for David and Ander. Faint voiceless music played in the background as a bartender put away clean glasses. They sat on swiveling stools at the bar, facing each other with drinks in hand. "I can't believe you're getting married, and you knocked her up. What the hell is wrong with you?"

Ander light-heartedly kicked the side of David's leg. "I've been planning on marrying her for a while. That baby thing, that was a complete surprise. I'd show you the scars, but Alma already cleaned me up."

David's days of pretending Dawn was his sweet little

redheaded daughter ended some time ago. Katie forced him to watch her sword videos. Making matters worse, Alma filled him in on her ravenous and violent sexual appetites.

"Alma definitely doesn't want to get married. Not the religious way at least. Something about religion shuts her down. Thankfully, Sunna has my last name. She wanted some confusing Iceland name thing."

Ander slammed his empty glass on the counter-top, waiving to the bartender for another. "I'm glad to hear you win one once in a while. I can't imagine a real fight between you two. I wonder how many times she's killed and resurrected you, but you don't remember."

"That joke is getting old. She's never really been mad at me. Frustrated, yeah, but not wrath of God angry." David slapped the bar. "Let's talk business."

Ander didn't think it was a good idea to discuss military matters when drinking, but he let him continue and prepared to cut him off if necessary.

"If they take her, we're screwed." David drunkenly looked for people listening in. "With her, it's going to be bad. Without her, we don't stand a chance." He waited for the bartender to give Ander his drink and walk away. "We keep telling people there are hundreds of thousands of ships near Earth. It's millions, and it's not just Sol. Daneln, Yeset, they're all surrounded."

Dread swept across Ander's face. "We can't fight millions of them. They already destroy our ships five to one. We'd be overrun in hours." He tapped his empty glass against the counter-top, trying to get the bartender's attention.

"It gets worse." Dawn was great at compartmentalizing military secrets. Not even Ander was aware of the depth and futility of the things David urged her to keep hidden. "Something's wrong. Either with Dawn, Ymir, or our AI." His eyes darted around. "The AI is telling us there are more people on Earth than Dawn and Ymir count."

Confused, Ander asked, "Is that a bad thing?"

"There are people Dawn can't hear. People who could be planning things." David mistrusted AI, but accepted their math as beyond reproach. "Ymir can't warn us if they're plotting something. The same problem exists on Cartara and all the Trey planets."

It took a moment for the information to sink in. "They could be Æsir spies or insurgents!"

"Yep. They can create fake histories, and take human names. They can even alter themselves to look like us." He eyed the bartender. Paranoia and alcohol made for a dangerous combination. "I'm going to let you in on another secret that no other ordinary human knows. Can I trust you like I trust Dawn?"

"You can trust me to keep a secret, but I doubt you can trust anyone as much as you trust her."

David stood to whisper into his ear. "They're all Æsir. The Kohor, the Trey. All of them. That's why Surtr hates them so much." He stumbled against Ander's shoulder. "The Kohor don't even know what they are. The Trey probably know, but they haven't said anything."

Ander's brain fast-cycled through his time spent with Raven and training Trey sailors. "I have Trey crew members!" His stomach churned at the thought of Trey terraformers cataloging every square centimeter of Earth.

"Dawn can hear all the Trey on Earth. They were the first ones we checked." He fell to his seat and shooed the bartender away. "Stacey was an Æsir using a real human body. Dawn could hear her but didn't know what she was. They're probably humans, or look and sound exactly like humans."

David lifted himself onto his unsteady feet. "You won't be getting married anytime soon. I'm sending you on a mission. Let's go for a little ride. I have something incredible to show you." He staggered to the door where he turned around to see Ander, stunned, resting one arm on the bar. "Come on!"

Ander's Q9 felt big and empty without his crew. David hovered over a console and brought up the navigation controls. He plotted a course taking them to a protoplanet in an asteroid field near the inner edge of Proxima Centauri's Oort Cloud.

That region of the solar system was a known classified location. Ander tried picking Dawn's brain about what could be there, but she pretended not to know. He was tempted to check it out himself. If he did, they'd probably kill him and restore him around Múspellsheimr with no memory of his trespass. He assumed this had happened once or twice.

When they reached the rocky debris field, Ander couldn't believe his eyes. Swarmed by thousands of Q9 warships, an enormous silver machine drifted among the rocks. "That thing has to be at least five kilometers long!"

Mesmerized, he walked to the front of the bridge and ran his hand over the largest vessel humankind ever created.

David's tipsy brain relished the thought of Ander taking in the magnificent sight. "We made it without any help from Alma. She's a handmade work of art. Well, we did get some help from the Kohor." He pointed into the distance. One hundred kilometers behind the glimmering American capital ship floated the final two Kohor generation ships, dwarfing the human craft. "We had to modify their engines quite a bit to get them here. The buoys didn't like their mass."

Ander traced his finger around the ship's giant head. It measured about four kilometers across, one kilometer deep, and stood at least fifty stories tall. A four kilometer tail resembling twisted metal ropes projected from her back to end in a huge tangled sphere. He turned toward David with his palms pressed against the screen. "You built this to fight them?"

David put a hand on Ander's shoulder and gave him a sturdy pat. "No. She's made with a specific project in mind. We call her the Hammer of God. She's your new ship."

"You're pregnant?!" Katie exclaimed with absolute disgust in her voice. She finished adding some unnecessary flare to Dawn's Destroying Angel ensemble and took a step back. "This isn't going to have the same impact when we let out the stomach."

Dawn rubbed and patted her belly, pushing it out as far as possible. "I don't know, a pregnant girl wielding a bloody sword? What could be scarier than that?" She recalled how miserable Alma was during her emotional pregnancy. "Unless I cry all the time."

Katie whispered under her breath, "I don't see that happening."

"Yeah, me neither." Dawn admired her slender body in a full length mirror with a pompous smile. "Now don't say no. Ander proposed to me, and I know you don't like me, but I want you to be my Maid of Honor. It's hard to imagine me getting fat, right?"

Katie's nose scrunched at the repulsive thought of spending more time with this horrible woman. "What? Why would you force me to do that?"

Dawn turned to the side and adored herself from another angle. "Alma and Raven are my only female friends, and they're both boring. Well, Raven can be fun, but that's something different. I want you to plan everything. It's kind of what you do all day anyway."

Katie looked away. "I'm guessing I don't have a choice."

Dawn's demeanor sobered. "We're not in too much of a hurry though. Should be a month or two, hopefully. I'll be getting chubby by then so keep that in mind." Cupping her own breasts with a little wiggle, Dawn said, "A lot of women want big boobs. I like my little girly ones the way they are."

Katie didn't want to ask, but it was rare for Dawn to display any emotions besides arousal or disdain. "What's wrong?"

"Trauger's sending him on a mission far away. It's one of those, succeed or we all die, kind of things." She grabbed Katie by the hand. "Let's go tell Raven."

Katie's eyes widened. "What?! Right now?" Before she could say no, her surroundings changed.

At Dawn's request, Alma deposited them outside the entrance of Raven's village. Katie froze at the sight of Bondi filling a small portion of the bright greenish-blue sky. Her body shuddered with adrenaline. "I haven't even been to Australia before." She couldn't take her eyes off Cartara's mother planet.

Dawn led her into the village and down a dusty path to Raven's home. "I've only been here a few times.

Everyone always stares at me." The inhabitants were doing just that, staring at the two women wandering through their neighborhood. Most of them had grown accustomed to humans, but Dawn's presence was different.

Like Alma, Dawn earned the title of demigoddess with the Kohor people. Rumors of her unimaginable violence served to make her seem more godlike to many. They worshiped, respected, and feared her.

Dawn pointed at two children clinging to their mother's leg. "Apparently, they're not allowed to talk to me. I wouldn't understand them anyway."

"Maybe walking through their town with a sword is a little off-putting?" Katie shook her head, wondering how Dawn could be so disconnected from people's hearts when she hears everything in their minds. "Don't you speak their language?"

"Eir and Ymir talk to me in feelings and pictures, not words. I only understand how they feel about me." Any normal person would be traumatized knowing they were feared by three distinct species. It did bother her a little, but she was able to pack those undesirable emotions deep down, where they withered and died.

When they reached Raven's modest home, Katie smiled at its simple twigs and clay construction. Dawn pulled her in close and warned, "If she offers you food, tell her you already ate. Kohor food is disgusting."

Before her knuckles could hit the door, it swung open to reveal Raven carrying Sunna against her body in a sling wrap. The tiny Kohor woman holding a gigantic human baby made Dawn laugh. "She's almost as big as you!"

Raven scanned Katie up and down. "Who is this?" She didn't find Katie attractive, but understood what humans considered appealing. "She does not look like one of your military soldiers."

Dawn leaned in and kissed Raven on the cheek. "Calm down. This is Katie. She runs all those doom and gloom broadcasts of Alma's. I think she's her Press Secretary or something."

Katie didn't know if kissing was a normal Kohor greeting, but to be safe, she thrust out her hand instead. "I help Alma and Dawn with their speeches and try to make them more appealing to people." She smirked at Dawn. "I'm not great at that last part?"

Raven looked down on Katie's outstretched hand, curled her upper lip, spun around, and walked inside.

Katie whispered to Dawn, "Did I say something wrong? Do handshakes mean something rude here?"

Dawn laughed. "Jealousy is a new emotion for her. She hasn't quite got a handle on it yet."

Katie followed them into her home and wondered, *jealous of what?*

Again, gesturing to Katie, Raven asked, "Why are you here with her?"

Shaken by Raven's hostility, Katie took a submissive step backward. *She really hates me.*

Dawn waited for Raven to place Sunna in her crib, then rushed in behind her. Raven turned to find her human companion wild-eyed and excited about something. Dawn blurted, "I'm pregnant."

Raven grabbed Dawn's head with both hands, and kissed her more than a few times on the lips. "I am so happy for you."

Oh. Katie's expression soured upon realizing why Raven didn't like her. *You have nothing to worry about there.*

Raven's sensual kissing muffled Dawn's words. "We

need to find a good Kohor man for you. I want us to be pregnant together. It would be so cool if I could get you pregnant myself. Does it take nine months for your people too?"

Unable to stomach this any longer, Katie interrupted. "Okay. Someone else is in the room you two. Please stop that. Please." She winced at Raven's irate gaze. "Dawn has some more great news to tell you."

Dawn dragged Raven by the hand, forcing her down onto a pillow. "Ander proposed to me, and I want you to be a bridesmaid. That's why she's here. She's going to measure you for an ugly dress and teach us what we need to do."

Raven had attended many human weddings on the military base. From her limited knowledge she deduced that their males propose marriage after impregnating a female. She looked up to Katie with a confused expression. "Why an ugly dress?"

The Operations Center onboard a garaged X9 warship was empty except for Alma, David, and an inexperienced engineer. She swiped through specifications for their new AI power and cooling control system while waiting for the young man to locate the correct cabinet door. "These things consume more energy than our Marines do."

She already knew which cabinet it was in but didn't want to make him feel foolish. David glanced at her tablet and said in an irritated tone, "Captain." He pointed toward a narrow door labeled, H7.

David shook his head and took a seat at a powered-off monitoring station as the embarrassed engineer made his way to locker H7 and opened it for Alma. "This is the new controller core. The power couplings are thicker, so they'll need replaced from the cabinet through to the inverter."

He reached into the locker and opened a small maintenance door on the front of the device. "These green lights turn on when you've properly connected the power."

Alma's annoyed huff made him nervous. "I am aware of what green lights mean."

Startled by a series of muffled pops, she spun around to witness David's head splintering open to paint the workstation with his blood. She froze in horror, giving the engineer enough time to pull a stun-gun from the cabinet and force it against her lower back.

One hundred thousand volts of electricity seared every nerve in her body, seizing her muscles. She recoiled into a fetal position as her eyes locked onto David slumping lifeless over the desk. A frustrating darkness, a veil, cascaded from the ceiling and enveloped the room as Alma fell to the floor with her mouth landing on a large wet piece of David's skull.

The engineer dragged her to cabinet H7, where he struggled to fold and cram her inside. He locked the door, leaving her alone in the dark cage.

Alma shouldered and kicked the door for an hour before she was released. Powerless and soaked in sweat, she tumbled out to the feet of her captors standing near David's remains. She looked up at the small group of men, all of whom appeared human. "Where are you taking me?"

The pirated ship's Captain raised a cattle prod,

pressed it into her side, and pulled the trigger. Alma screamed as it let out an unforgettable series of cracks. He moved the weapon's metal prongs to her cheek and demanded, "Stand."

Alma lifted to her feet, shaking with fear.

The Captain displayed disgust as he tapped his prod against the American flag sewn into the arm of her jacket. "Remove that trash. Now."

Terrified of being electrocuted again, she complied.

The men marched her into a bedroom in the ship's crew quarters, where the Captain spun her around and shoved her inside. "We need you alive, but not comfortable. Don't force me to restrain you." He pushed the prod into her stomach and pressed the trigger, dropping her to the floor, writhing in agony.

Alma remained alone on the ground for an hour before mustering the will to sit. She searched the room for something that could end her life with as little pain as possible. Her imagination saw her slamming her head into a table's sharp corner.

She crawled to a bed near the wall and climbed onto it where she stood in the middle, looking down at the table. *This is going to hurt so bad.* She worried the only thing she'd accomplish was harming herself, but couldn't think of anything better.

Her breathing accelerated. She bounced on the mattress like a child working up the nerve to leap off a diving board for the first time. In her head, she repeatedly ordered herself to do it, but her body wouldn't comply.

Alma turned around and focused on the bedroom wall, emptied her mind, and launched backward into the air. On her descent, she spun, smashing face-first against the table's corner. She fell to the floor with blood streaming from a deep gash across the bridge of her broken nose.

Her captors were watching this curious behavior the entire time. At first, they didn't understand what she was attempting to do, until she jumped. Panicked, they hurried into the room to make sure she'd survive.

The Captain entered and stood angry over her bloodied body. He shouted to his crew, "Restrain it!"

Two men rushed in carrying an orange portable medical gurney and dropped it to the floor beside her. They put on thick rubber gloves before picking her up and throwing her on top of it. With her body facing the ceiling, they strapped down her arms, legs, and forehead.

The Captain threatened, "If you cause any more problems, I will remove your hands and feet."

Alma could barely breathe through the blood running from her throbbing shattered nose. The pain she caused herself was worse than their cattle prods. She wanted medical help, but their leader terrified her, so she laid on the gurney, crying and bleeding, whimpering David's name.

Dawn and Katie sat cross-legged on woven pillows facing a bewildered Raven. They tried explaining the concept of marriage, but in different ways. Dawn's take was a bit cynical. "It's just an old human legal thing. It kind of makes you responsible for everything the other one does."

Raven couldn't resist making a bad joke. "Then Ander is surely getting himself into serious trouble." Dawn chuckled at Raven's terrible sense of humor.

Katie butted in. "There's a religious aspect to it as well. Religious people see marriage as a spiritual bond between two people who love each other."

Dawn admonished Katie with upturned eyes and a derisive head shake. She had long since abandoned her tenuous belief in a single God. Alma and the military resurrecting people, as if death were only an inconvenience, was the final straw.

Before Katie could continue, Dawn leapt to her feet screaming, "They took Alma, she's gone!" Seconds after her announcement, sirens blared from Joint Base Cartara in the distance. Dawn spun around, about to say something else, then vanished.

Katie shrieked, "What just happened?! Where the hell did Dawn go?!"

Raven stood from her pillow and walked to Sunna's crib. She reached inside and stroked her blissful, unaware face. "The Æsir have taken Alma, and now they are coming to burn the air and water from our worlds."

Katie didn't understand Raven's apparent calm, but before she could say anything, Raven also vanished. Her frozen panic melted at the sound of Sunna fussing in her crib. She lifted Alma's child, cradled her tight against her chest, and swayed back and forth as they cried together under the ominous din of air-raid sirens.

Chapter 22

The Hammer of God

Across the four solar systems, millions of Æsir warships entered what would have been Alma's spheres of influence. Human and Trey navies rushed in to engage as many enemy ships as their numbers would allow.

General Hanna Shaw led the main Navy battle group in Sol, confronting an Æsir fleet as it breached the Oort Cloud on a trajectory to Earth. Æsir ship numbers were far greater than anyone calculated, or admitted. Flustered, Shaw yelled, "Kill as many as we can." She didn't bother trying to hide her rattled nerves.

Shaw's X9 strike group left their Q9s behind and materialized thousands of AI antiparticle suicide drones on their way into battle. These drones distracted and slowed the Æsir advance, forcing them to use conventional close-combat weapons to defend themselves.

Her Q9 battle group resurrected lost X9s as they were destroyed, but the Æsir front continued pushing toward Earth. "Fall back ninety-million kilometers." Shaw found herself praying to God for Alma's safe return.

An Æsir warship jumped into the center of her X9 lines and detonated in a brilliant antiparticle explosion brighter than the sun. Without the annoying distractions of drones and small Navy warships buzzing around, they overran Shaw's position.

In deep orbit of Earth, a Kohor generation ship worked as the primary resurrection hub for multiple battle groups. It recreated Shaw's fleet and placed them near an advancing Æsir armada. Shaw's tenuous confidence crumbled. "We're not going to win."

Immediately after being resurrected on a Q9 warship orbiting Cartara, David commandeered it and demoted her Captain to Executive Officer. His first order was to collect Dawn, Raven, Katie, and Sunna from the moon.

Dawn emerged on the bridge with an angry finger pointed at David's face. "Craig failed." Her face was as red as her hair.

Raven appeared disorientated beside Dawn. Her entire body shivered as she struggled to make sense of her changed surroundings. "What am I doing here, and where is Sunna?!" She whipped her head back and forth, scanning the bridge.

"Sunna and Katie are in crew quarters. I'm not losing any more people I care about." David addressed his Executive Officer with an authoritative growl. "Commander Christou, Dawn is in command of this ship." He looked down into Raven's dark watery eyes. "You and I need to talk, alone."

No one on the bridge cared for the idea of a celebrated assassin and rumored psychopath taking charge of one of humanity's most powerful warships. David's second in command gave him a blank stare. "Just do what she tells you." He wrapped his arm around Raven and led her away to the Captain's stateroom.

Dawn waited for them to exit the bridge before turning to her Executive Officer. "Scoop up as many New Kohor males as you can fit into this ship's data storage."

He hesitated.

"If that's a problem, I'll replace you with someone who understands we're already losing this war. When we lose, our beautiful species will be erased from the multiverse, forever."

The apprehension in his voice was obvious to everyone. "You heard our—Commander. Pick any of them, my gut says it doesn't matter which ones, and make it quick."

Dawn nodded with a satisfied grin.

In the stateroom, David sat with Raven on a small sofa and draped his arm around her tiny shoulders. She couldn't imagine why he would put Dawn in command of a warship or why he wasn't standing beside her. She presumed Cartara was lost, and he was attempting to console her. "I have accepted that my home will be destroyed. You should not feel the need to comfort me."

David's tone hinted at his unease with Dawn's fallback plan in the event Craig couldn't reverse engineer the Æsir Voice Machine in time. "Earth will be gone in about twelve hours, overrun by Æsir forces. There's just too many of them. Seleen will fall soon after that. I'm ordering all fleets in Sol to retreat back to Yeset where they'll fight to protect Cartara. Raven, we've run out of options. I'm sorry."

His rare inability to say what's on his mind troubled her. "Tell me. I will do anything for Alma."

"I'm not sure if you already know this, but your people and the Trey, you're all Æsir. Descended from colonists." Her distressed expression made it apparent she was not aware of her lineage.

"Do you know who Surtr is?" She nodded with a blank stare, still processing his revelation. "He has the only weapon we know of that can push the Æsir back. We've been trying to replicate it, but we've run out of time. Our AI can run the machines, but we need something inside, like a key to a lock. We need a specific part of a brain with Æsir genetics."

"A specific part? Why can you not put a Kohor or Trey at the controls while your machines give them orders?" She believed her people were safe from being sacrificed by more advanced species.

"There aren't any controls. The machine runs by orders from our AI translated through something in an Æsir brain. Stacey called it a Vogt Mass. If we had more time we could maybe implant a chip in them." He dropped his face into his hands. "It hasn't been a full day, and we're losing two worlds. There are so damn many of them."

David's disposition colored dark. "We're collecting as many Kohor men as this ship will hold, and we're taking them to Múspellsheimr. Surtr and Craig will start the process of extracting what we need."

"Extracting? You mean murdering them, because we are your enemy?" Raven hadn't stopped crying since Alma's abduction. "I volunteer myself in place of another."

"You know I'm not going to allow that, and you know Dawn won't either. Without these men, we're dead. Hate me. Hate Dawn. I can live with that as long as we push them back. This isn't human selfishness. If we somehow win, we'll be able to restore your men once we find a way to make our machines work without them."

Raven looked down at the floor, away from David. A growing acquiescence tempered her sorrow. "Can we get their names before they are slaughtered?"

"We'll have their DNA. We can locate their families after we stop these assholes. They won't feel it, they're not going to be fully restored, just the sections Surtr and Craig need. We don't want them to suffer in any way."

Raven collapsed against him in exhaustion. "I don't like this." He held her in his arms and gently stroked her hair, as he would have with Alma.

Intelligence gathered from Stacey before she was imprisoned by Alma suggested Gliese 581 was the nearest star system harboring a bustling Æsir colony. The Hammer of God appeared surfing in its bow wave as a team of humans, Trey, and AI calculated their final jumps.

Ander stared out at the tiny pink splash of light. "There she is. If that colony has a Protector, this is going to be a painfully short mission." He loomed over his navigation team and squeezed his Deck Officer's shoulders a little too hard. "Hurry this up. We have zero time to waste."

The Hammer of God was massive, as was her Hallberg Reactor. She traveled three times further than the buoys could move her, but there needed to be ample matter at the target location for a successful jump. This slowed calculations by limiting available destination points.

After some threatening encouragement, the vessel was underway. One of their way-points brought them within scanning distance of the Æsir planet. It was a small world with thousands of ships and satellites in her orbit. His Deck Officer pointed out the obvious. "Sir, those aren't military ships. We could destroy that whole planet in minutes."

"That's not the purpose of our mission, Lieutenant. They need to know there isn't a line we aren't willing to cross." Ander smiled as Æsir vessels scattered at the unexpected site of his capital ship near their home.

They left the colony behind and anchored in close geosynchronous orbit of the dim red dwarf star, Gliese 581. Falk opened communications with the Q9 warships tucked into the HoG's hangars. "Captains, ready your ships and move into positions on my mark."

Ten thousand large doors split open at the back of the Hammer's head, releasing a swarm of Q9s scrambling to reach their posts around their mother. Once in place, they targeted a preselected area of

Gliese's surface and applied inertia to atoms in her photosphere, coercing them together into a loose clump of stardust.

The HoG grabbed hold of the developing pile, ripping each atom apart and rearranging their particles to form osmium. The giant Hallberg Reactor worked to force the ball of osmium into a tighter and tighter sphere. This tedious process went on for quite some time.

Ander was growing impatient. "Why is this taking so long?" He wanted something to distract his mind, so he loaded a poorly rendered chess game on the main display and waved his Executive Officer over. "Beat me slower this time, I need to get out of my head." During their match, many crew members wondered how he became a Navy Admiral as he, again and again, made terrible moves.

At ninety-two percent complete, there was a noticeable visual change in the star's appearance. The fiery randomness of her photosphere dulled as gravity pulled her winds toward their moon-sized ball of osmium. Gliese's apparent intensity faded.

Their super-dense protoplanet began feeding itself. It grew more massive with every passing second, disrupting the star's convective balance, and shifting her radiant energy from center mass. Unable to maintain her structure, Gliese expelled a large section of her corona.

Ander's armada jumped away, leaving their baby singularity to feed off its unwilling mother. The Hammer of God arrived at the Æsir planet moments before her Q9s. What Ander found was a world in the process of panicked evacuations. Transport ships escorted by small groups of warships darted about, scooping up their people from the surface.

When his Q9s arrived, a devilish grin accompanied his orders. "All Captains, fire at will. Make sure nothing leaves that planet."

His warships swarmed into and around the planet's exosphere hunting for prey. Braggadocios voices, influenced by their thrill seeking Admiral, morphed the theater of operations into an arcade-like competition. Ship Captains called out their kills with Ander keeping score.

He arranged for an AI to display a kill count and leader board on every view screen in the armada. None of the ship Captains cared that the majority of these vessels were simple transports. Massacring Æsir colonists didn't bother his people in the least.

It wasn't long before they decimated their enemy's ill-prepared fleets. They mopped up any remaining stragglers, but allowed one transport to escape and report what had happened to their colony.

With every Q9 docked inside their mother, the HoG jumped away as the star's ejected coronal mass blanketed the planet in a tsunami of charged fire. Radiation swept over the Æsir world, stripped off her atmosphere, and left behind nothing but a lifeless ball of incandescent rock.

Gliese 581 blinked out of existence.

David cleared hours of distraught sobbing from his throat in an attempt at regaining his authoritarian cadence. "All fleet Commanders, fall back to Yeset. It's over." The thought of billions of unsuspecting human lives about to be snuffed out overpowered him.

The vast majority of Earth's inhabitants had no idea a hopeless war was raging above their heads. Unaware their new military leaders abandoned them, leaving them to die, their final seconds would be awash in confusion and feelings of betrayal, but not for long.

Æsir warships filled the voids left by retreating human forces and entered into close orbits of Mars and Earth. No sirens blared, no reporters gave panic-laden play-by-plays on their imminent deaths. No one suspected a thing.

Unlike predictable villains from movies and television shows, this enemy didn't announce their presence or taunt their victims. They didn't hesitate for dramatic effect before saturating each planet's atmosphere with balls of densely-packed antiparticles evenly spaced in a spherical grid around the globes.

For a moment, Earth shimmered brighter than her sun as white-hot explosions vaporized her skies, land, and water, leaving massive craters across her once beautiful face. Now glowing embers, Earth and Mars orbited their mother star, beaten and lifeless.

Trey and human navies were losing ground in Daneln as well. Æsir warships swarmed Seleen, ignoring Daneln's other worlds, and finished off any remaining ships protecting the planet. With no chance for victory, the defenders fell back to the fourth habitable world, Olnae, to continue their struggle. The sight of Seleen burning again was difficult for the emotionless Trey people to accept.

"This isn't good at all." Craig poured through the documentation for Stacey's living storage device. He looked up at Surtr's statuesque avatar. "Her compression algorithms make this impossible, everything's encrypted and mingled together."

Dawn hovered over his shoulders. "So you can't do it. Great. Restore one of them down here."

"General Trauger made it clear we are not to do that." Unable to look her in the face, he didn't know who to fear more, her, David, or Surtr.

"Do it now." She placed her hand on the back of his neck and squeezed as hard as her fingers would allow.

Craig relented without a fight, and a Kohor man appeared in front of them. His gaze darted around the room as he tried to make sense of his new surroundings. He fixated on Dawn with wide black eyes and spoke in frantic streams of unintelligible New Kohor.

Surtr's gravelly voice startled them. "American General David Trauger is in the hall with an Æsir. No Æsir."

Dawn pointed at their Kohor victim cowering against a wall. "He's Æsir." She turned to Draugr with an outstretched finger. "Draugr's Æsir too."

"No Æsir."

"Raven is harmless, and adorable. Let them in." She tipped her head to the side like an angry girlfriend and repeated herself, enunciating every word. "Do what I say and let them in." The thick stone barrier disintegrated.

David charged the room, motioning to the Kohor man. "We weren't going to restore any of them!" Surtr assumed an animal-like defensive posture between him and Dawn. David stared unfazed into Surtr's giant avatar face. "Don't force me to give the order to kill your puppet." Surtr slinked away from David's intimidating glare.

Dawn had never seen David this mad before and she kind of liked it. She smacked Craig on the shoulder. "His AI can't figure out were their brains are in the backup data. If you want, we can wait a few hours or days while Craig teaches it." Dawn's sarcasm in the face of a callous homicide made David furious.

Raven walked to the trembling man and held both his hands. She spoke to him in their native language, but whatever she was saying didn't make him calmer. She yelled at Dawn with tears streaming down her face, "Don't take longer than necessary! Get this over with now! This man should not be forced to wait in fear."

Dawn found herself affected by seeing Raven so upset. It triggered new or suppressed emotions, which she didn't care for at all. "I'm sorry. Tell him to lay down, please."

Raven led him down to the floor, where she knelt beside him, crying.

Inside her head, Dawn ordered Surtr to take what Craig needed and put it in their machine. The crying man's eyes popped open, and then he died. Raven collapsed onto his chest.

"We can't do this with every one of them. I'm so sorry." Dawn sat next to her and rubbed her back. Consoling a friend wasn't something she had ever done with any measurable skill. Her feelings for Raven added an unwanted level of complication to her personality.

Craig's machine fed off the Kohor sacrifice and sprang to life. The AI recognized its new component and initiated a series of diagnostic test, sending and receiving encrypted challenge/response signals through the living specimen. Several agonizing seconds later, they got a green light. He kept his scientific exuberance to himself. "Sir, we should test this before we make anymore."

Powered by a large subterranean Hallberg Reactor, his machine's range extended thousands of times further than Surtr's. A rudimentary command interface displayed a long list of ship clusters for him to choose from. Craig selected a small fleet outside Surtr's sphere of control. "Sir, I'm ready."

David pushed his relentless grief down into his stomach and ordered his warships away from Craig's Æsir test subjects. He locked eyes with Craig and commanded, "Do it. End this."

Craig tapped a few buttons on his tablet, prompting his machine to start its assault on the unwitting Æsir fleet. The enemy ships turned on one another, saturating each other's positions with dense clouds of antiparticles. These brilliant explosions were so bright they could be seen in the daytime Múspellsheimr sky.

Excited by the success of his machine, Craig made his way to David who had joined Dawn and Raven huddled on the floor. "Can you have all our ships pull back, Sir?"

After ordering the ships in Proxima Centauri to fall back to Múspellsheimr, David growled, "Kill them all." He was barely able to get that out before his voice broke. "You've done a great job, Major. It's too late for our home though."

Craig fumbled his tablet, almost dropping it to the ground. He mashed down on its digital buttons, giving his machine's AI the green light to assault every Æsir cluster it could reach.

Anxious sailors erupted in cheers and celebrations

as they witnessed the Æsir on Æsir carnage. It was a beautiful site to behold.

David lifted himself to his feet. "This needs to be on Cartara and the Trey worlds, ASAP."

While Craig and David were discussing plans to sacrifice additional Kohor citizens, Raven stroked her fallen brother's arm. "You did it. If you have a family, you have saved them all. We are so proud of you."

Raven comforting a man she ordered killed, snapped something inside Dawn. Empathetic crying strangled her, making it difficult to breathe. In a hyperventilating panic, she ran from the room and down the dark hallway. The echoes of her intense wailing faded as she moved further away from her team. No longer able to stand upright, Dawn collapsed to the floor.

Alma needed to use the bathroom, but her captors ignored her desperate pleas. Unable to hold it any longer, she wet herself. She closed her eyes and sobbed as the acrid smell of urine flooded her nose.

She cried herself to sleep only to be awoken by the angry Captain kicking at the side of her gurney. "You smell disgusting." He motioned to his crew. "Unstrap this animal and take it to the shower."

Two crew members rolled on heavy rubber gloves, unfastened Alma's bindings, and lifted her by her armpits. They dragged her into the bathroom and threw her against the shower wall.

The Captain ordered, "Strip, animal. Clean yourself before you make me vomit." He raised his cattle prod in front of her face and pulled the trigger, allowing her to hear and see that terrifying crack of electricity, then left his crew in charge of getting her showered.

One of her guards stabbed his cattle prod into her stomach and pressed the trigger. Alma yelped in pain, but didn't collapse this time, she was growing accustomed to the electrocutions. Uncomfortable disrobing in front of these people, she turned to face the wall and rushed to remove her clothing.

The guard nudged his partner, then pushed his cattle prod between her buttocks and pulled the trigger. They laughed as she lunged against the shower wall, howling in agony.

He forced it deeper inside her and squeezed the trigger again. Alma clenched her teeth hard enough to shatter one into pieces. She drooled bloody tooth fragments onto the shower floor and begged, "Please stop." He electrocuted her one more time.

Alma couldn't endure their torture any longer. She spun to face him, grabbed his arm and yanked him toward her. With her hand wrapped tight around the back of his neck, she repeatedly slammed his head into the water handle until his skull yielded to the bloodied fixture. She released his lifeless body and reached down for his cattle prod, but was subdued by a team of men rushing into the bathroom.

They beat her into submission and dragged her, naked and broken, back to the gurney where they struggled to strap her down. The Captain squatted beside her swollen face. "Animals should all be destroyed since they serve no useful purpose. I told you not to cause problems." At this point, Alma would have welcomed death.

Two men donning rubber gloves braced her head while the Captain hovered a scalpel above her right eye. Alma begged, "No! No! No!" Another man placed layers of medical tape over her mouth to muffle her shrieking. Terrified, she closed her eyes as tight as she could.

He slid his scalpel across her eyelid, slicing through the delicate skin and opening her eye socket to the drying air. A thick mixture of clear oozing liquid and blood ran down the side of her face. Her screaming grew shrill as he cut open her other eye. The excruciating pain was more than she could tolerate. She passed out.

Annoyed, the Captain checked her for a pulse. "Good. That noise was irritating."

He discarded the scalpel and pulled a long thin barbed spike from his pocket. He worked the spike deep into her ear, rupturing her eardrum and tearing the middle ear bones from their connective tissue, then repeated the damage in her other ear. The blood soaked barb dripped onto her forehead as he glanced up and said, "Watch it and make sure it wakes."

The Captain stood and motioned toward their dead comrade on the bathroom floor. "You two clean that mess up." He looked down on Alma's bloodied, tear-soaked face in disgust. "It smells even worse now."

She woke minutes later, blind and deaf, in more pain than she ever imagined possible. Sobbing into the tape, she begged for David as tears burned in the open wounds of her eye sockets.

The man watching her vomited a little in his mouth. He dragged a blanket from a nearby bed, covered her body, and rested a pillow over her face to muffle her crying.

Not once did she yell out for Ymir or any other deities, they never crossed her mind. She repeated, *David, please.*

Chapter 23

Happy Hunting

Craig's objectionable personality and tendency toward anxiety attacks didn't detract from his skills and ingenuity. "It's more of a hack than a fix, Sir. The normal restore decompresses an entire body into an extremely massive data matrix, this program halts that process and restores only what we need. I call it the Part Picker."

David was growing jealous of Dawn's cold cruel side. He had done and ordered others to do things normal people couldn't or wouldn't, things Dawn would do without hesitation. "As long as we don't have to murder any more Kohor men while they cower in fear, I don't care what you call it."

The Æsir Voice Machines were working better than Craig had envisioned. "Admiral Pruitt and Commander Engel have an AVM installed on their ships for testing in Proxima Centauri. If all goes well, they can help clean up Yeset and Daneln."

Glassy eyed and haggard, David was suffocating under the stress of fighting this war absent Alma. "I thought you were sending a data feed to the planets, so they can restore their own." Surtr hovered over them like a dark foreboding sand storm. "It's not as if they have a lot of time."

"The data transfer is happening as we speak, Sir. It's a ton of information, but these planet-side AVMs have a limited range of less than ninety million kilometers, and they'll need warships to remove any remaining Æsir fleets."

David turned his head down and away, trying to hide his watering eyes. "This is great to hear, but, Craig I need you to find her. I don't care what you have to do. You have to find her. This is your only project now."

Craig feigned empathy by patting David's arm. "Sir, I understand, and I won't fail you. I promise."

Admiral Pruitt's small armada entered the Daneln system on a trajectory to the Trey world, Olnae. Upon their emergence in Trey territory, they encountered a cluster of Æsir warships. "Lieutenant, confuse them just enough to slow them down, then strip their hulls. I want to watch them suffer."

They jumped into the middle of an AVM disoriented Æsir fleet. To her dismay, after breaching their hulls, each ship self-destructed in a spectacular antiparticle explosion, leaving behind no trophies for her to collect.

"If you're done playing games Admiral, would you please assist us?" Trey Commander Durn was not amused by Pruitt's pointless theatrical violence.

On her orders, her fleet of Q9 warships separated with each ship acting as an AVM lead to forty different Trey parties. "Happy hunting, Captains. Field promotions for anyone who gets me an Æsir head, or arm. I'm not picky." After she dismantled her armada, her flagship jumped away on an unauthorized vengeance mission to Sol.

The augmented Trey fleets did their best to distract Æsir ships from their wolds while they waited for the data transfers from Múspellsheimr to complete. The planet Olnae was first to restore an AVM. Deep below her surface, engineers configured the new weapon and brought it online.

Planet-side operators, careful not to target Trey warships, let loose their gruesome monster, flooding enemy minds with paranoia and nightmarish delusions. Eager Trey and human forces swooped in to take advantage of the tumult, decimating muddled Æsir fleets. It wasn't long before the balance of power in Daneln shifted.

In the Yeset system, Cartara and Fennar had already implemented their planet based AVMs with great success. Shaw's enormous fleets huddled in their orbits, picking off Æsir ships brave or stupid enough to enter these protected bubbles.

Commander Engel's forces reached Cartara as news

of Daneln victories trickled in. General Shaw breathed a sigh of relief at the beautiful sight of his AVM equipped fleet. "Commander Engel, I'm too tired for formalities. Get rid of these assholes." Alone on the floor in a corner of her dimly lit stateroom, Shaw turned her eyes to the ceiling and prayed, *thank you, God.*

Engel's fleet dispersed with each AVM outfitted ship leading smaller packs of hunters from Shaw's group. The dramatic pivot from cowering around protected worlds, waiting to be slaughtered, to obliterating their enemies with little effort, reinvigorated the human and Kohor crews.

Kohor soldiers serving on human ships found it difficult to accept that their outlook had changed so spectacularly. It was exhausting trying to keep up with the wild mood swings of their human colleagues, but witnessing Æsir forces falling apart before each battle helped.

A plethora of Æsir fleets carrying human quantum signatures outside Proxima Centauri kept Ander and his crew busy. Now equipped with their own AVM, these battles lacked any hints of real danger or excitement, or fun. "Sir, the Q9 AVM installations are complete."

Ander huffed, "It's about damn time. Tell the Captains to prepare their ships." He muttered under his breath, *Time to delegate this boring shit to someone else.*

Half his fleet assembled into one hundred parties, each led by a single AVM equipped Q9. "Happy hunting Captains. Don't come back without a kill."

Ander switched his focus to a short list of AI pings Craig compiled during his search for Alma. There were American warships somewhere out here. He waved for his XO to follow him from the bridge to reconvene in his luxurious stateroom. Ander stared at Commander Hagen with lips pursed as he breathed out a heavy sigh through his nose. "I have five targets from Major Halvorson. They're all American military AI, probably from our ships."

"How the hell did human ships get all the way out here?" Hagen sneered as a queasy feeling churned his empty stomach. "Are they traitors?" The idea of human traitors helping the Æsir destroy Earth enraged him.

Ander shook his head. "I don't know, and we won't be interrogating them. I plan on surprising and destroying them. I don't want to give them a chance to jump away."

"If General Trauger doesn't know who they are, they have to be bad actors of some sort. What else could they be?" Hagen realized the Admiral was fishing for an opinion to back his plan, which may involve killing humans. "The AVM won't work if they're human. I don't see any viable alternative, Sir. They shouldn't be out here."

Their first jump landed them bow-to-bow with an Æsir armada. No American ships accompanied them, but their AI sensed one of its own somewhere in the cluster. Ander leapt to his feet and shouted, "AVM!"

The Æsir weren't expecting a giant human warship, and before they could engage, they were overcome with terrifying hallucinations. The enemy ships drifted from their tight formation as if someone snapped a solid tether holding them in place. One ship opened fire on another, prompting a confusing and brief battle to transpire.

"Someone please finish them off. We have somewhere else to be." The overwhelmingly successful AVMs dampened Ander's fighting spirit.

Their second destination contained only one ship, an X9 warship. Deep down, Ander knew this was Alma. "That's her!"

Hagen tightened his fists at the sight of an American flagged warship under Æsir control. His reddening face shuddered. "Sir, how will we know for sure?"

"Trust your gut, Commander. You'd be surprised by all the valuable insights churning around down there." Ander walked to the main viewing screen and turned toward his crew. "Destroy that fucking ship! Now!" His body shivered with a rush of adrenaline.

Alma's captors didn't notice the Hammer of God shadowing them. Their ship's computers ignored the friendly American military vessel, never alerting its crew to any possible danger. Warnings sounded only after their ship was surrounded by a dense fog of antiparticles, but it was too late.

The swarming particles chewed through the X9's shields and hull, disintegrating it into a burst of gamma radiation in front of Ander's teary eyes. The heart crushing realization that he ended Alma's life filled him with grief, dropping him to his knees.

Ander returned triumphant but humbled to Proxima Centauri. He wanted Dawn by his side, but she had been avoiding him since he killed Alma. He sat alone in his private office on the HoG, pleading with David through his console. "It's not normal for her to let things bother her like this. She knows I had to do it. They would've just jumped away."

David didn't realize Ander blamed himself for Dawn's worrying mental breakdown. "Honestly, it's something much worse than that. You wouldn't like her the way she is right now. She needs some time." He paused before letting Ander in on their horrible secret. "Those AVMs, we, we had to sacrifice a Kohor citizen to make each one work. Dawn ordered Surtr to kill a man in front of Raven. It was rough."

"There are too many details to explain, but seeing Raven crying over that man's body snapped something inside her. She just sleeps and cries all day and doesn't want anyone but Raven around."

Ander struggled with David's revelation, not about killing Kohor men, but Dawn crying. "She isn't comfortable being sad around me? I need to see her. I want you to bring her to me. She needs to know I'm there for her no matter what."

It wasn't difficult convincing the women to board a Q9. They both wanted to get away from Múspellsheimr and Archytas Station. Seeing them under a bright light for the first time in days, David cringed at Dawn's appearance. "Maybe you could freshen up a bit before we get there?" She tightened her lips and flashed him two middle fingers.

Raven seemed to be doing better, but she wasn't smelling great either. They laid about for a week doing nothing but sleeping, crying, and eating, when compelled.

On their approach to the Hammer of God, an AI took over and skillfully piloted their Q9 around the back of the gigantic ship's head. After trading encrypted signals, one of her thousands of hangar doors split open to allow access. The Q9 made her way inside and lowered herself to the deck where Ander was waiting in the hangar, eager to welcome his guests aboard.

The moment Dawn's eyes caught his beaming smile, she forgot about Raven and ran to him. He scooped her up off the floor and crushed her so hard she could barely breathe, but she didn't mind.

Upon losing the malodorous comfort of Dawn, Raven gravitated to David's side, took his hand, and laid her greasy head against his arm.

Ander fought a selfish desire to give them a tour of his ship during their silent walk to his cabin. Instead, he draped an arm around Dawn, leaned over and kissed her on the top of her stinky hair. A normal Dawn would have wandered from screen to screen tapping on things without concern, but she wasn't acting normal at all.

Inside Ander's extravagant private stateroom, they sat together in front of an ostentatious coffee table on a comfortable outcurved leather sofa. Dawn cuddled deep into him, abandoning her friend.

David held Raven close, like any father would hold his own grieving daughter. In time, he grew accustomed to their fetid aroma. "Do something to cheer them up, Ander. That's an order."

"I wish I could, but I'm here to listen." His eyes met David's. "To all of you."

A tinge of guilt washed over Dawn for abandoning Raven. No longer wanting to be her crying partner, she wiggled her fingers in front of Raven's face and said, "Fix her first."

Raven wished her friends would stop trying to comfort her. "Please don't try to make me happy. I'm tired of humans thinking words can repair things that hurt inside."

Ander leaned over the coffee table and flaunted a pretentious smirk. "Oh, don't worry. I'm not like that. These past few weeks have been one shit show after another. The only advice I have for everyone in this room is this: You aren't special, your pain isn't special, suck it up."

He motioned to David. "He's my best friend. He's also the person who ordered our ships to abandon my home, so they could protect yours. Billions of humans are dead, gone forever." Ander didn't mind crying in front of people. "I'm not mad at him. I'm not mad at the Kohor. Shit happens. Scrape it off your shoes and keep walking."

Raven heard variations of that metaphor from humans many times. Ander's graphic addendum helped her understand it a little better. "I know that you are correct. I would like to keep walking, but I can't stop thinking about him dying in my arms." Even though his death was only temporary, it didn't lessen her agony.

Ander pulled a couple of tissues from an ornate wooden box and wiped his nose. "Then just do what I do. Smile and lie to yourself. Tell yourself everything's going to work out. I find that if you lie to yourself long enough, your brain starts believing it."

His simple words explained so much of what she had witnessed from humans. They ignore their own suffering or the pain they cause others, and they were good at it. "People don't need to see me upset. It serves only a selfish purpose." She didn't sound convincing to anyone.

Dawn unfurled from Ander's embrace and roamed

the room, then turned to her friends with energized bright green eyes. "Alma's alive!"

David burst into tears, not your average tears, sobbing, snotty, debilitating tears. The tension he had stuffed deep down inside exploded out of every opening in his face. Raven put her arm as far around his back as she could, and tried to comfort him.

Dawn labored to decipher the rush of crude feelings and images flooding in from Ymir. "She's in trouble. There's an egg, like on Jupiter. It's confusing her. Little monsters are chasing her, and she needs our help."

David grabbed a large handful of tissues and wiped his entire face. "What do you mean by monsters? Can you describe them?"

"I don't see them. It's like that telegraph game. A Jötunn is describing something it doesn't understand to Ymir who's trying to describe it to me."

Ander reached over and patted Raven on the knee, attempting to show her they hadn't forgotten about her. He flashed her a sorrow filled smile as he talked to Dawn. "Does Ymir know where she is?"

"She doesn't show me maps, but there are two suns, if that helps."

Ander picked up a tablet from an end-table and called his astrophysics department. "Two stars with at least one habitable planet somewhere nearby, where is it? Quick!"

A woman's voice responded. "We're in a ternary system. There are two more stars right next door, Rigil Kentaurus and Toliman."

Chapter 24

Alone

Alma awoke, face up and naked on a warm sandy beach, screaming in pain. It took a moment for her to realize her torture had ended, and her body restored. She sat upright and gazed across a gentle ocean rolling onto a smooth, endless shore.

Please, not this again. She scanned her surroundings for pretty little alien women in beaded tan dresses offering her a woven sack of awful food. Her shoulders drooped upon finding no one whispering behind her.

She moved her focus to the clear baby-blue sky and tried to shake off the feeling of that scalpel slicing into her eye. "Why do I remember everything, Ymir?" She shuddered at vivid memories of her torture, then turned her attention back to the ocean waters in an effort to distract her mind.

Crystal-clear waves swirled around her ankles and buttocks as a mild surf encircled her body. Two suns warmed this world. One a blindingly bright yellow, the other, dim and orange. The orange star rested on the horizon and seemed further away or smaller than her sister. She followed its elongated reflection back to shore where she found no tiny fish darting about and no seashells decorating the sand.

Her thoughts kept returning to the gurney, and images of that angry man staring down on her. Her captors appeared to be human, but something told her they weren't. "What happened, Ymir? Did I die? How?"

She chuckled through her nose while fantasizing about the Captain going too far and killing her by mistake. The notion of him being tormented by her Æsir counterpart for failing to deliver her alive brought a smile to her lips. "I hope you suffer immensely."

As on Cartara when she first appeared, her worlds and friends were hidden from her, or gone. Alma walked for what seemed like hours. At one point, she paused to make a castle in the sand and daydreamed of Sunna playing with David on the beach. That sweet fantasy soon turned into crippling depression. She pleaded, "David, where are you?"

Her sphere of influence increased to more than a kilometer. There was still no bugs, people, or animals, unless worms count as animals. She laughed at her naked body and the memory of that one Kohor woman on the plateau who couldn't stop staring at her. She never saw her again after the first day.

Tired of meandering the coastline, Alma laid in a pool of water resting motionless between two ridges of sand. She tipped her head back and shouted to the sky, "Ymir, this planet is boring. I am ready to go home now."

Visions of David and Dawn scouring the universe, searching for her, consumed her thoughts. She didn't know how long she was dead. It could have been a month, a year, or a million years. Maybe her friends have been gone for quite some time. Perhaps the Æsir murdered everyone she cared about.

Selfish dreams of recreating her family on this world needed to be restrained. If they weren't dead, replicating them would harm them. She'd need to wait at least a hundred years before feeling confident they passed away. The thought of living alone for so long, again, was distressing.

She wanted to create a Q9 and pilot it home, but had no idea how to fly one of those things. *Craig was right. I should have paid better attention to what they were trying to teach me.* "I will only wait a few days, Ymir, and then I will leave this place."

Her sphere of influence continued to grow, but it was taking much longer than it did on Cartara. Saving the damaged Kohor women and slaughtering the Trey seemed to be the tasks she had to complete in order to reconnect with Ymir.

She spoke as if this world's Jötunn was standing in front of her. "I am so bored. Please show me what I need to do for you to accept me."

In an instant, she longed for her boredom to return. At the edge of her power, deep inside a lush green forest, the cold presence of a super-dense Æsir egg shook her. This one wasn't anywhere near as big as the one on Jupiter. It was less than twenty meters between its widest points.

Alma made her way into the forest to investigate, now clothed in jungle military camouflage. Trees and bushes cleared a path as she power-walked toward the shiny egg. Her eyes darted around hunting for anything that could be hiding a veil or an annoying man with a stun-gun. Paranoia strangled her thoughts. The path cutting in front of her widened.

Her target was at least ten kilometers into the forest. Frustrated by her speed, she remembered she could move herself and jumped to within fifty meters of the shimmering silver egg. Seeing it with her own human eyes somehow made it scarier than the other one. She froze.

It sat dormant among the shadowing trees, doing nothing. She assumed it could be dead or broken, but approached it with caution. When she was thirty meters away, it hummed to life. Every muscle in her body tightened.

She disappeared and reappeared behind a giant tree surrounded by thick underbrush. *I am no longer bored.* She was petrified. Her barely blinking eyes dashed back and forth over the egg's surface waiting for it to hatch or do whatever the Æsir created these things for.

That unsettling humming intensified as a loose patch of dirt near the egg began to dance and ripple, then disintegrated into a cloud of churning particles. The particles recombined, molded and shaped until a small reddish-brown creature materialized in a clay-like ball pivoting in random directions as if it were trying to unfurl.

The wobbling ball eventually opened, revealing an

ugly pointy-nosed animal covered in palm-sized scales, struggling to roll off its hunched back. She fought a profound desire to run over and help. A few seconds passed before the creature righted itself to stand as tall as it could on two stumpy legs. It stretched out its hairless body before inspecting the forest.

Alma found the odd thing's long scale-clad arms and rough human-like hands amusing. She laughed to herself at its thick scaly tail sweeping the grasses behind it.

The little creature lifted its nose into the air, sniffing with intent. Alma pried apart some branches in the leafy brush and peeked through a tiny hole to observe it teetering in her direction on stout inwardly-turned legs. It made random loud clicking noises as it neared.

It stopped about ten meters away and flattened its nose to the side. The egg hummed much louder, creating forty-nine more rolling scale coated balls unfurling their plump bodies as if they woke from a deep sleep.

They grouped behind their leader, joining him, or her, their genders weren't obvious, in pursuit of an unexpected scent. Alma no longer believed they were cute, or harmless, as they toddled toward her hiding spot. Her breathing grew rapid and shallow.

She released the branches and stepped backward. They heard and saw the underbrush move, snapping their heads in unison in Alma's direction. They trained their focus on the tree, sniffing at the air. Her eyes widened. She turned to run.

Her mind played scenarios, fatal and not so fatal, for dealing with them if they attacked. An ear-piercing chorus of powerful clicking noises echoed throughout the forest, distracting her from disappearing to another location. She ran faster.

Frustrated and unfocused, she headed for the beach. These little creatures looked heavy and probably couldn't swim, or float. She sprinted as fast as she could through a patchwork of trees and bushes.

The creatures galloped after her, using their long arms as forward legs. They moved more fluidly than their lumpish appearance suggested possible. Thunderous sounds of leathery flat feet thumping against dirt and pebbles, accompanied by that tormenting clicking, filled the air. The bounding herd was closing the gap between them.

They were fast, too fast to outrun. She shook off the fog clouding her mind, opened a deep trench behind her, and continued running until the stampede fell silent. The animals were no longer chasing her, but those dreadful clicking noises persisted. She stopped to catch her breath.

Alma followed the clicking to the edge of the trench and peered down inside. She was horrified at the sight of them building a ladder with their bodies. "Please do not make me do this." Three tiny claws reached over the ledge, compelling her to bury them under dirt and boulders.

Regardless of how many times she had done it, resorting to killing troubled her. She placed a mournful hand on their fresh grave as a single tear rolled down her face. "I am so sorry." She tipped her head back and looked to the sky. Her crying stopped, replaced by a new fear.

A shadowy bluish silhouette of a hammer orbited high above her. "Please no. Why is it always two things?" A loud clicking sound shattered her concentration as a lone creature stood across the rocky tomb with two beady round eyes trained on her.

Still on her knees, she lifted a hand and yelled, "Stop!" It didn't understand her word or her gesture, but it did stop. The creature continued sniffing at the air as it twitched its head back and forth with its chin pressed tight against its chest.

Alma stood and took a few apprehensive steps toward it, holding her palm down like she would for a strange dog. Its eyes sharpened and focused on her hand. Its clicking noises increased in speed and pitch as it stumbled backward. Something about the way it reacted forced a shiver up her spine, covering her body in goosebumps.

Her mind replayed the Captain's voice expressing his revulsion at her smell and none of the crew would touch her without gloves. She obsessed over a single sentence. "Animals should all be destroyed since they serve no useful purpose."

"You are not an animal, you are Æsir." Unable to contain her rage, she lunged at the monster and wrapped her arms around its dense chubby body. She grabbed hold of a scale and tore it from its back. The Æsir made an audible scream as blood spilled from its large open wound.

Alma gripped the scale in both hands and stabbed it in the face until it laid dead at her feet. She spat on the Æsir carcass, tensed her body, and screamed into the trees. There it was again, that menacing hammer floating overhead.

"Where the hell are you, Ymir?!" Echos of her screams rolled through the forest then dissipated, replaced by the roaring sounds of another Æsir horde galloping in her direction.

She clutched the bloody scale and waited for them

to come bounding over the rocks. A sole Æsir, probably the same one she murdered, jumped into the air where it plunged impaled on its own sharp scale. The force of its heavy body knocked Alma to the ground.

Stunned and breathless, she pushed the writhing creature away and jumped to her feet, ready to kill more. They stopped on top of the rocky grave, lined shoulder-to-shoulder, and surveyed her carnage. Alma growled through clenched teeth with spittle flying from her lips. "I will kill you all!"

She crouched, never breaking eye contact with the monsters, and ripped another scale from her second lifeless victim's body. With two blood-dripping weapons in front of her face, she yelled, "Come On!"

Before her opponents could react, the forest erupted in an ear-piercing barrage of rapid popping noises. She dropped to the dirt under a terrifying rainstorm of tissue and bone as the line of Æsir beasts exploded. Soaked from head to toe in blood, she turned in a panic.

Alma broke down, sobbing tears of relief at the beautiful sight of an American Marine unit emptying their weapons above and around her. She collapsed onto a dead Æsir with her face in her shaking hands. "Thank you, Ymir." She didn't notice Dawn and David standing behind the soldiers.

David weaved through his team, dropped to his knees, and wrapped Alma's bloodied body in his arms. Barely able to speak, Alma warned, "There is an egg."

He buried his face into her matted hair and kissed her on the head. "They took care of it."

Dawn, disappointed at the thoroughness of David's Marines, held her sword in her hand ready for battle. She sheathed her weapon and joined them in the soup of glistening entrails. "You look kind of hot covered in gross meat chunks." They cried together as David enveloped them both in his arms.

Alma struggled to speak through their oppressive hug. "Where is Sunna?"

"She's safe with Raven and Katie on Ander's ship." David pointed up at the hammer that had been haunting her.

A single laugh escaped her snotty tear soaked lips as she followed his finger upward. "How long have I been gone?"

The Marines swarmed passed them, over the rocks, and into the forest in search of more monsters. Dawn wanted to join them as they swept their weapons from side to side and disappeared into the brush. "Not as long as last time."

Alma pushed them away as a heavy breath escaped her mouth. This world's Jötunn, impressed by her and her human military, surrendered to Ymir. The three sister stars, Rigil Kentaurus, Toliman, and Proxima Centauri also succumbed to Ymir's will. Her voice was a fragile whisper. "Our home." Overwhelmed, she melted into David's arms.

Visions of Earth's and Seleen's smoldering lifeless bodies seared into her mind. "No. All those people. No." She clutched at David's chest as he stroked her hair.

Dawn placed a hand on Alma's back. "We saved a billion humans and almost all the Kohor and Trey." She concealed her happiness over losing so many useless garbage people.

The absence of Æsir ships in Sol, Yeset, Daneln, and Proxima Centauri made it obvious they won the war, but at an enormous cost. She surveyed an unrecognizable Earth. "We will breathe life back into her. Promise me this."

David responded, "Trey terraformers are already making plans, and they could really use your help." He focused on the dead Æsir beside them, sniffling against his tears. "Is this what they really look like?"

"Probably not." Dawn had seen many iterations of Æsirs in crude mental renderings from Ymir. "They're a little different depending on the world they're colonizing."

Brilliant antiparticle explosions twinkled like stars across the clear blue sky as Ander's fleet racked up more points removing any remaining Æsir ships from Alma's latest acquisition. Seeing him on the bridge of the Hammer of God, Alma chuckled. "What is that thing?"

Chapter 25

Mockingbird

"Push them? You want me to push them, all of them?" Alma scoffed at a crude hologram of Sol's main asteroid belt playing a sequence depicting giant rocks merging together then making their way to Earth as a single, much larger rock. "This will take months."

A company of Trey terraformers stood with her and David around the display. Engineer Rhey responded, "Our worlds lost too much mass, and you cannot make something from nothing. You can only convert existing matter. If you'd prefer, we could redirect our efforts toward making Venus habitable. Why your people wasted so much time with Mars is perplexing given your poor level of technology."

"I will do as you ask, but what is a planetesimal?" She pointed at a circular label anchored to the northern pole of a combined rock on its long journey to Earth.

Rhey, annoyed by her questions, replied, "They are larger celestial objects which will allow you to focus less on moving and guiding billions of smaller objects from the belt into Earth. This is for your benefit."

"Could I not squish the moon into Earth and make a new moon later?" They ignored her latest query, turned in unison, and left the room.

"What did I say?" She flashed a demure smile at David and bumped her shoulder into his. "I assume they regret their dismissive attitude toward Shan."

David ran his hand through the low-resolution moon hologram. "I don't like them, never have. Maybe when I see our world alive again I'll change my mind." He studied the planetesimal as it merged into the charred Earth.

"They grow on you, like surly old dogs. Just like you!" She kissed his cheek and replaced the hologram with a solid display of touchable rocks, then motioned to a large cluster floating in front of them. "I am currently moving these. Do you think they will be angry I started without their permission?" She nudged him again.

He huffed with a rolling grumble. "Yes. Can you actually tell when they're not angry? Do they have any other emotions?"

The display updated to an image of Earth and her moon, Luna. "Trey engineers show a happy smile on occasion. It looks strange, not quite right." Playing with Luna like Raven or Dawn probably would, she poked it closer to Earth. "I have to keep moving this giant thing, or it will escape. Apparently, it is important for breathing life back into our Earth."

A lone Trey terraformer returned with a tablet in his hands. He was smaller than his team members, probably younger. He sheepishly looked up at David. "General Trauger, I understand Earth is our priority, but it will take much longer to move matter from Daneln's Oort Cloud. We do not have an asteroid belt." He held the tablet in front of David, making sure not to look at Alma. "When time permits, these are the masses necessary for us to begin rebuilding Seleen."

Alma reached out and touched his shoulder. He was terrified. "I will make a deal with you. If you tell us how much mass Mars needs to become a viable terraforming candidate, I promise to fatten up Seleen at the same time." She crouched down and peered into his giant fear-filled eyes with a smile.

The young Trey man presented the tablet to her and loaded a Mars project plan created by Trey and human terraformers over a year ago. He stared through her instead of at her. "This is what you will need. Thank you, Guardian Alma." He handed her the tablet, turned, and fast-walked away.

She clutched the tablet to her chest and spun around with a coy little smile. "That was kind of adorable."

David tried maintaining his scowl, but couldn't. "They do sort of grow on you, I guess."

From the bridge of the Hammer of God, Alma, Dawn,

David, and Ander witnessed the first planetesimal combine with Earth's lifeless body. Alma scraped this one together from nearby asteroids months ahead of the others, which did anger the Trey. They had to recalculate everything.

Dawn looked disappointed at the controlled collision. "So, no huge explosions?" She tugged on Alma's arm. "You know you could drop a nuke or two in there to make it a little more exciting."

Ander lifted Dawn's hand and kissed her fingers. "She's rebuilding entire worlds. This is the most amazing thing I've ever seen." Dawn recoiled in disgust at the sight of water pooling in his emotional eyes.

"Do not give me so much credit. Without our engineers, I would fail to understand what to do or how to do it." She wondered if her Æsir counterpart had teams of intelligent engineers helping him as well.

When Alma allowed nature to take over, Raven appeared disoriented on the bridge. Dawn ripped her hand from Ander and launched toward Raven. She embraced her with an overpowering hug, raised her from the floor, and twisted their bodies in a violent dance. "I've missed you so much. When are you going to move in with us?"

Raven spoke through Dawn's crushing embrace, "My people have been traumatized by the revelation of our Æsir heritage. Many of them are unsure of my allegiance to humans. I am no longer universally respected. Regaining my former status will take time, and great effort." She looked around the empty bridge, frowning at Alma. "You will need to trust your own people eventually."

"Eventually." Alma forced her hands between them,

peeling Dawn's arms away from Raven. "Katie is waiting for us to try on dresses."

Carved from a small area of several decks on the HoG, Alma created a cozy private village containing large rooms and a homey common area. The two couples lived there with Katie, who acted as Sunna's nanny and Alma's reluctant therapist.

They entered the living-room to see Katie holding Dawn's wedding gown up to her body, admiring herself in a mirror. Dawn laughed. "There's about ten million men on this ship. Just pick one, or two."

Katie rolled her eyes with a subtle head shake and waved the women over. She held out two whimsically different sized bridesmaids dresses for them to model. "Put these on. Let's see if we need to make any adjustments."

Alma left the area with her new gown in hand while Raven pulled on the string securing her tan beaded dress and let it fall to the floor. She stood naked and unashamed in front of Katie and Dawn.

Dawn's nostrils flared. "Oh God, I've missed you!"

Raven presented a sweet smile to Dawn, dismissing Katie's disgusted expression. "I have missed you as well." She balanced on her tiptoes and kissed Dawn's lips more than a few times.

Katie wanted to stop them before this became too graphic. "Dress fittings first. You two can wait a few more minutes. She'll be naked again after I get it back."

Alma returned wearing her dress in time to see Raven lifting hers up over her nude body. She glared at an aroused Dawn. "What is wrong with you? You are to be married in less than a day."

She failed to understand Ander's tolerance of their

physical and quite open relationship. Although, if she were being honest, the fantasy of watching David and Katie was not unpleasant. She shook off that unwanted, likely Ymir inspired image.

"Are you nervous?" David glanced down on Dawn's glowing face. In their years together, he had never seen her grin so wide. It looked painful. They waited, arm-in-arm behind two giant ballroom doors guarded by Navy personnel in dress whites. Dawn was a breathtaking vision of maternal beauty.

She bumped her shoulder into his arm. "No, but you sure are—dad." Dawn smiled at her handsome escort standing strong and tall in his stylized military dress blues. Everyone else, except Craig, was wearing white.

David concentrated on those ominous closed doors. "I'm petrified." She cuddled against him, forcing his eyes to water.

The two rigid officers swung open the doors as a symphony orchestra played a dramatized version of the Wedding March. Dawn surveyed the crowd. "There are thousands of them, and they look so nice." Her eyes welled with tears, making David cry.

Dawn's protruding belly didn't look out of place in her lacy gown. She scanned the long carpeted aisle and melted at the site of Ander waiting in his crisp white Navy uniform covered in colorful medals and ribbons.

It had been over a year since Alma wore a dress in front of David. She was stunning, and he couldn't help but smile at Raven. He hadn't seen her in anything but that beaded gown or a camouflaged military uniform.

Her bridesmaid dress and styled hair helped him see her as the woman she was, instead of as a daughter, like Dawn.

Admiral Kathryn Pruitt stood proud in her medal clad Navy dress whites as she officiated their wedding. Behind her, the American Navy Orchestra roused the audience to their feet as they turned to watch Dawn and David walking the aisle.

Halfway up, the orchestra transitioned into the Navy fight song, Anchors Aweigh! David shook his head and let out a breathy laugh. He whispered to Dawn, "You're marrying a dork."

A wave of emotions flooded Alma with a powerful desire to have her own wedding. She leaned toward Raven. "I hate that I want to do this so much now." She couldn't stop fantasizing about herself in a long flowing gown with everyone's eyes trained on her. Those fantasies didn't include a giant belly, but Dawn carried it well on her petite frame.

"He would like that." Raven didn't understand the purpose of marriage, but she still wanted Alma to marry David.

Dawn and Ander stood side-by-side, facing their audience. Admiral Pruitt stepped forward as the orchestra faded and placed a hand on their shoulders. "I'd like to begin by welcoming everyone, and thanking all of you for being here on this incredible day."

"I can't think of a better venue than this awe-inspiring Navy vessel orbiting an Earth on the threshold of rebirth. It is a great privilege to be here today, among you, as witnesses to their life-long commitment of love for one another. And we know a lifetime for them is a serious commitment." Muted laughter rolled throughout the audience.

"So, without further delay, dearly beloved and honored guests. We are gathered here together to join Dawn Rosemary Branagan and Ander Theodore Falk in the holy union of marriage..."

After the ceremony, they sat around a decorated table in an enormous banquet hall filled with officers and their guests. Ander rapped his knuckles on the table. "My chefs have been working all month with Kohor cooks." He stared into Raven's eyes. "I hope this tiny symbol of respect helps you understand how much we appreciate your incredible sacrifices."

No one knew Raven found human food as disgusting as they found Kohor food. Human food contained way too many spices, and salt, so much salt. Her relationship with Dawn helped her open up about these annoyances, and others.

Waitstaff swarmed their table, placing gratuitous amounts of food in front of everyone. Raven hunched over her plate with an unenthusiastic grimace and forced herself to taste the human-made Kohor dish. "This is quite good." She shoveled forkfuls of it into her mouth.

Dawn stabbed her fork into a brown mushy blob on Raven's plate. "This gross looking stuff is the best."

Alma turned her attention to her irritable and hungry daughter. She tried forcing spoonfuls of mashed vegetables between her angry little lips, but Sunna resisted.

David empathized with Sunna. "You should let her try feeding herself."

"I am not ready for that. I have missed so much time with her." She kissed Sunna's forehead to distract her while stabbing at her mouth with a spoonful of something yellow.

Alma and David fussing over Sunna prompted Dawn to rub her belly. She leaned into Ander and said, "I can't wait."

They finished dinner and briefly mingled with their guests. Relieved to get back to the comfort and safety of their private home, Alma whispered to Katie, "I think I am getting better around the crew. I do not feel so scared." Saying that made her worry she was letting her guard down too soon.

Katie and Dawn walked Sunna to a giant pile of colorful stuffed animals laying in the middle of the common area floor. Once a cold assassin, Dawn was now a soon-to-be mother playing with anthropomorphized toy animals on a living-room carpet. Everyone was envious of her ability to segment off her different personalities, locking those powerful versions of herself away in little cages until she needed them.

When the group seemed distracted, Ander left and returned holding a gift-wrapped box. He and Dawn presented it to Raven with a spirited bounce. "Open it!"

Gift giving was not a Kohor tradition. She observed many humans trying to impress Kohor women by giving them weird gifts they had no use for. Telling herself to pretend she liked it, she opened the box and wept. Inside were several new toy ships, including the Hammer of God and Archytas Station.

Teary-eyed, Dawn waved her over to the floor with Katie and Sunna. "Let's play with them."

The moment Sunna got her hands on the replica of Ander's ship, it went straight into her mouth. The four of them played on the carpet for an hour before Sunna curled against Katie's stomach and fell asleep.

Alma scooped her up and carted her away, hugging and kissing her while laying her in a crib. A gentle lullaby warmed Sunna's tiny body. *Hush little baby, don't say a word...*

In close geosynchronous orbit of a lifeless starless world twenty-seven light years from Earth, an X9 warship carried out its pre-programmed tasks. Sporadic skilled quantum mutations added to and altered Sunna's neural structure. Stacey's comforting voice continued, *mamma's gonna buy you a mockingbird.*